TALES OF THE
HEXAGONVERSE
1. MUTATIONS

IN THE SAME SERIES

TALES OF THE HEXAGONVERSE

1. MUTATIONS

Stories by
Cédric Burgaud, Nelly Chadour, Fabien Clavel, Tepthida Hay, Julien Heylbroeck, Romain d'Huissier, Jean-Marc Lainé, Jean-Marc & Randy Lofficier, Ghislain Morel, Alex Nikolavitch, Yohan Odivart, Frank Schildiner and **Krystoff Valla**

Translated by
Michael Shreve

Edited by
Romain d'Huissier
& Jean-Marc Lofficier

BLACK COAT PRESS

TABLE OF CONTENTS

Homicron by Christian Gossett

Introduction

Since the beginning of time, tales about larger-than-life heroes have fascinated humanity. Exceptional beings living extraordinary adventures are found in all cultures and often follow the same patterns, punctuated by similar events, fulfilling an essential need in the safeguarding of their societies, as Joseph Campbell brilliantly analyzed in his *Hero with a Thousand Faces*.

The superhero is the modern avatar of these mythological figures who have always made people dream by offering them an ideal designed to inspire them.

A true shared universe inhabited by colorful superheroes, the Hexagon Universe is a French creation the origins of which go back to 1950, with the founding of Editions Lug, a publishing house that did a lot for the popularization of comic books in France.

Reinvented and modernized over the past twenty years, the Hexagon Universe is featured in this anthology of tales that bring together many of its heroes.

It was in 1950 that writer Marcel Navarro decided to create his own publishing house, which he did by teaming up with businessman Auguste Vistel. Together, they created Lug Editions, based in Lyon—Lugdunum being the Latin name of that city.

At first, Lug was content to publish reprints of Spanish and Italian comics, but very quickly, Navarro decided to create his own characters, which he entrusted to French and Italian artists. We owe to him the creation of the first shared universe of French superheroes in comics.

His most successful creation was Zembla, a jungle lord inspired by Tarzan, but many other characters followed: Rakar, a masked western avenger, Silver Shadow, a vigilante from the future, Max Tornado, an astronaut with Herculean strength, Tanka, another jungle lord, the Sea King, an amphibious hero, the Dark Flyer, a techno-hero, Gun Gallon, an adventurer exploring a fantasy world, etc.

In 1969, Claude Vistel, Auguste's daughter, returned from a trip to New York and convinced Navarro to publish the very first Marvel comic in France, *Fantask*, with The Fantastic Four, Spider-man and The Silver Surfer. Inspired by their success, Navarro launched *Wampus*, featuring the eponymous alien monster, and CLASH, a UN-sponsored counter-terrorist organization.

Alas, French censorship had Lug in its crosshairs and both Fantask and Wampus were forced to cease publishing. The following year, undaunted, Navarro relaunched the Marvel characters in *Strange*, then *Marvel* (which was also censored) and various other titles. In 1972, a new wave of French heroes emerged under the pen of sci-fi writer Claude in *Futura*: Homicron, Jaleb (an alien telepath), the Time Brigade, The Man of Brass, The Other, Sibilla, Aster, etc. Then in 1974 came the magazines *Waki* (a young post-apocalyptic hero) and *Kabur* featuring the eponymous sword & sorcery character and another superhero, the Bronze Gladiator.

In 1980, Navarro launched more superheroes, including Ozark, an Indian shaman, Phenix, a female crime fighter, Starlock, Kit Kappa (a master of kung fu), Jaydee (a metamorph), Motoman (a super-biker), etc. This gallery of characters coexisting in various magazines created a universe not unlike that of DC, pre-Crisis.

After Auguste Vistel's passing, Navarro decided to retire and Editions Lug was sold to a Scandinavian publisher in 1993. The creation of new stories stopped until the late 1990s when it was resold to a French company. From 2000, under the editorship of Thierry Mornet, the characters once published by Editions Lug returned in new stories. Under the aegis of Jean-Marc Lofficier, Zembla, Wampus, Kabur, Phenix, Sibilla, the Bronze Gladiator and many others returned, sometimes in new versions. It was formally established that all these characters lived in the same shared universe and there was a real effort to create retroactive continuity and coherence between the various elements introduced over four decades.

This was when *Strangers* (bringing together Homicron, Starlock, Jaleb, Tanka, Jaydee and Futura) was launched and published in the U.S. by Image Comics, making it the first French superhero comic published in America!

But despite the dynamic approach, this revival ended with the publisher going bankrupt at the end of 2003. Fortunately, the writers and artists who had contributed to the creation of this unique universe banded together and reclaimed their rights to form Hexagon Comics.

Since then, Hexagon Comics has launched an ambitious policy of reprinting the original classic stories in thick omnibuses, as well as continuing the publication of new stories in *Strangers, Strangers Universe* and *The Guardian of the Republic*. *Tales of the HexagonVerse* is the latest in this modest effort to bring recognition to this section of French popular culture—over half a century old—virtually unknown in America.

It turns out that, like their American cousins, French superheroes may well be immortal!

Romain d'Huissier

The Bronze Gladiator by Jay Stephens

The Bronze Gladiator, aka Prince Starko, is the heir of King Arkadin of the warrior world Arena, located in the Constellation of the Trident. Starko was forced to flee his home planet because of the usurper Kahezar who killed his father to seize the throne. With the help of his sister Lyvia, he stole an experimental hypership, Polyvac, with an artificial intelligence drive. Once on Earth, after having hidden Polyvac at the bottom of a Pennsylvania lake, Starko rescued young Lorna Logan, who allowed him to "borrow" the identity of her late brother, Mike, as well as his job as a special ed teacher in Brooklyn. This new story takes place before Kahezar locates Prince Starko on Earth...

Cedric Burgaud: *Mutations*

Like every time they came back from Christmas vacation, the students in the reform school where Mike Logan worked seemed less interested in what they were studying than in what they had done during the few days of relaxation with family or friends. The bitter cold that assaulted New York this year did not make things better, and Mike had a hard time focusing their attention on the daily math equations.

"Come on, gentlemen, calm down, please."

Mike Logan had quickly gotten in the habit of treating his students (all of them, male) like responsible adults and not like delinquent teenagers. Thus he had got a reputation among his colleagues (but also with the students) of being an open, understanding, patient and attentive teacher, so that teachers and students alike would often confide in him. Important bonds were forged this way, which Mike Logan appreciated because he was one of the few teachers who thought that his work did not stop at the classroom door.

"Please! I know it's the first day back, it's cold and you're thinking more about the past few days than the ones coming up, but a little concentration on what we're doing today will help everyone. So, let's get back to this tricky equation I tried to explain ten minutes ago…"

The class calmed down a little. Logan was familiar enough with this problem that he had seen since he started teaching years ago in this school for troubled kids. He was not bothered much because he knew that, by the end of the week, they would all get back to being serious when PE and shop class would start up again.

No, what bothered him was the absence of two students in the second and third row: Ted and William Balsam, brothers who were three years apart and whom Logan had taught now for three years. He had never seen them miss a day of school. Being their teacher, Logan knew their story: raised in a big family, beaten by their alcoholic father who made them beg on the streets to buy his booze, they'd run away together to end up in a gang that attacked couples coming out of movie theaters late at night. Luckily for them, they'd been arrested before committing any serious crimes and, thanks to their youth and their intelligence, they'd been assigned to this school where Mike Logan taught. A kind of cliché life, but one similar to a lot of students at the school, and many of them, like the Balsam brothers, took this second chance very seriously, and would follow through all the way to their diploma. Some even came back to teach at the school and share their experiences, good and bad.

The Balsam brothers' absence, therefore, was abnormal and it worried Mike Logan.

"Are you listening to me? You don't look like you heard a word I said!"

Jane Mason, Mike's girlfriend, looked furiously at him over the table at the café where they met after work.

"Sorry. There's just something bothering me at work. Two of my students didn't come to class. You know, Ted and William, I've talked about them. No note, no phone call. Nothing. I asked their friends but none of them has heard from them since the start of vacation."

"Maybe they just took a few extra days with their family? Or…"

"Unlikely! Their father is still alive and as tough as ever."

"How do you know?"

"I checked. I also went to the police. No word. Just like the hospitals. I don't know…"

"Don't worry, they're probably just late coming back, really."

Since she had been with him, Jane Mason knew how involved Mike Logan could get in his work and how protective he was of his students. Sometimes he lost sleep and had to go out to quiet his mind. The first few nights she had been surprised and worried but now she was used to it—as long as he did not come back stinking of booze and cigarettes.

She took his hand and kissed it gently. "I guess you're going to run all over town looking for them?"

"You know me. Don't wait up tonight."

They kissed and then Logan dashed out, disappearing on the crowded New York sidewalk.

Like every time that he felt upset or worried, Mike Logan took his 4X4 and drove to Pennsylvania. The narrow, dirt road he turned onto from Highway 78 led to a deserted lake on the banks of which stood a small shack used for watching migratory birds when they stopped off here on their journey south.

In spite of the absence of tourists—eight inches of snow covered the road—Logan hid his car under a white tarp that he kept by a tree stump, then, with peace of mind, he entered the cabin that he had the only key to. The place was simple, containing only a cot, a folding chair with a writing desk, a telescope pointed out the big, rectangular window across from the door that looked out upon the frozen lake, and a big army footlocker that he opened right away with the second key on the ring. Canned food, a can opener and folded blankets were laid inside. Logan searched until he heard a click and the bottom of the trunk lifted up to reveal a stone staircase leading down and under the lake.

At the bottom of the stairs, Logan put both his hands on a door that had a shiny, purple, metallic sheen. Right away his palms started glowing, then the door swung open and a voice came from inside.

"Welcome back, Prince Starko. I wasn't expecting you so soon."

"Hello, Polyvac, not too cold for you?"

"You know very well that I don't feel that kind of thing, Prince Starko."

"And you know that I don't like it when you call me that. Here, my name's Mike Logan."

"As you wish, Prince Starko."

"Ah, you're so pigheaded! Maybe I should try to reprogram you."

Polyvac was a supercomputer and the pilot of the experimental spaceship in which Prince Starko had crashed into this lake after escaping a plot against him on his home planet. Since then, the interstellar ship had been the earthly refuge for the prince who had taken on the identity of Mike Logan to live among humans.

Sitting in his command seat Prince Starko felt better.

"Polyvac."

"Yes, Prince Starko."

"We have work to do. Two of my students have disappeared. Ted and William Balsam. I want to know everything about them. Search through their past, their files and if you find anything interesting, let me know immediately."

"Very good. I'll take care of it."

Thanks to Polyvac, Starko had access to all the databases in the world, and no governmental site could block out the supercomputer. In less than a minute, Polyvac had run through billions of bytes of data, sorted the pertinent information in order of priority, and was ready to give his verdict.

Starko listened closely until Polyvac said, "James Curley, 21 years-old, incarcerated on Rikers Island, released for good conduct two weeks ago. Member of the Last Show gang."

"Like the Balsam brothers. Find me his address. I'm going to pay him a visit tonight."

"It's already downloaded on your GPS."

The building was lit by a blinking street lamp and a 24-hour porno theater marquee. The snow, which had started falling again about an hour earlier, kept the night owls off the streets. Everything was calm and quiet. Nobody noticed a shadow slip between the walls, jump onto the second floor balcony, grab the fire escape ladder and climb up onto to the roof.

In his room on the fifth floor, which faced the street and the red neon sign, James Curley was dozing in an armchair, cap on head and beer in hand, in front of the TV that was re-broadcasting a baseball game.

All of a sudden a deep voice whispered in his ear, "So, James, what's the score?"

Before he could answer or see who was talking, James Curley was lifted from the chair and plastered against the wall upside down. Two black eyes, barely visible through the slits in the golden helmet, stared hard at him, just a few inches from his face.

"You scream; I kill you. You call for help; I kill you. You don't answer my questions; I kill you. You understand; nod."

Curley nodded with conviction "I... I'll tell you everything, but... but don't kill me, okay?"

"Polyvac? You there?"

Mike Logan, alias Prince Starko, was in constant communication with his supercomputer thanks to a microphone and earpiece. He only had to call on Polyvac and he was answered in a split second.

"Of course, Prince Starko. Did you find James Curley?"

15

"In his room, but he won't be staying long. After the fright I gave him, he should leave New York tonight. I have some information concerning a bar. The 7th Gear Bar. Give me the address and hook up to a satellite to watch the place."

"The Steeplebush III is just over us. I'll send its images to your phone."

"Perfect."

"I also ran through the recorded NSA images. Ted and William Balsam entered the bar on December 30, but they never came out."

"And it's January 2. Uh-huh. How many people have gone into this bar and were never seen again?"

"Going back two weeks, there were eight people including the Balsams. All young, healthy men."

"I think we've hit on something, Polyvac. Let's go see what it's all about."

"The building across the street has a wonderful view of the bar and the backyard. The fourth floor apartment was cleared out by the police yesterday morning."

"A lucky break we can't turn down."

Although he was still shaking, James Curley quickly stuffed a gym bag with some clothes and a few personal items before hopping down the metal steps of the fire escape. The deserted streets of the neighborhood he knew so well looked menacing to him tonight. He jumped at the slightest noise, hid from any moving shadow, kept glancing behind him, and finally went every which way to make sure he was not being followed.

After a long, hard, hour-long walk in the snow he disappeared down a small alley. He found a metal door and knocked twice before it opened.

"Hey, James."

"Hey, Marlow. Can I come in?"

The giant guarding the place looked the sweating young man up and down, scanned the empty alley, and then decided to let him in. The door slammed shut.

"Wait here. I'll get Mr. Tikanochi."

Curley sat on a case of beer and wiped his dripping forehead. His t-shirt and shirt were soaked despite the cold, and he could not tell if he were shivering from fear, or running, or the snow melting down his neck. He barely noticed the shelves full of canned foods in the faint green light coming from a small office in the corner of the big storeroom. When the guard suddenly appeared in front of him, he jumped as if the devil himself had come calling on him.

"Follow me."

The office he was almost pushed into could not have been more different from the storeroom. A carved, heavy, solid wood desk took up most of the space. The hand-woven wool carpet cushioned the nervous steps of James Curley as he approached one of the armchairs for visitors. He cast a quick look at the two modern paintings that brightened the white walls, and then focused all his attention on the little, round, Asian man who was scrutinizing him from behind his half-moon glasses. In two cases behind him stood the account books squeezed between cast-iron bookends.

"Hello James. Make it quick, I still have work to do tonight."

"I... Hello, Mr. Tikanochi. I... I had a visit tonight and, uh, I'm wondering if..."

"Not again about one of those bitches from the movies across the street..."

"No, no. It's that..."

Curley's mouth was suddenly dried out and he had trouble voicing his worries, which were even worse than before. Why did he come here? Why didn't he take the advice and leave town right away? He made up his mind to tell everything.

"It's that... I had a visit from a guy in a suit..."

Before he could finish, yelling broke out in the bar. Shots were fired, then the door opened and closed quickly behind two thugs in suits holding guns.

17

"Mr. Tikanochi, we have a big problem. A guy bust into the bar dressed up like a circus acrobat. Burt tried to kick him out because he was scaring the customers. He didn't see it coming and he paid the price: the guy had him whipped in no time flat. Me and Will hesitated, but got our pieces out. I swear we didn't miss, right Will? We emptied our clips into him, but it didn't do a thing. There's something screwy."

Will nodded, "It's the suit. Must be Kevlar or something like that."

Mr. Tikanochi leaned forward and very solemnly asked for a detailed description of the costume.

"No doubt about it. It's the Bronze Gladiator."

James Curley turned pale and shrank down in the chair, but the little Asian man had already forgotten him.

"Where is he now?"

"In the bar, I guess. When we saw he didn't even flinch at the bullets, we ran back here to warn you."

"OK. We take the emergency exit. Knock this guy out and burn the place."

Before he could react, Curley was hit on the head and collapsed. The other thug pulled a gas can out of a hiding place and poured gas over the carpet, desk and bookcases.

As the fire spread quickly and the smoke filled the room the three men hurried through a trapdoor under the desk and landed in the sewers.

When he saw James Curley entering the backdoor, Prince Starko knew he had to act quickly.

"Polyvac, I have to go in there. Scramble the police radios, I don't want to be disturbed during my interrogation."

"A piece of information that might interest you, Prince Starko. The bar was bought by a dummy corporation belonging to CRIMEN, and it is run by a Japanese called Tikanochi. Despite their suspicions, the police haven't been able to gather enough evidence to bring any action against him."

"No need to put on the kid gloves then."

The biting cold of the New York night poured into the fourth floor apartment. This did not prevent Prince Starko from leaping off the balcony and soaring off to the entrance of the bar where he landed softly. A drunk was relieving himself in the alley across the street and could not believe his eyes— he would wonder for a long time whether an angel really did fall from Heaven.

But this was obviously no angel. Prince Starko, in fact, had inherited his formidable armor, which gave him the ability to fly and to alter the molecular structure of his body. While wearing it, he was known as the Bronze Gladiator, upholder of justice, fighting the crime that infested New York City.

Using the powers of his suit, Prince Starko made his fist harder than stone and, with a simple punch, the wooden door went flying across the bar, crashing into the tables of the stunned customers.

"Hello everyone. Is Mr. Tikanochi here tonight?"

All he got for an answer was the bouncer kicking him. His foot would have taken the head off a normal person. Fortunately, the helmet cushioned the blow and, before the thug's foot was back on the ground, Prince Starko had already unleashed his own that swiped his other leg. With nothing to stand on, his opponent dropped to the ground. However, his professional training in Russian combat got him up and facing his foe again, wary now of this nutcase dressed up like a weird Roman fighter.

"Don't push it. You're going to get hurt," said Starko.

Behind the tables and chairs, the customers did not run away, but watched on silently as the two men faced off. Nobody was listening to the radio playing old rock. Nobody watched the TV showing images of a Middle Eastern country in revolt.

The bouncer lunged first with a shower of fists and feet. Thanks to his armor, the Bronze Gladiator took the beating easily. Then, he got tired of the game and grabbed the bolas hanging from his belt. His opponent was shackled in no time.

All of a sudden, shots rang out, but his armor protected him as the bullets flattened against his body like balls at a carnival game.

The room emptied instantly. Prince Starko stood alone. The shooters had also vanished. When he opened the door to the storeroom, thick black smoke was pushing out of a second, metal door.

The police and firemen did not take long to arrive at the site of the brawl. Prince Starko had to leave, so he did not have time to search the bar for clues.

"Polyvac, I need all the addresses of Tikanochi as well as those of all the businesses he operates. Get information about the fight clubs, too. The bouncer had an unusual technique. I hope you filmed the whole thing."

"Got it, Prince Starko."

Unseen in his 4X4, Starko watched the street that was soon filled with onlookers despite the late hour. Witnesses with blankets around their shoulders and cups of hot coffee in their hands answered questions by the police. Two ambulance drivers were carrying the unconscious bouncer on a stretcher. Firemen were rolling in the hoses just used to put out the fire that had ravaged the office and storeroom. Among the rubberneckers behind the police line, a few journalists were recording their version of the facts with the little information they had managed to gather.

A refrigerated delivery van turned the corner and slammed on the brakes, skidding over the layer of snow on the ground. The driver, a dark figure in the cab, leaned forward to get a better look at the blue and red flashing lights at the end of the street. A few seconds passed, then his bearded face was lit up by a cell phone.

Prince Starko jumped out of his car, but did not have time to hear the short conversation. What he heard was that the driver was about to leave, which was not to his liking. So, he moved silently up to the driver's door, yanked it open and sent the driver into the passenger seat with a right hook to the jaw. He climbed into the empty seat and pulled away slowly to avoid attention. A couple of blocks later, he grabbed the phone of the motionless driver beside him.

"Let's see who you were calling, friend. Ah, apparently it's blocked. Polyvac! You should have my location. When you've got the number, check the last call."

While waiting for an answer from his AI, Prince Starko searched the man (no papers), the cab (gun in the glove box and GPS) and the van (three empty, blue plastics bags and two black ones big enough for a human body).

"Hmm. I hope I get luckier with the GPS. Bingo! Polyvac, I'm sending you an address. Tell me everything about it."

"It's a meat processing plant registered to a company that is a front for CRIMEN. It's run by a Mr. Hijikata, the son-in-law of Mr. Tikanochi."

"Now we're getting somewhere. I think I'll pay a little visit to that plant."

Driving the van through the snowy streets was no walk in the park because the packed down snow had frozen in places, despite the salt poured on by the city. But finally the plant appeared, lit by two spotlights on top of the two buildings that flanked the locked entrance to the place. The guard in the shack blew on his hands and shuffled from one foot to the other to keep warm. His coffee had gone cold a long time ago and the electric heater sitting on a chair was not helping much.

Parked at a discreet distance, Prince Starko watched for several long minutes, as he did so often when admiring migratory birds on the lake under which his spaceship lay hidden. The lack of deliveries could be explained by the heavy snow, which made it hard for business. But if no vans were expected, why was the guard so alert in his shack, and why were the buildings lit up?

With more than just a hunch to go on—the hair on the back of his neck stood up as always when he suspected shady business—Prince Starko took out a pair of night-vision glasses from a black bag. He saw infrared rays sweeping over the grounds to prevent any unwanted visitors from entering undetected.

"Polyvac, I'm at the plant. I'd like you to examine the place for me."

"Impossible. An electromagnetic field is interfering with the satellite image."

"What?"

Starko was expecting something weird about the factory, but not this ultra-sophisticated protection like some nuclear power plant.

"It's impossible to get a clear image of the site. A strong electromagnetic signal is being broadcast by the main building and is disturbing all frequencies above 30 kilohertz."

"Hmm. And with the lasers swinging around, I can't fly over the fence."

Starko watched the entrance and the guard who had just come out to get some feeling back in his legs.

"So, I'm looking at the only way in."

He got a quick glance at an Uzi clip peeking out from under the guard's thick coat.

"I have an idea to get in here, but I don't think she's going to like it."

On the fourth ring a woman's voice came through.

"You better have a good reason for waking me up or you're going to be…"

"Hello, Lorna. You know I'd never pull you out of the arms of Morpheus for anything trivial."

"Stop beating around the bush and get to the point."

Several years before, Prince Starko had saved Lorna Logan's life. In return, she had let him "borrow" her brother's identity, Mike Logan, who had died. A special relationship had been formed from this agreement.

"OK, listen, I need your help."

"Right now? You've got to be kidding…"

"Really, if I could do it alone, do you think I'd be disturbing you at this time? I'm really stuck here."

"Hum… Will it be dangerous?"

"Maybe."

"Ha, you're really a pain in the…! Can't you find someone else? A friend who likes to play medieval knights with you, or a masked girl all dressed in leather?"

"You know you're the only girl I've got."

"Right, I get it. I'm coming. But this is the last time, I swear!"

Lorna Logan always said this when she helped her "brother" in dire circumstances. She gave in every time, all the while knowing that he would never put her in danger if it were not absolutely necessary and if he could not protect her.

"I'll come pick you up. With the snow falling again, it'll take you forever."

In the shack with non-existent insulation, the guard's teeth were chattering as he cursed the weather of this coldest January in years. He could not concentrate on the magazine he had brought that detailed the latest innovations in American weaponry. When the headlights of a van drove up, it took him a minute to understand that a delivery was arriving. The honking horn startled him.

"What's this all about?"

The guard came out of his shack, one hand stuck inside his coat pocket, which had been cut so he could reach his hidden automatic weapon. His first reflex was to scan the van's plate as it sat in front of the gate: it was on the list that he had memorized and could therefore enter the site without being searched.

Still standing back, he shined his flashlight through the window and blinded the driver who was wrapped up in his coat and whose face was half-concealed behind a scarf. He hesitated a moment because he could not recognize the driver, but he did know the Yankees baseball cap that belonged to a regular delivery driver. He felt reassured.

Finally easing off, he pressed the button to open the gate so the van could enter. Then went up to the driver's side window and said, "Hey, Steve. Kind of late for a delivery, isn't it?"

"You kidding? With all this snow…"

"Yeah. Your voice sounds funny."

"Damn strep throat from the cold. My throat's killing me."

"Stop by on your way out. I've got a great cure for a sore throat."

"Will do. Later."

Without giving in to the panic that was running through her bones, Lorna Logan steered the van calmly into a loading dock. Her hands were shaking when she let go of the wheel.

"Never again! Never!"

"You were great!"

"Are you listening to me? Never again! I thought he was going to kill me when he came up to the window."

"There was nothing to worry about. I was watching him the whole time. Now calm down and just sit here and wait for me. I won't be long."

Prince Starko left her and snuck into the plant through a window that was left unlocked. As he went through some cold rooms where animal carcasses hung silently from their hooks, he could barely see in the semi-darkness and cold steam. His infrared goggles came in very handy to avoid bumping into the sides of beef or any unexpected encounters.

After a few minutes of looking around, Starko could see that the single floor of this building was used as a slaughter-house—nothing but cutting and slicing the meat brought in. And yet, in spite of the high price of meat, it was hard for him to understand such security measures to protect a few tons of proteins.

He went back to the little reception room for deliveries. Three trapdoors, like the garbage chutes you see in some buildings in Harlem, were set in one of the walls, not far from the metal sliding door that led to the loading dock outside.

At first, he thought they were just ordinary garbage chutes for animal waste, but on closer inspection he saw no trace of blood. On the contrary, they looked too clean and they were big enough to fit a full body bag into, for example.

As opposed to the ground floor, the basement was lit by lights protected by grills. The white-tiled floor was spotless— no traces of footsteps, or even dust, like a ship's deck scrubbed clean by the cabin boys every day. And there was not a scratch on the light blue walls. Starko glanced back toward the tube he had just come through, and he felt a current of air escaping the cold sterility, as if any intrusion was sucked out of the place. The building therefore was under light pressure. All this made him think of a hospital, and right away he thought of his two missing students.

His premonition was confirmed when he followed the conveyor belt that moved under the three chutes and that had started working as soon as he landed here—an automatic command must have triggered the system when a body was sent down—and, at the end of the corridor, he ended up in a big room equipped with everything modern medicine could ask for: scanners, MRIs, ultrasounds, gamma cameras, X-ray machines and chromatography equipment, Raman spectrometers, sterile chambers and other scientific instruments that he did not recognize.

"...are ready but I need more specimens. I... I'm doing the best with what I've got. Look at the tests. There are too many failures to start a new series..."

The voices Starko heard were coming from a corner of the room hidden behind a big, blue, plastic curtain.

"I understand, professor, but CRIMEN is not a charitable organization. I've put a lot of money into this facility. So of course I expect results. And what do we have after months of waiting? Nothing!"

"I... With all due respect, Baroud, there has been some progress, and I'm on the right path. I just need a little more time to refine the..."

"There's no need for further development. You've already managed to get viable specimens."

"I... Yes, but... with too many failures."

"That doesn't matter. Be happy with what you've got. We'll worry about how many bodies it takes."

"Er... OK, very well."

The curtain moved and Prince Starko dove between two big machines to keep out of sight of the three people walking toward him: a man around fifty, bald, wearing a white lab coat buttoned up, and a couple in black, tailored suits wearing sunglasses.

The woman pointed to the conveyor belt.

"Look!" she said. "The belt's moving. Are you expecting a delivery?"

"No, nothing," replied the man in a lab coat. "With the snow outside, everything's on hold."

The couple looked at each other. They had heard about the fire at the 7th Gear Bar and the appearance of some guy dressed up like a superhero.

"It's him!"

The man in the suit pulled out an automatic pistol. The woman ran to a computer terminal and set off the alarm.

"Gladiator! That's your name, right? If you give yourself up, I promise not to kill you."

"I doubt that. And it's 'Bronze Gladiator, not just Gladiator."

Knowing that he could not hide, Prince Starko stepped out. Right away, the man fired, but the bullets bounced harmlessly against his suit.

"No! My machines!"

The professor wanted to intervene, but the woman blocked him off.

"Get out of here, professor."

"But I don't know if I can control them."

"Now—or I'll kill you."

The woman backed behind the curtain. Meanwhile, the man was keeping the Bronze Gladiator at a distance. The bullets flew, ricocheted off his armor, and struck the walls or the machines, which started falling apart.

Soon, the air began smelling of gunpowder, melted plastic, and fried electronics. Sizzling short-circuits could be heard under the screaming alarm and the rattle of gunfire. The man swore again and again; he knew he could never get the better of an adversary like this before he ran out of ammo.

"Rowena! Hurry up!"

The words were hardly out of his mouth when someone screamed behind the curtain, followed by the sound of broken glass and a big splash of water.

"Let's move!"

The woman, whose sunglasses had been replaced by a slit across her forehead, rushed out from the curtain and pulled her partner as she headed down a corridor to their left.

The Bronze Gladiator, who had grabbed his bolas to knock his enemy off the trigger, held back when he saw the curtain fall down to reveal the experimental part of the lab: in three big tanks, floating like jellyfish, were bodies hooked up to respirators, purifiers and dialysis machines; a fourth tank was still spitting bluish water while a body lay in the broken glass; two others were intact but empty, their occupants standing around the professor and playing with his torn lab coat like cats. They were laughing at his indifference.

The professor talked to them like children:

"Come on now, that's enough… I know, I know, you're happy to be out of the tank and you want to have some fun, but this is really not the time. Be nice and stay here while I find you something to play with, OK?"

The two men looked alike, but not identical, like brothers but not twins: clean-shaven and bald, tall and muscular. To tell them apart, Starko dubbed them "Blue Boxer" and "Green Boxer," this being the only piece of clothing they wore.

Like two children ignoring their parent's advice, the two giants kept playing with the professor, hitting him harder and harder, hurting him worse and worse. The professor did not know what to say to save his life.

Then seeing Prince Starko he cried out:

"Bronze Gladiator, help me! I can't reason with them!"

Turning to look at the same time the two men in boxer shorts saw another fun toy to play with. They immediately forgot all about the professor who went scurrying behind Starko. The bolas flew at the legs of Blue Boxer, but he leaped away with cat-like agility. In his surprise, Prince Starko did not have time to dodge the first blow from Green Bower. He fell back several feet and knocked over a table with a computer on it. The screen popped out when it fell.

"My laboratory!"

Despite his wounds, the professor buried his face in his hands in a gesture of grief worthy of a Greek tragedy.

Barely on his feet again, Starko got kicked in the chest by Blue Boxes. This time, it was a cabinet full of glassware—test tubes, pipettes, round and conical flasks—that crashed onto the floor. Starko protected himself by rolling under a metal desk, then he jumped up again, keeping a little distance between him and his opponents.

"What did you do to them, professor?"

"No! Not that!"

Green Boxer swept his hand over the desk to clear off the laser printer, monitor and all the clutter.

"Professor! What did you do to them?" Starko had to yell to be heard over the shrieking alarm.

"Uh, well... just a few genetic improvements."

The metal desk was being folded in half when Blue Boxer took his turn to leap up and land behind the Bronze Gladiator. Starko dove to avoid the double attack. Unless he figured something out quickly, the only possible recourse would be to run away from these superhuman furies. His armor absorbed the blows and protected him from serious injury, but he could not hold out forever.

I have to catch my breath and think. And above all question the professor.

"OK, boys, let's go!"

The Bronze Gladiator launched himself through the wreckage, dodging the punches from Green Boxer and rolled a breathing apparatus into Blue Boxer's legs to slow him down. He caught the professor by the collar and dragged him into the room next door, slamming the heavy door shut. Fists started pounding on it right away but it seemed to be holding. But it was very cold inside.

"We're stuck now. We can't escape."

"Can't you reason with them?" asked Starko.

"Not at all," the professor replied. "They haven't finished evolving. They have the mental age of a two-year-old child. I didn't have time to finish the tests. I warned them about this."

"What modifications did you make?"

"I... I tried different hybrids of animal muscular cells. A lot didn't work. But the tests aren't finished. I need more time."

"What animals?"

"Oh, all kinds. For these guys, I mixed cat, bear and kangaroo in different proportions."

Prince Starko remembered how they had attacked: Blue Boxer jumped like a cat and kicked, whereas Green Boxer used only his arms and hands.

"So if I can neutralize the feet of one, and the hands of the other, they'll be harmless."

"I guess so..."

Only then did Starko look around the room and at the wall opposite the door, which was still being pummeled by the bratty children. It was covered with big, metal drawers, the highest accessible by a rolling ladder.

"This is where I stored the bodies they brought me."

Prince Starko glared at him.

"I had no choice. They didn't give me the opportunity to..."

"Later. You can answer all my questions later. I just want to know if they brought you two young men."

He gave the description of the Balsam brothers.

The Professor pointed to two drawers at chest height. Ted and William were lying in them.

"I promise, they're just sedated. I didn't have time to do... any... thing..."

"Wake them up. In the meantime, I'll take care of your successful experiments."

When he opened the door, Starko dove between his adversaries and plowed through the lab to lure his muscular foes as far away as possible from the professor. He managed to pick up his bolas that were lying like a snake between two loose slabs. Again, some instruments, tables and cabinets went flying. A liquid spilled on the floor streamed toward a frayed electrical cord and set the sparks on fire when it touched it. Thick smoke added to the chaos. The stench of burnt plastic was stronger.

Using the panic that hit the two giants, the Bronze Gladiator sprang at them, grabbed Green Boxer's arm and kneed him in the ribs. As expected, the shoulder was dislocated.

"Sorry, old boy, this was the only thing I could think of to keep you from swatting me like a fly."

The guy looked ashamed and bent over, searching for a corner to hide in so he could lick his wounds. He did not know what pain was, and it terrified him. Seeing his brother in trouble, Blue Boxer howled out and bounded toward the Bronze Gladiator, who dodged this new attack.

Now that he only had one opponent to worry about, it was easy to study his moves and spot his weaknesses for an opening. And he found one on the third charge. His bolas flew and cut down Blue Boxer in mid-air. The giant crashed into a desk that was crushed under his weight.

"Evacuation procedure commenced. All personnel go to the nearest emergency exit. Evacuation procedure commenced. All personnel..."

"Now, what's this all about, professor? Can you hear that? What's going on?"

"I don't know. It's the first time I've ever heard this message."

The professor was in a panic and barely dared a peak out of his hiding place. When he saw the two wounded giants scared and harmless, his heart sank.

"Where are you? We have to hurry."

"I just gave your two kids a big dose of adrenaline. They'll be up in a couple of minutes."

"We don't have time. Help me."

Prince Starko brought over a rolling table on which he laid Ted and William Balsam, then the professor pointed the way to the emergency elevator.

"No, it's guarded for sure," said Starko. "We'll go out the way I came in. Come on."

"And my children? We can't leave them here."

"Sure, it'd be a crime to abandon them, but they won't fit in outside, and you can't control them as you yourself admitted."

"I know a special institute in Pennsylvania that can take them. Let me redeem myself by rescuing them."

Prince Starko watched the professor attentively. His eyes looked sincere.

"Let's not drag it out. That message sounded like a bad omen. So how are you going to convince them to follow you?"

"I've got a serum in my office that will turn the fiercest tiger into a pussy cat. I was keeping it for a moment just like this."

The alarm went off again, more menacing than ever.

"I think the time has come. Hurry up because I don't know how long we have."

Starko was right. Just as the professor had finished giving the serum to his two creatures, the conduits hidden in the false ceiling opened and the pungent smell of gas replaced the unsettling smell of burnt plastic.

"Uh-uh, they're going to burn the place down. Run, professor, I'll take care of the others."

The Bronze Gladiator, who was last in line, had just come through the trapdoor when a tongue of fire shot up and licked his feet. The gust of hot air threw him to the ground.

"The men who hired you don't mess around," he said. "You really didn't know about this plan?"

"I assure you, I was told nothing."

The three trapdoors shut out the waves of heat coming from the basement.

"In a furnace like that, your laboratory will soon be just a bad memory. Come on, my driver is waiting."

"The van is there. Load up the two sleeping beauties, put your creatures in the back seat, and stay down. I'll tell my partner that we're back."

Prince Starko dashed around the van and knocked on the driver's window, ready to smile at Lorna Logan. No one. The hairs on the back of his neck stood up.

"Bronze Gladiator!"

A man's voice, loud, called out to him from the top of the factory. A dark figure stood out against the bright spotlight that was pointed at the van.

"Who are you?" Prince Starko asked.

The voice paid no attention.

"I didn't think I'd see you get out of alive from the hell let loose because of you. You have earned your reputation. Be that as it may, you have something I want, and I have something you want. Therefore, I propose a fair trade between gentlemen."

Another spotlight flashed on Lorna Logan, hanging off the building by her hands, unconscious and gagged.

"The professor for this woman. What do you say?"

Prince Starko gritted his teeth without knowing what to say. He felt a movement behind him and turned around. It was the professor coming forward with his hand held out.

"Don't forget: Kerr House, Belfast, Pennsylvania. Thank you."

Prince Starko shook his hand, resigned to his fate.

"Who are they?"

"If I tell you, you and the others won't get out of here alive. Leave me."

Reluctantly Prince Starko let him go.

"Release the woman. Be seeing you."

"Thanks, professor."

The professor went into the building without looking back.

With a swift movement, the dark figure in the light pulled out a knife and cut the rope holding Lorna Logan.

Forgetting for an instant everything around him, the Bronze Gladiator soared off to catch the unconscious girl and put her gently on the ground.

The projectors switched off; the site was drowned in darkness. For a moment Prince Starko thought of chasing the dark figure who had just kidnapped the professor, but a gasp from Lorna changed his mind. This was not the time to play hero.

A few minutes later, he was driving the van through the open, unguarded entrance and through the sleeping streets of New York City.

The snow had finally stopped falling.

"You're back at last. I was cold tonight."

Half-asleep, Janet Mason wrapped her arms around Mike Logan who had just lay down beside her in bed. Despite all his precautions he had woken her.

"Did you find them?"

"Yes."

"And?"

"They're fine now."

After bringing Lorna back home, still unconscious—he would hear about this when she woke up—the Bronze Gladiator had left the brothers at the emergency entrance of Jersey City's Medical Center, with a short note of explanation, before heading to the address the professor had given him: Kerr House, Belfast, Pennsylvania.

There, to his great surprise, he found a curious boarding school that accepted the two giants without questions, despite the unusual time and circumstances. They were safe now, sheltered from the world and well treated. The professor knew what he had been talking about.

"Yes, everyone is fine."

Morgane by J.-M. Arden

A descendent—or possibly, a reincarnation?—of the original Morgan Le Fey, young Morgane Gorlyer is a budding sorceress who does not yet control the powers of her famous ancestor—nor does she have all of her occult knowledge. She is in love with Faust, a young nobleman from the past who has been doomed to live in the form of a black cat by an ancient curse. In the tale that follows, Morgane lives an adventure at the edge of two worlds, ours and that of the fairies of ancient Brittany...

Nelly Chadour: *A Fairy's Night Dream*

A veritable human flood streamed into Glastonbury for the festival. Morgane Gorlyer felt like a little fish struggling against the current. She slipped between two sharks burned like lobsters by the early summer sun.

"Hurry up, Jeff!" she shouted over her shoulder. "The concert's starting soon."

"Calm down. I'm not an eel."

Jeff Ferin, tall and strong, with curly hair, carried his adorable two-year old son, Galaad, on his shoulders. He was a beautiful child with chubby cheeks and hair like a raven's wing. Blue, noise-reducing headphones covered his ears. He spent the day babbling and clapping at all the shows.

The trio finally got in view of the stage where the singer Laura MacKin was supposed to show up. Morgane jumped for joy. Her long, straight, black hair swung like a hypnotizing pendulum. With her pleated skirt, white blouse and black tie she looked like a high school student.

A high school student able to change a pumpkin into an Austin Mini with a simple snap of her fingers.

A high school student in love with Faust, a beautiful sorcerer transformed into a black cat.

But Jeff knew nothing about these details. He just saw her as a wonderful friend. A little eccentric, sure, but she was there for him when Anna, Galaad's mother, had died. A wonderful friend.

They found a perfect place in the shade of a refreshment stand.

Three characters with outrageous makeup and colorful clothes came out on the stage.

Applause.

"My friends, we have some bad news," one of them spoke into the microphone. "Laura MacKin, who you all came to see, has left on a belated honeymoon and won't be able to perform tonight. So, go drink a few pints to her health because she's probably making a baby for us."

Boos and hisses flew out. Laughter too.

At the same time they pushed out on stage a statue covered in a white veil and the apology continued.

"You're probably thinking: it's pathetic that we, who do not sing so well, are standing before you. But look! If I paint my eyebrows like this, I'm the spitting image of Laura!"

With more shouting the public expressed its skepticism.

Meanwhile, they set up the mysterious statue at a piano and with a grand, theatrical gesture they pulled off the veil. The thin fabric was drifting over the audience when Laura MacKin, dressed in a lacy wedding gown, launched into her first song on the piano.

On his father's shoulders Galaad imitated Morgane, who was yelling, "Lau-raaaaaa!"

The kid squealed, "Lau-waaaaaa!"

The concert started off in a cheerful mood. A violinist with long hair played around. Laura greeted her public and made jokes.

In the middle of all the crazy musicians, a young man appeared. Morgane noticed him right away. He, too, looked a little crazy, but not in the same way.

He was around sixteen years-old, skinny and sprite. Nobody on stage paid any attention to him. However, he was unmistakable with his flaming red hair and weird clothes that looked like a patchwork of dead leaves and flower petals. His legs were scrawny and feet bare. His attitude was also different. Instead of dancing with the others, he watched them with an amused, puzzled look. He even made fun of a pudgy guy before tripping him.

"Drunk already?" Laura joked.

The pudgy guy jumped up and spun around wildly. The audience laughed, believing he was clowning around.

"That kid's got some nerve," Morgane said to Jeff.

"What kid?"

"That kid who just tripped the fat guy."

Jeff raised his eyebrows. He could not see the bratty kid who was sabotaging the concert.

"*By the pricking of my thumbs, something wicked this way come*," Morgane muttered. "I'll be right back, Jeff." The young father did not even have time to argue; his friend had already disappeared into the crowd.

On stage the intruder continued his pranks. He spun around the violinist whose instrument screeched into the mic. To the musician's utter amazement, all the strings had been unwound.

"Sorry, friends," Laura laughed. "The spirits have decided to make it harder for us."

The kid bowed low. "Spirits? No, sweet minstrel, just the rascally Robin Goodfellow… Hee-hee!"

The brat jumped. An electric shock had stung his calves. He looked around furiously. Another flash crackled by his ear. He spun, ready to pounce on his attacker. And he froze at the sight of Morgane.

Squeezed up against the barrier that separated the audience from the stage, the young woman was making sparks fly off her snapping fingers. She was staring at the kid with the smile of someone who has just exposed a bad joke. But far from getting angry, the rascal smiled back, baring all his teeth. Morgane thought they were a little too sharp.

"Exquisite girl," the kid's voice could be heard over all the noise, "I am your humble servant. Your powers and your beauty could rival the fairies'."

Once his speech was finished, he leaped into the crowd. Perched atop a head that was taller than the others, he winked at the sorceress before leaping onto another, like crossing a river by jumping on rocks.

"Oh, the little weasel," she hissed and went after him, elbowing her way through the crowd.

Jeff looked for Morgane, but there were too many people. He hopped from one foot to the other, peering into the crowd. His bear-dance made his son laugh.

"Sorry to bother you, my good sir, but your child is one of the most adorable creatures I've ever seen in this part of the Earthly Realm."

The girl's voice, like a pleasant breeze through freshly bloomed flowers, lightened Jeff's foul mood. The girl was watching him intently. She was thin and wore a pink and gold dress that looked like a rumpled poppy petal. Her triangular face framed by long strands of milky blonde hair.

The girl bowed slightly. "Don't be frightened, I'm Iris, at your service."

Jeff quickly got over his surprise. She was one of performers having some fun and she would drop the act when the festival was over. "Well, then, Iris, my son and I thank you for your kind words."

"Not kind, just the truth. What's the cute prince's name?"

"Galaad."

The girl pronounced the name studiously and put her pale index finger on the babbling baby's nose, murmuring, "We'll see each other later, Galaad."

And with a final bow she skipped around Jeff like one would a tree. The young father turned round and round expecting a prank from the performer but the next thing he knew she was gone.

Unseen by Jeff a butterfly with pink petal wings fluttered above them and darted off to the ruined abbey.

Morgane had a talent for slipping through a crowd like a swift eel. But the kid was putting distance between them. It was like swimming after a person who was running on the shore. The trickster was fast and agile. His steps were airy as he leapt from one head to another. He was not human, that was sure.

The crowd finally thinned out. The rascal jumped, twirled in the air like a top and landed gracefully. Then he scampered toward a purple tent. He turned around to make sure Morgane was still on his heels before slipping between the velvet curtains.

Morgane swore at him. The little tease was going to regret it!

She rushed after the brat to nab him before he could ruin another show. Past the curtains she was in near darkness. They had decorated the place to look like a forest at night: bluish lights depicted the starry heavens. Artificial ivy wound up the metal arms supporting the tent. The spectators were sitting on cushions and on the raised stage there were actors bathed in golden light.

Morgane recognized *A Midsummer Night's Dream.*

She had come in just when the Athenian laborers met in the woods to rehearse a play they wanted to present to Duke Theseus on his wedding day. Quince was played by a tall, gangly fellow with curly hair. He gave orders and gesticulated. An actress entered. She was thin and her short, brown, mussy hair was sprinkled with fake dead leaves. She had black lines under her big eyes and she wore a khaki tunic. With hands on her hips and a mischievous sneer she made a convincing Puck:

"What hempen home-spuns have we swaggering here, so near the cradle of the fairy queen? What, a play toward! I'll be an auditor: an actor too, perhaps, if I see cause."

Morgane tensed up because the redheaded kid just showed up on stage. He dogged the steps of Girl Puck all the while staring into the audience. The huge grin that lit up his face when he saw his pursuer made Morgane shiver.

The Boy Puck pointed to the Girl Puck and said, "What smug mortal is this, prancing around on stage, counterfeiting my image? There's a price to pay for aping Robin Goodfellow."

Morgane knew right away what he planned to do. She ran toward the stage but a simple movement of his index finger exacted his fee. Before the eyes of the spectators and the stupefied performers, the false Puck was changed into a chimpanzee. She looked at her black, hairy hands and whined in fear.

"I believe," the little wizard went on, "if I'm not mistaken, in this play, this rogue here is changed into an ass."

Another twist of his finger and the actor playing Bottom started braying. He dropped on all fours and the horseshoes on his hands clopped across the boards. A wave of panic shot through the public.

When the kid turned to Quince, Morgane snapped out of her trance, "Stop this right now! Leave them alone, demon!"

"Demon, Miss? What a thing to say! And here I am just a simple little devil."

Morgane hopped on stage to grab the kid, but he vanished at her touch. The donkey slipped on the floorboards and bumped into Morgane. When she grabbed the long ears to keep her balance, the bratty kid popped up behind Quince.

"I'm doing them all a favor, pretty lady," he snickered. "Besides, don't you think his old glasses could use a new perch?"

He raised his finger. Quince's nose stretched out farther and farther. His skin turned gray. His braying turned to trumpeting, as he grew bigger. Within seconds an elephant stood in place of the actor and the stage cracked under his enormous weight.

The kid blew a kiss to Morgane, "With compliments of Robin Goodfellow, *ma belle*. We will see each other again very soon I am sure."

With that he disappeared into the panicking crowd fleeing from the terrified elephant.

The head of the huge beast was touching the top of the tent. Morgane took a deep breath and pointed her two index fingers at the animal.

"By the powers vested in me I order you, elephant, to become human again! A skinny human with glasses and ugly hair!"

The young lady concentrated. The elephant shook so hard the tent almost collapsed. But in the end the magic worked: the actor gradually took on human form. Morgane felt something tugging at her skirt. It was the little chimpanzee girl begging for her help.

"Yes, yes, one minute and it'll be your turn, and the donkey's."

After Morgane had finally got everything back to normal, she ran out without waiting for thanks. She only wanted one thing now: to get back to Jeff.

She could hardly believe that she might have just met the real Puck

Morgane told Jeff nothing. She pondered in silence. But this did not stop her from falling into a deep sleep, lying on the belly of her black cat, Faust, when she got to her friend's house.

In the meantime, in Galaad's room, the window opened without a sound. Two shadows, undeniably human and unquestionably feminine, slipped into the darkness. One of the intruders was Iris. In the palm of her hand she was holding a caterpillar. The other was a tall, haughty woman. She was beautiful like a statue of snow. The thin strips of her dress floated around her slender form. Long, crystalline eyelashes half hid her purple pupils. A crown of silver wires strung with pearls as delicate as dewdrops encircled her brow. Her black hair, tied into an elaborate braid, fell all the way to the ground.

"You see, my Queen," Iris said, "how adorable the little cherub is!"

The Queen leaned over the child. She stared at it for a long time until a smile stretched across her lips, which sparkled like frost. "This infant is just as lovable as sleeping Cupid."

Iris jumped for joy at the verdict.

The Queen picked up Galaad. She hugged it gently to her breast without waking him up. She took a minute to enjoy his silky black locks and the scent of his skin.

Frenzied scratching at the door followed by a long, menacing meow interrupted the moment of tenderness.

"What's got into you, Faust? You're going to wake Galaad," an irritated voice whispered.

The door handle turned.

"Hurry!" the Queen hissed. "Put the larva in the crib!"

Iris did as she was told. The critter writhed on the white sheet and cooed. At the same time, the door opened onto Morgane in her nightshirt and the cat Faust, a black shadow with blazing eyes who pounced on the two intruders with a screech.

A bright flash, a puff of smoke and they were gone.

Faust leapt onto the windowsill. He scanned the night through the open window and sniffed the scents on the wind. Morgane ran over to Galaad's crib. She sighed in relief when she saw the little boy sitting on his blanket. Then he opened his mouth...

...and he let out an ear-splitting howl straight out of hell, wailing of the damned that was humanly impossible for a baby's throat to produce. The walls and windows shook. Morgane plugged her ears and yelled in pain. Galaad howled and howled. He did not even stop when his distraught father burst into the room.

"What happened?" He had to scream to make himself heard.

"I don't know," Morgane screamed back. "Try to calm him down, please!"

Jeff took the little thing in his arms and started rocking it. His face turned ashen. "This... this isn't Galaad."

Morgane guessed more than heard what Jeff was saying over the infant's roar. She started biting her nails with gnawing anxiety. What evil forces had she attracted?

"You're right. It's not the flesh of your flesh. It's a Changeling."

It spoke from the darkest corner of the room. A dark hand rose up and made that movement with a finger that Morgane knew so well. The howling stopped. The little impostor lay quiet for a minute. Then it struggled, over and over, but all that came out was a squeak. The veins in its neck pulsed. Its cheeks turned purple.

"You again!" Morgane hissed.

Puck stepped out of the shadow. "Gently, pretty witch. I'm innocent of stealing the kid. That was Titania's doing. The Fairy Queen needs a baby."

"Titania..." Jeff could not believe his ears. "And you are..."

"They call me Robin Goodfellow, Hobgoblin or even Will, but my good King prefers to call me Puck." He bowed but straightened up right away when sparks singed his toes.

"Where's Galaad?" Morgane demanded.

"What a tigress," Puck mumbled, wiggling his injured toes. "And I was just going to offer you my help. See, my master, the tenebrous Oberon, doesn't much like Titania's whims. Just like he hates these wailing larva that are the babies of our race."

"Huh? All the children in the Fairy Kingdom are as noisy as this thing?" Morgane asked.

"All! And their shrieking drills and splits the eardrums until they get their first tooth after about two hundred years. That's why some fed-up fairies exchange their child for a human baby that's less grueling."

"So rather than wait two hundred years Titania stole my son." Jeff was disgusted by the creature writhing in his arms. Hastily he put it back in the crib.

He's taking this well, Morgane thought to herself.

"Our Queen's heart is like that," Puck sighed. "But if you follow me and trust me, I'll bring you to the kiddie. The bear will get his cub, the sorceress will discover the beauty of fairy flowers, and all's well that ends well!"

Morgane looked at Faust. The cat snorted in contempt. But what choice did they have?

Ten minutes later, they were moving through the streets guided by a leaping Puck. Faust was with them. He trotted along keeping an eye on the hobgoblin. Morgane felt the pocket of her coat fluttering. She had changed the fairy baby into a mouse with the idea that it would be eaten by Faust if it tried to escape. So now it was stuck deep inside the quivering pocket.

The majestic outline of a big oak tree loomed into the night sky. Jeff stopped. His wife was buried near that tree.

"You're bringing us to the cemetery, aren't you?" he asked.

"The cemetery lies next to the ruins of the abbey," Puck stated. "The majestic stone arches are a perfect passage, I dare say, between our two Kingdoms."

Coming back to the place where Anna lay was a painful reminder for Jeff that he might also lose Galaad if they failed.

They entered the cemetery like thieves in the night. Puck pointed to a stone arch that was missing its keystone. "And here's the door."

But Faust left the group. He went over to the oak tree and sniffed at its roots.

"What do you smell, Faust?" Morgane asked.

"Let the pint-sized panther do his dirty work," Puck said.

Morgane did not listen: Faust was pawing at the roots. She went and helped him dig up some dirt and clumps of grass. She ended uncovering a slab of stone as smooth as a headstone. Faust meowed again and put his paw on the slab. It would take magic to bring up what was beneath.

Jeff, who had paused a moment by Anna's grave, came over to them.

"Don't come any closer, Jeff. I'm going to invoke what's buried here."

Puck brooded a safe distance away.

"By the powers vested in me," Morgane intoned, stretching her fingers toward the half-buried slab, "you who lie under these roots, come out of your sheath of soil and breathe the night air."

Faust leapt back when the ground rose under his paws as if the earth itself was breathing. A column of dirt and grass lifted off the ground. Morgane, Jeff and Faust watched it slowly rise almost seven feet high. The thing wiped off the dust and dirt that covered it, revealing rusted armor. It was a gigantic knight whose face was hidden behind a helmet topped with a crown. A heavy, musty cap hung on his wide shoulders. His iron gauntlets gripped the handle of a monstrous, double-edged sword whose metal shined coldly in the moonlight. The knight put a hand to his heart and bowed before the dazed group. Then he turned to help another form, much more frail, rise out of the freshly dug-up grave. The face of the second, all dressed in black, could not be seen behind her dark veil.

"We are the guardians of the Door between the two Kingdoms," the woman said. "This is the Knight-King. And I am Lady Parturia."

"Uh... We are Lady Morgane, Sire Jeff, cat Faust, and sassy Puck," Morgane responded.

"Will you help us find my son?" Jeff asked.

The veiled woman turned to him and stood silent for a moment before answering. "The Knight and I have foregone eternal rest to come to the aide of the mortal victims of fairies. The Knight will guard the door, preventing any other intrusion into this world and I will keep the passage open during our expedition."

"*Our* expedition?" Puck scoffed. "But they already have a guide, Lady Parturia."

"Can we call someone a guide who would get lost just for the fun of it?" the Lady replied coldly.

Puck mumbled under his breath and scowled. Then he sighed and clenched his fists, "So be it." And without even seeing if the others were following he jumped through the ruined arch.

On the other side he was just a faint shadow. The veiled woman waved Jeff and Morgane to follow. The young lady took her friend's hand and Faust stuck close to his mistress' leg. The Knight strode behind them, his armor clanking at every movement. And they went through the stone arch.

It felt like going through a cloud of odorless, tasteless smoke. But on the other side the landscape was very different. It was a forest so dense and thick with trees that sunlight had never touched the long, purple leaves of the bushes or the huge black trees as smooth as obsidian. All kinds of mushrooms lit the forest with intense phosphorescence.

Morgane turned around. Instead of the stone arch was another arch, huge and wide, formed by a gaping hole in a baobab. Standing before the opening the Knight-King nodded reassuringly to Morgane. She was bitterly sorry that such a force of nature was not coming with them.

A hand fell on her shoulder. She knew the gentle touch. She turned slowly and saw the handsome, smiling face that she always hoped to see again someday.

"Faust!"

Her lover was back in human form. In this world he was no longer under the spell that changed him into a cat. Morgane hugged him. She felt their two hearts beating as one. It had been such a long time. Tears of joy clouded her vision.

"Faust, I can't believe it! I missed you so much!"

"Being a cat has its advantages but I have to admit that not being able to hold you in my arms has been torture," the handsome sorcerer said, kissing her forehead.

The others watched the scene in silence. Puck's face was completely blank, but his eyes darted from Faust to Morgane and back again.

Jeff was lost. "Where... where's the cat?"

"He's still here," Morgane laughed, putting her hand on Faust's shoulder. "When we've found Galaad, I think I'll spend the rest of the night explaining some things to you."

It was Puck at the head when they started off. His step was so light that it left no trace on the ground. Morgane and Faust followed him holding hands; Jeff was looking all around, fascinated by the strange plants. Lady Parturia was the last in line. Her black dress glided silently over the leaves and flowers. Puck was all ears. He kept turning around to motion the others to make less noise.

"What? Playtime's over?" Morgane snapped.

"Know, sweet sorceress, that my master Oberon and Titania, although bound by marriage, are committed to a fierce, mutual hatred. As servant of the King of elves, I am not welcome in the Queen's realm."

"This is not the right way," Lady Parturia whispered. "Why the detour?"

"Approaching from the rear we can stay concealed," Puck whispered back.

Lady Parturia did not reply but under the veil she kept her eyes on the boy.

The road opened onto a clearing with a huge dead tree covered in gray lichen. All the vegetation in the area was rotting.

"We're not far, mortals. Take a short break before continuing," Puck murmured.

Faust frowned, "I don't like this place."

"Ho, ho!" Puck mocked. "Is the pretty, noble wizard scared of a sterile clearing and a shriveled up tree?" Snickering, Puck jumped onto a high branch in the dead tree. "See? No danger. We're the only ones here, you, me..." He showed them a nasty smile and kicked the trunk. "And this good old Arboleus."

The dead tree pulled itself out of the ground bellowing dreadfully. Two bulging eyes opened in the middle of a monstrous face covered with knotty bumps. Morgane and Faust raised their hands crackling with magic for a counterattack. But leafless tentacles were already winding around their arms. Other lumps and bumps were springing from the ground in a cloud of gray dust. The four mortals were quickly shackled.

"Hold the arms of those two there so they can't use their magic," Puck ordered the tree monster. "But don't squeeze that mortal girl too tight. I'd be very upset if you tore the skin of my beloved."

Arboleus opened a gaping mouth full of slobbering teeth and rumbled, "Eat!"

"Let me take care of the charming girl first and then you can feast."

Puck took a red flower from a small pouch hanging on his belt. The petals were a little withered but still radiated a blood-red brilliance. He tilted back Morgane's head. She closed her eyes as hard as she could when the demon rubbed the flower juice on her eyes.

"What are you doing? Leave me alone, you little snot! Faust!"

"Morgane!" Faust was twisting and turning but the tentacles held him fast. He winced in pain.

Despite her panic Morgane felt a gentle freshness around her eyelids like a cool breeze after a heat wave. It tickled her eyeballs, made her optic nerves vibrate like a zither being delicately plucked. All of these feelings created an enchanting music in her brain that sped up her heartbeat and warmed her veins.

"Don't open your eyes!" Lady Parturia shouted.

At the same time Faust groaned with pain. Then Morgane opened her eyes. And the first face she saw was Puck's. She thought him so beautiful she could cry.

"Who are you?" she panted. "It's like I've been waiting for you all my life."

"Let her go, Arboleus," Puck was quivering with joy. Cupid's Flower was working its spell.

The tentacles freed the prey. Morgane fell forward into the arms of her new prince. She breathed in the heady scent of her love. He was no longer a little imp in a kid's body. He was a prince, a splendor, a god whose glittering eyes pierced her to her very soul.

"I think I'm going to die."

"Love is a delightful little death," Puck whispered. "Let me revive you with a kiss."

The traitor's lips moved slowly toward Morgane's. Faust was shaking with rage. He struggled to free himself, called out to Morgane, begged her to wake up. Tired of the young sorcerer's theatrics, Arboleus lifted him off the ground and carried him toward his huge mouth.

While Faust was looking at an ugly death, Morgane offered her lips to the demon. Puck's lips intoxicated her and she got dizzy. Faust felt tears in his eyes, hoping that the tree monster would swallow him quickly.

Meanwhile Jeff felt the tentacles' grip on him relax. The monster was focusing all its attention on Faust. So, he took the opportunity to grab the Swiss knife in his pocket and, with all the desperate strength he could muster, he stuck the blade in the tentacle. The vegetal leviathan hurled in fury. It dropped Faust and turned its anger on the insolent little human who had scratched it. This insect with its ridiculous spine would be its feast.

Faust was free, but in pain. Black spots danced before his eyes when he stood up. Still, he lost no time. Arboleus was about to swallow Jeff who was screaming in terror.

The young sorcerer cried out as loud as he could, "By the powers vested in me, dead tree you seem, dead tree you be!"

Arboleus roared one last time, then froze. Its eyes sunk back into the bark and closed. Its tentacles dried up, broke off under Jeff's weight and he fell into the gaping hole. But he landed safely on a pile of earth and dead leaves, all that remained of the monster's tongue.

Lady Parturia shook off her brittle binding and ran to the tree corpse to help Jeff.

Morgane hugged Puck while watching her former love with fear. Faust walked up to them slowly. His jaws were grinding, his fists clenched.

"Free her from the spell!"

"Or else what? What are you going to do, mortal? Kill me? You'll have to dodge this spell first!"

Puck raised his finger and scowled at the sorcerer. Faust felt invisible hands all over him. He focused on his memory, recalling the image he saw in the mirrors before his curse.

"I am Faust. I will stay Faust," he chanted, feeling the hands knead his flesh, pinch his skin, trying to remodel him into whatever the wicked elf desired.

Faust's form was rippling and blurring like a reflection in troubled waters.

"My beloved," Puck was getting angry that he could not break his rival's defense, "come and help me. Together we will subdue this fiend."

"Your wish is my command, my love," Morgane whispered.

She pointed at Faust. He felt his heart break at the cold determination of his beloved. Oh, how much he hated that horrid kid! He felt himself being brutally attacked by two magic forces. They gripped him and whipped him. They were going to tear him to pieces.

A stick hit Puck hard on his head.

Startled, Morgane lost her concentration. She turned to Jeff who was picking up another stick. Morgane did not have time to avenge her seducer because Faust was using his magic.

"By the powers vested in me, Puck, change into the animal you are like."

Puck's cry turned into a feeble yelp. Red fur covered his body as it shrank. In short time he was just a little fox trembling at Morgane's feet. Her mouth dropped open. She looked back and forth from the animal to Faust.

"Morgane…" he started to say.

"You!"

She spit out the word so venomously that Faust recoiled, terrified. His girlfriend was raging mad. Her beautiful eyes were opened wide and flashing daggers. Her black hair twisted around her face deformed by hatred.

"You're going to pay for that!"

Sparks of fury jumped out of her fingertips. The magic bolt she unleashed surprised him with its strength. Hatred and anger had multiplied her powers. Hatred directed against him, Faust realized tragically. Getting back his human form after so long and seeing her stand against him was a kind of cruel irony. He managed to put up a magic barrier that made her bolt explode on impact. Blinded by the blazing spray, Jeff and Lady Parturia covered their eyes. Puck took the opportunity to scamper away.

Lady Parturia took Jeff's arm, "We can do nothing for them. Let's follow that lying trickster. He'll lead us to his master."

"But my son?" Jeff muttered. "He's with Titania."

"And he's safely guarded by the Fairy Queen," she said. "Oberon is the only one able to break the spell on your delirious friend. Put your arm around my waist and trust me."

Jeff had no choice but to obey. He hugged the slender waist of the veiled woman and felt like he recognized her fragrance. But he had no time to think about it: Lady Parturia soared off at full speed through the trees. The ground sped away under their feet. Jeff let himself by carried, the fast wind blowing through his curly hair. Ahead of them in the distance the little red fox was scurrying away.

Titania sat on a sumptuous carpet woven of countless flowers with perfumed corolla. Next to her Galaad was tapping on small, silver bells. They had a pretty ring. The music delighted the infant. Titania had the prettiest toys brought to him: a flute made of nymph reed, a tambourine with gold cymbals, a lily branch whose every flower was a crystal, a spinning-top that sparkled... Nothing was too precious for the little adopted prince.

A series of explosions jerked them out of playtime. Titania felt a poisonous wave wash over her, full of anger. She quivered and hugged Galaad close to her heart. "Tell the Howlers to go and see what's happening right now!"

All the racket might attract the attention of her hateful spouse who was only interested in destroying the Queen's happiness.

"Morgane, listen to me, that kid put a spell on you! A kid! You're just a toy to him, a whim, and when he's had enough of you…"

"Shut up! You have no right to talk like that about my Puck!"

Morgane accented her shouting with bolts of lightning that Faust blocked the best he could. Puck had bewitched her with an immature and impatient love. She was reacting like a teenager whose parents did not like her boyfriend. Except that normal girls could not wipe out their parents with a snap of their fingers.

Faust changed tactics, "Morgane, don't you remember our love? You were so happy when I got back my true form. You hugged me so tight! Our hearts beat as one in perfect harmony. Have you forgotten already?"

Morgane looked confused. Tears welled up in her eyes. Conflicting thoughts clashed in her mind. She remembered the warmth of his arms (Puck!), his kisses (Puck!), she trusted him (Puck!).

PUCK!

Her memories shattered under the force of the elf's spell. The tears rolling down her cheek were now tears of rage.

"All that… is over!" she spit out.

Morgane picked up the remains of a tentacle and threw it at Faust. The branch turned into a raven with razor-sharp claws. The sorcerer raised his arms to protect himself from the bird trying to pluck out his eyes with its beak. Faust understood that this was just a diversion when a bolt hit him head on. The impact threw him into the bushes. He tried to get up but he felt like he had been hit by a train. The raven, however, had taken the brunt of the explosion. It stank of burned flesh. Faust shook it off him in disgust. Morgane was marching toward him, hands up, ready to finish him off.

Lady Parturia squeezed Jeff a little closer to her. "Oberon's castle," she said.

Jeff would have dropped to his knees from shock if the veiled woman were not carrying him like a baby. He saw a thin, black building whose summit was lost in the treetops. It was like a giant piece of carved onyx. Thousands of narrow windows filtered the opal-white light. Fox-Puck was already at the entrance. Jeff noticed that there was no drawbridge or portcullis. The entrance was a huge, elaborately carved mouth of a giant dragon's head. Its eyes turned red at the animal's approach.

Lady Parturia and Jeff stopped at a respectable distance and crouched behind some hawthorn bushes.

The dragon's stony mouth cracked open in a sarcastic smile bristling with unsavory fangs. It spoke in a rumbling voice that rolled out like an earthquake. "Who goes there, trotting around in a strange shape? Is it the one we call Robin Goodfellow? Greetings Renard Goodfox!"

The joke was delivered maliciously. Puck yelped.

"I don't understand that language. What do you want, little red bug?"

Puck lowered his ears, dejected. The little animal looked so helpless that Jeff almost pitied it.

The enormous stone head laughed at his calamity. "Should I let you in so you can go running up to our master's throne? Is that what you want?"

Puck looked up expectantly. The dragon was considering. Its red eyes suddenly fell upon Lady Parturia and Jeff. The latter fell backward, struck by fear.

"But first I have to decide if I'm going to burn these two intruders. Come closer, mortals, don't be scared. My fiery breath is so hot that you'll be reduced to ashes before you feel a thing."

"Thank you, noble gate of the royal palace, but you see, our presence here is justified," Lady Parturia walked up boldly. "The rules have been broken twice on *your* part. And Oberon needs to be informed about it."

The stony head raised a scaly eyebrow, "Really? And what are these infractions?"

"Kidnapping a mortal child whose father right here is under my protection. And…" Lady Parturia pointed accusingly at the fox who was cowering on the ground. "The spell that this clown put on the eyes of a mortal girl to make her love him. The magic disturbances you must have felt are nothing but the consequences of the enchantment."

The dragon seemed to weigh the pros and cons. In the end, the veiled woman's words won out. With a sigh he opened his mouth to reveal the dark entranceway. At the end of it shone the same opaline light as in the windows.

"Enter!"

Lady Parturia took Jeff's hand and they walked into the corridor warmed by the dragon's breath.

The closer Morgane got, snapping and sparking her fingers, the farther into the forest Faust backed up. He would never have suspected such sadism from her. She was taking her time; her face was contorted by hate. Then her expression froze and her eyes grew wide with fear. Faust turned around and lost his breath: women in white armor surrounded them. Neither he nor Morgane had heard them arrive. They were beautiful, in their way, their hair braided with pearls and their silvery skin. They were beautiful despite their too wide mouths and powerful jaws.

A little girl was at the head. "I'm Iris and you're in Queen Titania's territory, mortals. You're disturbing our Kingdom's peace with all your inconsiderate use of magic. In the name of our Queen, leave here or perish."

"We cannot leave here without the mortal child your Queen took," Faust said.

"And I'm not leaving without Puck," Morgane growled.

Faust shook his head. Great! Titania's warriors would think they were working for the enemy.

"I see. In that case, farewell. Be brave, the Howlers are going to hurt you a little." With that she disappeared.

The women surrounding them smiled voraciously, literally from ear to ear their mouths were so wide. And they let loose an inhuman, unbearable shriek. Faust thought his ears were going to explode and his guts were going to melt. Behind him Morgane was rolling on the ground with her hands over her ears.

"By... by the powers vested in me," Faust muttered inaudibly, "I command you... to become mute as fish."

The shrieking quieted down a little. One of the Howlers touched her throat. No more sound came out of her open mouth. But the others still had their voice. Faust grimaced. His magic only worked on one of them at a time.

He turned to Morgane, "Please help me stop them!"

She looked dazed. Tears rolled down her cheeks. "It's too loud! It hurts!"

She remembered the fairy baby and his piercing cries that made the whole house shake.

The fairy baby...

Puck said they were the most feared creatures in the Kingdom. Morgane stuck her hand in her pocket while trying to cover one ear with her shoulder. The fairy baby transformed into a mouse was trembling in her hand, its ears bleeding from the howls.

"Please don't be dead, little one."

Morgane lifted it up to face the Howlers who were laughing at her. Then she said, "By the powers vested in me, mouse, I command you to turn back into the insufferable baby."

Right away it was no longer a rodent but a wriggling infant that she was holding by its neck. Its pointy ears were still bleeding and it had a runny nose. It looked to be in terrible pain. But the Howlers stepped back when they saw it.

The fairy baby took a deep breath and shot them each a nasty look. The cry that sprang out of its mouth bent the bushes and blew leaves off the trees. Morgane advanced on the Howlers with her deafening little package. Titania's killers could not stand it. They turned tail and ran away.

Morgane put the baby down gently on the ground and he went tottering after the Howlers, determined to make them pay for what he suffered as a mouse.

Morgane dropped to her knees. Her ears were ringing as if she were standing in the middle of a symphony of bells.

Faust's muffled voice got through to her, "Well done, Morgane."

"I'm not finished with you," she mumbled. "I just have to get my strength back and then..."

"Come now, dear, don't be angry. I'm bringing back your lover." This voice was foreign to her. It was deep and soft like velvet.

Faust and Morgane straightened up and looked around.

Where Titania's guards preferred white, King Oberon's had a penchant for black. Some knights wearing dark, chitinous armor sat on heavily caparisoned horses who were pawing the ground. Faust saw Jeff and Lady Parturia riding behind two of the knights.

At the head of the group was King Oberon himself. He sat proudly on a huge charger with red eyes. He was all black, from the tips of his boots to the crown of midnight stones. Only his skin was white as marble. He looked the two mortals up and down as they stood there bewildered.

Then Puck popped up in front of Morgane in his old form and the girl embraced him.

"Oh, my dear, my love! I thought I'd never see you again."

Puck caressed her hair. His eyes pleaded with his master but the King was inflexible. Puck hugged her one last time then he took a flask out of his sleeve and poured a few drops into Morgane's eyes, murmuring, "A mortal girl for a mortal boy, leave Puck alone and unhappy, sweet ingrate."

Morgane stumbled back, rubbing her eyes. She felt a strange bitterness in her heart. Slowly, the music that had boiled her blood went silent. She turned to Faust and a new flame lit up her face. The heat of shame.

"Faust... I'm so sorry..."

Tears welled up in her eyes. Her friend wiped them away. His touch was gentle, his smile tender. He had his Morgane back even if the memory of the last few minutes still stung.

"There you go!" Puck said to Oberon and, without looking back, he fled into the woods like the shadow of a punished child.

Jeff and Lady Parturia got off the horses. Jeff went up to the King, hesitated, then spurt out, "What about my son, Your Majesty?"

"Patience, mortal, I hear the Grand Duke coming."

A huge shadow cut through the trees. It soared in, carrying in its claws a bundled up little shape.

"Galaad!" Jeff shouted with joy.

The Grand Duke dropped the confused infant into its father's arms.

"Papa!" the baby babbled.

Jeff covered Galaad with tears of relief and kisses.

In the distance they heard a scream so harrowing that everyone froze. To the sound of breaking ice the forest was covered with frost, the trees and bushes enveloped in ice.

"Ah," Oberon sighed, "Titania found out we took her little human. She's raging like a she-wolf. I feel a new war coming on. How annoying."

The King of Elves turned to the humans. His obsidian eyes were flashing.

"I deigned to grant your request, but I advise you to get away without delay. My knights love to hunt your kind. Let our paths never cross again. Farewell, mortals and be fleet of foot."

58

Oberon turned the bridle and his dark figure disappeared into the forest twilight.

"My friends," Lady Parturia said, "I believe we should run... *now*."

She took Jeff's hand, then Morgane's who had just enough time to grab Faust's, and they sped off. The veiled woman ran like a hare. Morgane felt like a kite being carried on the wind. Behind them the cavalcade of hell was stamping the ground with its ironclad hooves. They were lucky to be able to flee under the Lady's magic influence because the horses were hot on their heels. Morgane felt hot breath on the nape of her neck...

"We made it!"

They had arrived at the giant tree that was the gate between the two Kingdoms. And in front of the gate the Knight-King was marching forward. His step was heavy and determined. The blade of his sword gleamed. Just when one of the chargers was about to stomp on Faust, the Knight-King attacked. His sword split open the dark knight and his horse in a geyser of black blood. The rest of Oberon's guard stopped short. Fascinated by the sight Morgane did not realize that Lady Parturia had brought them over the threshold. Completely exhausted she collapsed without letting go of Faust's hand... or rather his paw.

"Oh no!"

The cat meowed sadly. Morgane picked him up and cradled him her arms. She cried. She cried for losing his human form. She cried for losing the time to enjoy it.

The cat snuggled against her cheek. He purred to comfort her.

Jeff was also cradling his son. But he was laughing. Tomorrow he would think it was all a dream.

The Knight stepped back into the human world. Its rusted armor was covered in blood. A sweeping wave of his huge gauntlet and the passage between the two Kingdoms was closed once more, showing only the ruined arch. He stood beside Lady Parturia and greeted Morgane, Faust, Jeff and Galaad. Then he lumbered back into his ditch.

Before following him Lady Parturia spoke to Jeff, "There is a way to keep the fairies away from your son. Go to the river that winds north out of the abbey. Search the banks and the running water. You will find a smooth, flat stone with a hole in the middle. It will keep him safe as long as he wears it."

Rain fell. Black clouds hid the stars. A cold wind kicked up. It raised the veil of Lady Parturia. Jeff caught a glimpse of Galaad's mother. Anna smiled at him before the veil fell back down. Another gust of wind and she was gone.

Tomorrow he would think it was all a dream.

In the Fairy Kingdom, Titania's court was frozen in frost and sorrow. The Queen wandered through the icy castle cradling empty air in her arms.

In Oberon's castle, Puck had lost his taste for jokes. He sat thoughtful at the foot of the throne. He could not forget the taste of the mortal's kiss.

Morgane went back to France with Faust. She had promised to do whatever it took to break the spell. She promised to never again waste precious time.

In Glastonbury, Jeff made a pretty necklace for Galaad with a woven leather strap and a smooth stone with a hole in the middle. He smiled watching his son play with a little silver bell.

Rod Zey by Christophe Ouvrard

Homicron is an energy being from Alpha, an advanced civilization of space explorers. He merged with the body of Apollo astronaut Ted White, transforming him into a superhero in order to fight the Kyrosians, war-like extraterrestrials who threatened Earth. He was eventually captured and tortured by them, and his energy matrix was then transferred to Ted's girlfriend, NASA physicist Rita Tower, who became the new Homicron. This story takes place between episodes 4 and 5 of the new Homicron origin story. Rod Zey is Head of Security for the multinational oil company Patriot Petroleum. He is their multi-talented "fixer", totally devoid of scruples and sparing no effort in order to please his employer...

Fabien Clavel: *Who Will Take Care of Rita Tower?*

Homicron sits with her hands on the table. She is shivering. Her long chestnut hair falls over her handcuffs. She does not look up until someone enters her cell. It is a Kyrosian, over six and a half feet-tall, covered in reddish scales. The door slides closed behind him.

Only then does Homicron realize how dark the room is. A single ray of light flickers over an elaborate machine that hums menacingly. Wires connect it to the young woman's arms.

"Don't try to escape," the Kyrosian mutters. "Klein magnetic fields will hold you back. And you're fully aware of what this prototype can do."

Homicron nods silently.

"Good," the reptilian humanoid continues. "So, you're going to tell us everything you know."

The young woman stares at him long and hard, her jaws clenched, her green eyes sparkling with defiance. After an endless silence her body relaxes and she says, "OK."

Homicron entered William Brown's office apprehensively. She was still not comfortable in her new super-hero outfit, skin-tight and purple with a big yellow H.

The director of CLASH[1] welcomed her with a big smile on his sharp face and he invited her to sit down, turning his back to the screens blanketing the wall behind him. He took off his glasses and asked her gently, "How are you, Rita?"

"I'm fine, thanks. The sedatives are still working."

"Are you getting used to your new powers?"

She nodded curtly. "I haven't noticed any harmful effects, if that's what you mean. I can sometimes feel a strange energy flux. That's all."

Brown put his glasses back on and the reflection hid the glimmer in his eyes. "You suffered through a lot lately. Ted White didn't make it, but your body absorbed an Alphan..."

She broke in, "Sir, my fiancé is not really dead. By fusing with Homicron, I've got all the memories of both Ted and the Alphan. We are one now. Even if I can still only access scraps of his memory, nobody has ever known such a degree of intimacy. And I'm fine," she repeated.

Brown nodded, apparently convinced. "Great. That's all I need to hear. As the director, it's my duty to take care of you. Therefore, I'm going to send you on a little mission..."

Rita was a little startled, "Already? Well, if you say so..."

"It's the best way to see if you're truly ready. Even if the battle with the Kyrosians seems to have ended, we're still purging our ranks of all the reptilians that infiltrated them. And we're trying hard to dismantle their bases that are still active on our soil. It's this second project I need you for."

He pressed a button and a map of the USA appeared on the main screen.

---

[1] Consortium for Law-Enforcement Action for the Security of Humanity. A UN organization.

"Our agents have spotted an old WSU[2] base on the Mexican border in Texas, smack dab in the middle of the desert. According to our latest reports, that base should have been evacuated, but we'd like to send in a team to secure the site. We don't want to take any risks. Do you think you're ready to lead a team?"

"Sure," Homicron answered. "Sounds like something I can handle."

"Great," Brown said. "You take off in 30 minutes with a squad from our task force. Mr. Song will brief you. Good luck. I hope to see your report on my desk tonight."

Homicron stood up. "You'll have it."

Rod Zey's blue eyes roam back and forth to the reptilian guards standing on either side of his cell door. "Boys, you sure don't look like good-luck charms."

He sighs and stretches his wide shoulders, in spite of the handcuffs around his wrists. Pearls of sweat sit on his brow.

A third Kyrosian comes in and sits in front of him. "Mr. Zey," he growls, "according to our information, you are an ordinary human, the dregs of this wretched pack. So you can't survive a long torture. Therefore, I'm asking you to tell us exactly what you're doing here."

Rod Zey runs one hand through his blonde hair and starts laughing. "Well, you really know how to negotiate, don't you? OK, relax, I'll tell you everything I know."

The Hummers from Patriot Petroleum sped across the Texan desert, raising clouds of dust that covered the vehicles.

Rod Zey turned to the squad leader, an old soldier with a rugged face who took a pretty dim view of the Head of Security trespassing on his turf.

"How long till we get there?" he asked.

"Five minutes, Mr. Zey," the veteran grumbled.

---

[2] World Safety Unit. Another UN organization, devoted to ecology.

"Relax, friend, I didn't come along to get in your way. I'm just making sure you don't miss anything interesting…"

"Interesting?"

"Yeah, if the base was really evacuated in a hurry, the Kyrosians might have left behind some scientific materials of utmost importance to us. Imagine what Dr. Tanaka would give to get a hold of some new weapons… We might find something useful for ourselves too…"

The jeeps came to a halt then. Rod Zey donned his sunglasses and climbed out of the air-conditioned cab. The dry heat invaded him instantly. He looked around. The sun was glaringly white and made the bright dunes ripple.

"Nothing but gypsum here. Not even a coyote. I don't know where you see a base…"

"There are all kinds of military zones in the White Sands desert," the squad leader replied, glad to be better informed than his superior.

"I know," Zey said. "You worked on them for three years before joining our ranks. If only you hadn't stolen government material, you'd still be cracking the whip." He smiled wryly at the squad leader. "I know my job too."

The soldier winced and brought the conversation back to their mission. "A satellite found an entrance a hundred yards from here."

"Let's go."

Twenty men marked off the zone while Zey and the squad leader walked forward. They came upon a metal door stuck in the ground and swept clean by the wind.

"Blow this up for me!"

The bomb specialists set the charges and scurried away. The explosion blew buckets of sparkling sand in all directions.

"C'mon! Let's go!" the squad leader ordered.

They dove into the gaping hole and hurried down the ramp. The interior was both cool and dark. Rod Zey had to take off his sunglasses to take in the huge underground room. Except for the crates at the foot of the ramp, the place was almost empty. The only things on the walls were big ventilation grills. But beneath the steel-beamed vault stood a weird-looking machine, a kind of huge, dark monolith with a plethora of antennas.

"There's nobody here," the squad leader observed. "What is that thing?"

"That thing, as you call it," said Zey, "looks a lot like a machine built by the Kyrosians. Search the site but this is all we need. This is worth a fortune!"

The Kyrosian comes into the room and faces Homicron. "From now on, we shall know if your information matches the other prisoner's."

"And if he's lying?" Rita asks. "It's a habit. You can see it in the eyes."

"We know our job and we'll know if he's lying."

She raises her hand loaded with cables and points at the prototype. "I don't really have a choice anyway."

"True. When did you realize that it's the kind of machine we used on Ted White?"

In response, she sneers silently.

"Homicron, we have a problem."

"What's wrong?"

"We've picked up movement around the entrance to the base."

Rita leaned over in the helicopter to see where the pilot was looking. Indeed, a half dozen big Hummers, camouflaged in white dust, were parked nearby.

"Set it down over there," she ordered immediately.

She would have liked to go alone, but the idea of flying out of a moving helicopter seemed a little dangerous. Not for her, but for the team. She would start her tests later. A desert was the perfect place for it; William Brown had thought of everything.

The copters landed a safe distance from the cars. Squinting, Rita tried to adapt her vision to use infrared rays. The cars were air-conditioned and therefore cold. But they had left the engines running, proof that the visitors did not figure on staying long. By concentrating hard, Homicron could detect that no one was in the vehicles. They had not even placed guards outside.

The task force jumped down into the pure white sand. It spread out in formation and slowly approached the door. Rita followed them, feeling both useless and dangerous to her team. Homicron's powers had no known limits. And she was not sure she could control them.

The doors had been blown off. The first comers were obviously not concerned with details.

Silently, the team entered the underground complex. Cooler air welcomed them. They snuck down a long ramp that ended in a big room with a vaulted ceiling reinforced by metal beams. They hid behind some crates. Voices echoed. In the distance, Rita recognized the tall outline of Rod Zey. So, Patriot Petroleum had gotten the jump on them!

But her attention was immediately drawn to the machine that dominated the center of the room. It was a chrome ball bristling with sharp, formidable spikes. Rita felt her body turn cold. She recognized the machine that had inflicted an endless torture on Ted White, on Homicron, and finally on her—until the pain was too great for the Alphan!

She stood paralyzed, unable to move. She concentrated and tried to rein in the part of her that was rearing up to flee.

"Drop your weapons!"

Two men had just appeared behind them. They were wearing *ghillie suits*, which made them completely invisible and undetectable in the desert. The rest of the men from Patriot Petroleum converged on the CLASH team.

Rita cursed her incompetence. She had missed everything! In the end, even with Ted's memories, she was still just a scientist, not a soldier.

"Ma'am? What are our orders?" a soldier asked.

When she didn't answer he asked again, more frenzied, "What do we do?"

The interrogator comes back and sits in front of Rod Zey. The Kyrosian and the human stare hard at each other.

"So far your information agrees with what we already know. Make sure it stays that way."

"This is the moment you promise me a quick and painless death, right?"

"Exactly."

Zey shakes his cuffed hands. His face is turning beet red. The heat is getting to him. "So, let's go."

The squad leader turned to Rod Zey after getting the message in his earpiece. "Sir, it seems we have visitors. Three helicopters just landed near the base."

"Did they see our sentinels?"

"No."

Zey smiled, "Let 'em in. We'll corner them in here. But I want this machine protected; it's our most precious booty."

The men surrounded the prototype while Rod Zey kept talking casually with his second-in-command. Nevertheless, he was wondering who could have found out this base so quickly. CRIMEN? CLASH? He would know soon enough.

"The sentinels are ready. We've got around twenty newcomers. By the looks of their uniforms, they're CLASH."

"Order them to surrender. We don't want a bloodbath in here."

A voice rang out in the distance, "Drop your weapons!"

Rod Zey and the other men slowly turned their weapons toward the ramp. The CLASH team looked totally surprised, especially the woman at their head. She was masked but superb with green eyes and long chestnut hair. She wore a skin-tight, shiny purple suit that showed off her whole body. A big yellow H outlined her curves.

"Could this be the famous Homicron? Or rather Femicron if I'm seeing right," said Zey, raising his voice when she froze staring at the machine.

He walked up to her, curious to get a closer look at the freshly honed superhero.

"As you can see, we've already got hold of what the WSU left behind. Please put down your weapons and wait quietly while we get all this stuff out of here. Then you can go home."

Homicron did not even look at him. She was clearly overwhelmed. Then he understood.

"That's the machine they used to torture the old Homicron, isn't it?"

He barely had time to gloat when gunfire broke out.

The Kyrosian watches Rita Tower whose face has turned white as death.

"Let's go back to when we attacked. The other prisoner gave us a very unsatisfactory version."

"I hope you made him sweat!"

"We did make him sweat."

She manages a faint smile, then replies, resigned, "The different version doesn't surprise me. Everything turned to chaos. Myself, I got it only after the machine...

Gunfire broke out, shaking Homicron out of her daze. She suddenly realized that she was surrounded by Patriot Petroleum men who, in turn, were surrounded by Kyrosians!

At the sight of them, she was filled with terrible rage. These disgusting creatures had tortured her despicably. No, it was Ted White, her fiancé, who had suffered the torment!

She was thrown off-kilter for a instant while bullets flew around her.

"Take cover, ma'am!"

She looked back and the machine was still there. She should not be afraid of it.

But, all of a sudden, a figure broke ranks and headed for the prototype. It was the damned louse from Patriot Petroleum. What was his name? Rod Zey! He apparently knew the importance of the machine and was trying to steal it from right under their noses. His henchmen were pushing it onto a wheeled cart.

The extraterrestrials were caught in the crossfire of the men from CLASH and from the multinational oil company, but this did not slow them down. On the contrary, with their superior weapons, especially those serpent-blades glowing green and some kind of magnetic net, they were plowing through their enemies.

A dozen men had fallen under the eerie crackling and more were dropping every second. The element of surprise was devastating. Where were they coming from? Homicron spied some hiding places hollowed out of the walls and concealed by metal panels that looked like ventilation grills.

Homicron forced herself to get up and leave her men. She felt her body rise from the ground on a cushion of antigravity. Energy flowed into her limbs. Throwing her fist forward to give her some momentum, she launched herself at the prototype. It was her first flight since fusing with the Alphan. She felt a dangerous thrill.

Rod Zey was already reacting! Spinning the cart around so the machine faced her, he aimed a kind of cannon and, before she could reach him, he fired.

Struck head on, she felt like she was cut in two and drained of energy. Her levitation failed and she plummeted to the ground, out of breath. But she had managed to grab Zey and drag him down with her. Seeing that the prototype did not have the desired effect, he pulled out his pistol as gunfire continued spewing around them. But he could not get away from Homicron and the two of them rolled around on the ground.

When she finally stood up, still groggy, all her men were dead. Those from Patriot Petroleum as well.

Only Rod Zey was still alive, in the hands of the Kyrosians.

"She really said that?" Rod Zey is outraged. "She said I shot at her?"

"Yes."

"That's ridiculous. How could I have time to aim when she was right on top of me?"

"She admits she doesn't have complete control over her powers yet."

The head of security straightens up, sounding skeptical, "Really? And how's that?"

"Her fusion was recent. So far, she's the only one to have survived such an experience."

Rod Zey screws up his face in concentration, "What do you mean?"

"From what we know, the fusion of an Alphan with a living being is forbidden because it causes massive explosions. Ted White's body was vaporized, but he could have wiped the Earth right off the cosmic map."

"And what were the warning signs?"

The Kyrosian suddenly becomes worried. "A luminous glow, why?"

Rod Zey holds up his hand. It is all lit up.

Rod Zey shoved away the table in front of him. He felt charged with an immeasurable power that was burning him up inside. He shot out lethal radiation that immediately consumed the two guards by the door. As the interrogator was standing up, he, too, was destroyed.

It only took a wave of the hand to blow out the door. Rod Zey hurried down the corridor. His heart was beating a mile a minute.

The Kyrosians came in droves and shot at him, but Rod protected himself behind a quantum field force.

He had no time to lose. "Homicron!" he shouted.

Information was flowing through him. Material flux and rays. The pain was unbearable.

"Homicron!"

He put one knee on the ground, unable to go any further. A figure appeared next to him. No, in fact, she was on the other side of the wall. Thanks to X-rays, his vision could penetrate matter. He saw Homicron fighting with some Kyrosians. She had a gun and was firing at them. It was like a shadow

71

play. He saw her kill two reptilians before trying to escape. But the door was locked.

With one last effort, Rod Zey pulverized the metal door with an ionic bombardment, then he passed out.

Hands slipped under his arms and raised him up. "Come on," a female voice said.

He stumbled forward, supported by the young woman. A little further and he could make out the big vaulted room.

"I'm going to try to reverse the operation," she panted.

He did not try to stop her. His body was a furnace. He could already feel his cells bursting in the heat, exploding into thousands of atoms.

Homicron sat him in a chair where he could barely hold himself up.

"Watch out," she said, "I'm turning it on."

As soon as he heard the hum, a ray struck him.

"Well?" Brown stares at her uneasily. "How did you get out of there?"

Rita looks away. "It wasn't easy, but I put everything back in order."

"And Rod Zey?"

"In a moment of weakness of mine, he managed to escape. He stole one of our helicopters and sabotaged the other two. I had to fly back here."

"What a bastard!"

Rita sighs, "Tell me about it."

"It was an error of judgment on my part," the director goes on. "You weren't ready. I should be as concerned about Homicron as I am about Rita Tower." Then more solemnly, "I'm sending you back to our space station. Dr. Kalamazoo and Dr. Malone will take care of you. Before any more missions on Earth, we need a lot more tests. And don't worry, this time, I'm coming with you."

He watches for her reaction, fearing she will protest, even refuse. But Homicron just nods. Her eyes stare absently but serenely. She grabs the glass of milk and swallows a handful of sedatives.

Rita felt the Alphan's energy body come back into hers. She also got her memory back. The shock wave had thrown her against the wall, which she hit hard before sliding to the ground. When she opened her eyes, she saw Rod Zey staring at her.

"Hello, princess," he whispered seductively.

Despite his calm exterior, there were beads of sweat on his forehead. The poor guy must have gone through hell.

"I see you finally got it," she replied without moving.

"I figured it out when I saw the Kyrosians didn't know about the gun you stole from me. And I felt the warning signs of the fate awaiting me if I didn't get you your powers back. But it was thanks to my own psychic powers that I got the reptilians to tell me the truth, right?"

"Who knows! I never tried them out myself," Homicron admitted.

He stood up, "What exactly happened?"

"You already know," she said as a trickle of blood ran down her lip. "By firing the Kyrosian prototype at me, you severed me from the Alphan."

"How's that possible?" Zey was honestly bewildered. "The effect isn't permanent?"

"The fusion was too recent. Usually the Alphans fuse only with corpses, dead things. Your little warning shot obviously was enough to break his link with me and take refuge in the nearest body: yours."

"At the risk of destroying me," Zey said with a smile.

"In a very short time, your atoms would have been scattered to the four corners of the galaxy. And the Earth with them."

The Head of Security whistled in awe. "Well, that was a close one!"

73

Homicron coughed. She had been injured fighting the Kyrosians. A serpent-blade had left a long, ugly wound on her side, which she was pressing with her fist.

Zey furrowed his brow and asked, "Are you going to be OK?"

"Sure. We... I can heal myself faster using my energy flux."

He nodded in disbelief. He ran his hands through his blonde hair and sounded more relaxed, "I thought the Kyrosians had psychic powers. I couldn't dare to fool them like you did," he admitted willingly.

"You just had to think about it. The fact that they separated us for the interrogation proved that they had no telepaths among them. They were scientists, not even soldiers. Their job was to develop the ultimate weapon against Homicron... against me. The soldiers assigned to guard the base must have been killed in the fighting. And the last survivors were taken out by our men. They only beat us because they caught us off guard. I was able to take out two of them with the gun without being touched. They didn't even think of throwing up a force field. As for the transfer, I knew the Alphan was out of me but I wasn't sure it was in you. I mentioned your eyes to find out if they'd turned purple. But no go. On the other hand, when I talked about you sweating and they confirmed it I knew you'd got the Alphan. I figured you weren't the type to panic in an interrogation."

Rod Zey nodded. "You're pretty clever," he complimented her as he looked around the room full of corpses.

"Leave now," Homicron ordered, "before I've got back all my powers. I can't stand you being here another minute."

"After all we've been through together? I think you're being a little rude to your prince charming."

"You're alive and free because you helped me. That should be enough," she said bluntly.

"I guess it's no use asking to share that tech with Patriot Petroleum?" he said, turning around.

"You've already stolen documents. That's enough."

He looked surprised. "How did you know?"

"I had access to part of your memory because of our... exchange. You saved my life by saving your own. This is my way of thanking you. Anyway, none of the files matches this prototype that I'm going to destroy very shortly. So, goodbye, Rod."

The man saluted her with a smile and walked slowly out of the Kyrosian base. He was still weak. Before leaving the base, he searched one of his men's dead body and pulled out a few papers that he stuffed into his coat.

Rita sat among the corpses for a long time.

It took her many long hours to recover control of her body and become one with the Alphan again. Rita Tower was about to slowly dissolve to be reborn as a child of the stars.

When the solar photons had finished spinning on the ramp, Rita headed for the machine, holding out her hands toward it. But before she made the final gesture, she froze. She could still try to free herself from the Alphan who was living inside her. It was impossible to predict what would happen, whether she kept him or cut him out. But she did not want to lose Ted White a second time.

"I am Homicron," she said.

Then a purple beam shot out of her eyes and started to liquefy the machine.

The Five-Pointed Star by Franco Oneta

The Five-Pointed Star is a group made up of four individuals plus a ghost, dedicated to the investigation of the supernatural phenomena. It includes the eccentric Professor Archibald Kay, his butler Otto, the medium Elizabeth Hume, and young Edward Bruce. The ghost of Pamela, Edward's deceased girlfriend, who died in mysterious circumstances, assists them in their inquiries...

Tepthida Hay: *The Cult of the Nautilus*

Inspector Brown closed his eyes, pinched the bridge of his nose and took a deep breath. He felt a migraine coming on, ready to seep into his sleep-deprived brain. There were days when he hated his job. That rumbling noise that was supposed to be a sob just annoyed him. With great effort the 40-year-old opened his eyes and put on a serious face.

"So," he spoke slowly, "in short, you arrived at 5:45 like every morning, went to your locker, said hello to your colleagues Janet, Piotr, Ali and Cathy, got your stuff and then went to the Green Zone. And there, you started cleaning the fossil room before you came to the fossils from Great Britain, where you saw... something unexpected, let's say. Is that right?"

The small, blonde woman sniffled before answering.

"Yes, Inspector! Oh, awful, it was just awful!" she replies in a trembling voice.

Again the witness fell apart, remembering her morning discovery. The inspector thanked her and sent her away. He slapped his notepad shut and went to the scene of the crime. The forensics specialists were finishing their work.

"Anything new?" he asked.

"From the looks of it, a hundred different prints from curious visitors," Graylin said while closing his case. "Not sure we'll get much from it."

Brown looked disappointed, disconcerted. Once again, he scrutinized the macabre picture he had before him: squeezed into the narrow space between the display case and the fossils was the body of Professor Walter Diggins, lying in a very unnatural way. The legs were folded at a weird angle, the right arm stuck behind his neck whereas the left arm hung down, dislocated. The head was thrown back, revealing an Adam's apple that bulged out so much that it hurt to look at it. The blue eyes were wide open in silent wonder.

But what was most disturbing in this scene was certainly the shirt open on his pale chest where, among the curly white hairs, was carved the figure of a spiral shell. The edges of the incision were swollen, making the inspector more nervous than he should be.

"Your thoughts on it?"

Graylin's question tore Brown away from his morbid reflections.

"The deceased is a renowned paleontologist from Cardiff, reported missing three months ago, described as a quiet, friendly person; there was no break-in at the Museum of Natural History; this mark on his chest is obviously the work of a lunatic; the position of the body indicates that *rigor mortis* had not set in when he was put here; and the window is sealed. I'm eager to hear what the coroner has to say. As for me, I hate to say it, but I'm stumped."

Mumbling to himself, the inspector went to get a cup of coffee. It would take hours for them to dismantle the window and extract the body. His migraine was not so patient.

The November air was more bitter cold than usual, so Liz picked up the pace. Her judo class had been canceled, but she wanted to work out. It had been months since she went jogging and she realized that she missed the streets of London at twilight. After running up Swains Lane along the old cemetery and by Waterlow Park, she turned to get to Highgate Hill and then headed down to her apartment.

As web editor at the *Londonear*, Liz managed the culture section, which introduced her to passionate people—and no lack of subject matter. But her natural curiosity had urged her to open her own blog about more personal things. Except that, for months now, everything had been too *normal*.

The journalist reached Junction Road. As she passed by the Archway tube station, she noticed that the blue sign had been tagged in orange: a convoluted circle with some wavy lines coming out of it.

It started drizzling, which forced her to head home as quickly as possible.

Friday was promising. But the coroner's report had to land on Brown's desk right before his first coffee of the day. He threw open the file and swore out loud. In a fury, he grabbed his coat and stormed out of his office as his colleagues watched on in bewilderment.

Liz waited for the final jolt of the elevator. She was late and rushed into her workspace. Her friend Sushmita, in charge of the literary section, said hello to her over the partition. But she had a hard time concentrating. When she had caught the bus this morning, she had spotted the same tag covering the name of the tube station in Camden. Then she'd transferred buses at Highgate. Too distracted to read her book, she'd looked out the window, streaming with rain, and had seen the same symbol for the third time. Intrigued now, she wanted to count them.

She watched for them everywhere—traffic signs, shop signs, advertisements—but the mysterious drawing only appeared at the entrance of tube stations. She was so absorbed in her task that she had not realized that she had reached the end of the line, a long way from her job.

While her colleagues kept busy, she did a little search on the net. It only took a few clicks to find it: the tag was a *nautilus*, a cephalopod, simplified of course, but picturing an eye with some tentacles.

Making sure no one saw her, Liz posted a short article on her blog *Hidden*:

Mysterious signs at the underground entrances. Pictures of nautiluses popped up at the entrance to some London underground stations this week. Tagged with fluorescent paint there are dozens of them around the city. What's the meaning of it? Is it a budding young street artist or some weird rallying symbol? I'm going to find out what's behind these tags.

After uploading a few photos she had taken, Liz logged out and forced herself to concentrate on her work. But her mind was already constructing the wildest theories.

The temperature had plummeted in the afternoon and, now that it was night, Liz was sorry she did not have her scarf. She was hurrying through Kensington. A strange atmosphere loomed over the city, as if some dark design was at work. Her senses felt in jeopardy; something was not right.

The young journalist used her meeting with an association for the historical reconstruction of Pont Street to take a trip to the museum. They would soon be stopping admissions, so she was in a rush. Since she had got the message on her blog around noon, she was on pins and needles. "Nobodybutme" had left a simple comment:

Green Zone, Museum of Natural History.

The zone in question contained the marine fossils, so she took the cryptic message seriously. Either it came from a skeptic who wanted to give her a lesson in marine biology, or else it was a lead.

As she turned onto Exhibition Road, a cold drizzle started falling. Liz ran the rest of the way. Despite her heels, she managed to fly up the stairs to the monumental entrance.

With her brown hair plastered over her face, she did not see the man in a gray coat coming out, and she bumped right into him. A firm hand grabbed her arm before she could fall back down the stairs. A little stunned, her confused eyes opened wide.

"Miss Hume!" the man steadying her blurted out. "What are you doing here?"

"The nautilus..." she muttered.

"Why doesn't that surprise me," Inspector Brown sighed. "Come, let's get some coffee."

He opened the door and nodded to the security guard. When Liz entered the building, she became violently dizzy and almost fell over. Brown held her up. Supporting her gently, he guided her to the café. After ordering for two, the inspector sat across from Elizabeth Hume, who looked pale and worried.

"Drink, it'll do you good," he pushed a steaming hot cup of coffee toward her.

"It'll pass,' Liz mumbled. "Tell me everything."

He did not need to be asked twice. Brown unloaded everything he knew about the Diggins affair: the mystery of his disappearance from Cardiff a few months ago, his reappearance—death—in the display case in the Green Zone, the absence of any sign of a break-in (even after carefully reviewing all the surveillance footage), and the nautilus carved into the victim's skin.

"But the icing on the cake," he frowned, "was the coroner's report. Our man drowned... in sea water, which looks nothing like any of Earth's waters."

"Seems you're leaning toward a supernatural theory, inspector."

Brown pursed his lips. "You haven't told me how you made the connection between the tags and the victim," he asked suspiciously. "Only the identity of the dead man was given to the press. Nothing was said about the mark on his chest. Is it your... third eye?"

Liz smirked. She knew he was not being mean. After all their collaborations, it had almost become a game. Brown was a skeptic, and despite the help given by the Five-Pointed Star in his difficult investigations, he refused to believe in the supernatural. For him, Liz was simply more intuitive than the average mortal.

"An anonymous contact of all things," she said with a wry smile. "It seems my screwy site attracts some people with a sensitive nose."

"It could be our murderer!" the inspector shot back.

"Come on, stop suspecting my sources every time," she was annoyed. "Don't you know there are others like me?"

"Like what? Rash and reckless?" he spoke flatly.

Liz clenched her jaw and snapped, "No, people with the gift. But it's obviously some reckless crank, so I won't bother you any longer."

The journalist swept up her wet things and stomped away. Brown watched her disappear into the silent museum. Obviously, this was not a good week.

Inspector Harding Brown was walking through the night, his collar turned up against the pouring rain that echoed his mood. His day was over. He had fiddled with the phone in his pocket for half an hour. Knowing he had hurt Liz's feelings, he did not want to send her a message. But when the phone vibrated, he answered right away.

"Brown, go! Oh, it's you, Hodgson... All right... I'll be there in twenty."

Will this circus never stop? The inspector was dripping wet and cursing inside. What's gotten into this city? Sergeant Hodgson had said enough to give him heartburn, but not enough for a heart attack. He was sure, however, that the final blow was coming soon. Maybe he was getting a little clairvoyant himself, he laughed bitterly.

In the storm drowning the London night, he marched against the wind. When he looked up, he saw The Shard and its shining tip. Although he was more partial to the old stone buildings, he had a soft spot for this brand new, steel and glass construction.

When he left Queen Street to go up Cannon Street, he was quickly welcomed by the blue lights that stained the shop front windows. Seven police cars formed a perimeter around the entrance to the London underground.

"I think I'm going to have to call you back, Liz," he grumbled as he slipped under the barricade tape.

"Ah, Inspector," Sergeant Hodgson was twisting his blonde moustache. "Right on time. This is the strangest thing I've ever seen..."

The inspector had had enough. After watching hours of surveillance at the Museum of Natural History that afternoon, he was now analyzing those from Cannon Street. The three cameras pointing at the entrance could not lie: at 7:52 p.m. precisely, the body of climatologist Lloyd Causton—46 years-old, recently divorced, reported missing eleven days ago in his native city of Cambridge—had *materialized* in the middle of a moving crowd.

He himself had questioned the twenty or so witnesses and everyone agreed: the dead man just *appeared* on the steps, right under their legs. Nobody had dropped him there; nobody had dragged him; he just simply *sprang up*.

The coroner immediately confirmed that he had been dead for hours, probably from the four-pointed mark "stamped" into his chest. The pictures were not cut and unless they were dealing with a very well organized criminal gang, this corpse should not have been there, just like Diggins in the museum display case. The nautilus carved into his forehead became almost banal in this context.

Exhausted, the inspector dialed a number.

"Liz, sorry for earlier. I need your help. There's another one. Brown."

At this point, he would get down on his hands and knees for help. When the answer came—"At the manor, tomorrow 11 a.m. Rest"—he felt less tired and more relieved.

The inspector straightened his clothes. It looked like he had not changed them in days: his light-colored wool coat, soaked through, had turned charcoal gray, his shirt was wrinkled and his pants were stained with coffee (a usual morning baptism). Being preoccupied by this crazy case, Brown had not even shaved.

He took a deep breath before using the sonic screwdriver knocker on the blue, checkered double door. Professor Kay was an original... During his last visit in March, he had had to go through a Hobbit hole. Today, he was going in through a police callbox—a little more appropriate...

The right door opened silently and Otto, the butler of Oneta House, stood there.

"Oh, hello inspector," he sounded surprised as he stepped aside to let him enter. "I was expecting to see the Doctor."

Brown started to laugh, but when he saw the imposing employee look politely offended, he changed the subject.

"It's bigger on the inside."

He detected a slight smile on Otto's face. To his surprise, he was led to the second floor. Going up the monumental staircase of the Edwardian mansion, he noticed that the young man had braided his frizzy hair in complex patterns. The thin stripes of his three-piece suit outlined his muscles. He made a clashing pair with his employer, who looked like an old English Lord.

When they got to the closed door, Otto gave two short knocks before introducing the inspector. Lying among a chaos of cushions and quilts, Archibald Kay was dozing in the dark. When the light from the hallway hit his face, he opened his eyes.

"Inspector Brown," his voice was hoarse. "Would you be kind enough to open the curtains?"

The inspector did so. "You should have told me to cancel, professor. I don't want to disturb you."

"Oh, this?" Kay sat up in bed. "Nothing but a rough evening."

"But Otto said you were expecting..."

"The Doctor, yes," he laughed. "Because I don't want to move, you know. I'm not so young anymore and anything goes with the eccentric Lord Kay."

The professor winked mischievously as he climbed out of bed completely dressed. His elegant gray suit had not even a single crease and Harding suddenly felt like a schoolboy caught being naughty.

"Is everyone here, Otto?"

"Yes, Sir, Miss Hume and Mr. Bruce are waiting in the salon."

"What are we waiting for then? Let's go!" the old man put his spectacles on his long nose and repeated, "Let's go, hop to it!"

And as spry as a young man, he hustled down to the ground floor while fussing with his shock of gray hair.

In the small salon in the west wing, the furniture was shaded with the dramatic light from the storm. Brown shuddered as he looked around at the strange decorations. White, chiffon curtains framed two high windows with dark woodwork. At times, an unsettling ripple stirred the wispy fabric. Where the walls were not covered by shelves full of books on parapsychology or with weird objects, there were old baroque tapestries with vague colors—or here big, purple dahlias printed on an olive background. A grand chandelier spread its panorama of red crystal pendants above a small, round table.

Liz was sitting in a wing chair, her legs crossed and her back very straight. Her thick, brown hair created a silky stream on her right shoulder. The inspector nodded discreetly when she looked up from the steaming hot cup of tea.

Leaning against the backrest, Edward Bruce gazed at the officer with penetrating eyes. As usual, the lawyer dressed casually: a mustard-yellow sweater with a round collar, blue jeans and a pair of brown derbies. His thick, black jacket and motorcycle helmet lay at his feet. His expression, for years, had had an unfathomable severity that he often had trouble hiding.

The inspector's gaze fell upon the table on which a crystal ball sat in claws of exotic wood.

"Don't worry, Harding, you're not here for a séance," Liz said as she raised the porcelain cup to her lips. "I brought you here to tell you about some new developments."

Brown suddenly felt crushed by the weight of his wet coat. He took it off without saying a word and sat down to keep his composure.

"You know," Liz continued, "the nautilus graffiti that I listed on my site? Well, tonight, something was written under each of them. No exceptions."

"What was it?" the inspector was troubled by the intensity of her stare.

"*Reversio*."

"Go back, in Latin," Otto translated in his calm voice.

"Latin, shellfish drawn on victims and at tube stations, questions with no answers, we have all the ingredients of a very complicated mystery," the inspector sighed and slumped in his chair. "A mystery that only the Five-Pointed Star can help unravel..."

"And we're counting on you to help us," Liz tried to loosen him up a bit.

Professor Kay stroked his beard, "Perhaps you can tell us what you know about the second victim? Liz told us everything she knows, but we'd like to know what killed the poor man."

"Internal bleeding after an injury to his rib cage. It seems—and this is where it gets really weird—that it was caused by a kick from a giant bird that's been extinct for forty million years—a so-called *Gastornis*. How it could have occurred with such force we have no idea. No skeleton has been stolen from any museum in Europe. But the horrible bruise on Lloyd Causton's chest leaves no room for doubt. We're dealing with some really twisted lunatic..."

"So we have two victims who did not know each other, kidnapped with no demand for ransom, one from Cardiff and the other from Cambridge," Edward summed up in his warm voice. "What connects them?"

"Science? Maybe they specialized in a particular study," Otto offered as he drew the curtains.

The group thought about his comment. The trees outside that bordered the calm banks of Little Venice were letting their red leaves flutter down into the canal water.

"Let's call Pamela now," Liz said. "I want some answers. Harding, would you leave us alone?"

The inspector picked up his coat and waved to the group. During his three years of collaboration with the secret organization, he had never been allowed to attend any of their séances. At first, he 'd been a little irked, which later turned into frustration, but now, he was only tired. Maybe his skepticism closed the doors of the supernatural, and especially that of Liz...

Outside, clouds were gathering. A rain shower was probably going to hit the Maida Vale district, so the inspector hurried to his car. He had to go back to the office and comb through the Diggins and Causton files like Otto had suggested.

Edward, Otto, Liz and Professor Kay stood around the table. The double curtains were drawn and only a three-branched candlestick lit the room from the mantle above the fireplace. In the muted silence, Liz Hume prepared herself. With her head hanging forward, her face was buried behind her brown, wavy locks. Her breathing became slower, heavier. When she brought out the small piece of crystal that she wore as a necklace beneath her green blouse, a soft light glowed from it. Slowly the journalist reached out over the crystal ball, which started to tremble and move to the edge of the round table between her and Otto. Then she muttered some quick words, too low to be understood.

The flames of the candlestick danced on the ball. All of a sudden, they flickered, on the verge of going out. The journalist/medium slowly separated her arms to form a V and the others did the same. Then they all held hands. The flames sizzled for a moment, then rose up as if being breathed in. Bright rays shot out of the sphere and, in a few seconds, spread to each of the participants to form a pentacle.

"We are now going to engage the spirit world," Liz looked up and at each of her partners in turn. "Close your eyes, forget your surroundings, think only of Pamela, of what she represents for you. Invoke her with all your willpower."

Liz felt Edward's hand tremble in hers and squeeze hers encouragingly. She spoke again, more loudly and more slowly.

"Pamela, come join us. Rend the veil that separates you from our world, pierce the mists..."

A vibration crossed the room and a noise, like rustling silk, came out of the crystal ball.

"Welcome, Pamela," Liz greeted and opened her eyes. "We missed you."

Edward let go of the medium's hand and held back a gasp. "I see her silhouette!" he cried out to Liz.

The young woman nodded. She saw her such as she was in death: a gentle face framed by chestnut brown curls, a slim figure dressed in tight pants and a baggy shirt. Cut down in the flush of youth. With a halo of light that she alone saw in all its brightness. Otto scrutinized the space between the crystal ball and the candlestick, trying to make out Pamela, but he saw nothing but the glowing light, like the rest of his companions.

"Hello, dear Pamela," Professor Kay said, putting his hand to his chest. "We need your help in a matter that's beyond us. Walter Diggins and Lloyd Causton were killed this week. But their deaths remain unexplained. Can you help us?"

The ghost of Pamela, who came out of one of the points of the pentacle, turned to the medium. "Give me a moment, I'll be right back," her voice chimed.

And in a flash she disappeared. Only a misty light remained, like the dormant dawn.

"Is she still with us?" Otto asked Liz.

"Went to get some info," she apologized.

"As long as she finds some answers..."

"Otto," Professor Kay scolded, "the spirit world is not a search engine!"

"She's taking her time," Edward sounded worried.

"Concentrate!" the medium hissed and glared at them. Something in her voice betrayed her nervousness.

"There's a problem, isn't there?" the lawyer asked, turning pale.

"She's taking longer than usual, that's all," Liz tried to reassure them.

"And if she were in danger..."

"Did something happen to her..."

The parapsychologist stayed quiet, but the damage was done. Edward Bruce glowered and scowled at him. Liz tried to intervene, but she got dizzy and suddenly slumped down. Her forehead was covered in sweat and she could not get back up. Otto rushed over to an inlaid side-table and came back with a flask of whiskey, which he uncorked and shook gently under her nose.

"Concentrate," Liz groaned, pushing away the flask with a feeble hand. "Please..."

Seeing she was dead set on continuing the séance, Otto and Edward helped her get back on track. Despite her unstable balance, she wrapped her hands around the crystal ball and the others took their place at the table. An ethereal figure manifested after a while and Liz gasped.

"What's wrong?" Edward asked.

"Nothing... Now the connection!"

The panic in her voice could not be concealed. Suddenly she went stiff and looked up.

"I failed, Liz," Pamela looked disappointed. "There's like a... fog on the line. I can't reach those two spirits. It's baffling. I felt such a void... oh, such a gulf between us. I'm sorry, I... It's too hard."

"I have to stop the séance, Pam, for your own good. Thanks for everything. Take care of yourself."

And without a word, the medium took her hands off the globe. The mist vanished and she felt the other members of the Five-Pointed Star staring at her insistently.

"What does that mean?" the young lawyer asked anxiously. "How is she?"

"Come on, Elizabeth, speak up," Archibald Kay squeezed her hand gently.

"Pamela couldn't get in touch with the deceased."

"Miss Hume," Otto asked, "what's wrong. You're very pale."

"I... I could barely see her. As if I've lost my gift!"

"But you heard her," the butler said calmly, "which means you still have it. And Pamela couldn't reach our victims. The problem, therefore, isn't with you."

Liz nodded and seemed to relax a little.

"You said Pamela couldn't communicate with them," Otto contemplated, "like they were far away."

"It's crazy, you know," Edward Bruce said. "The spirits are in the same world."

"Are you sure?" the old professor smiled. "It's a very mysterious universe that..."

"As if their spirits were having trouble finding the land of the dead," Otto paid no attention to the others. "As if they weren't dead in this reality!"

"That's impossible!" Edward furrowed his brow in doubt.

"On the contrary, it's obvious!" the professor exclaimed. "Go on, Otto, please, you've got a captivating idea there."

Despite his imposing size the butler seemed to shrink with shyness. "The inscription *reversio* means 'Go back' in Latin. Now, Professor Diggins was found in the room of fossils, drowned in a type of sea water that's not found in our oceans. And the climatologist had his chest caved in by a bird that's been extinct for millions of years. So if Diggins drowned in an ocean that no longer exists? And if Causton was killed by a real, flesh and blood, giant bird?"

Nobody said a word. But everything seemed a little clearer in their minds.

"We have to see Brown to find out what these men specialized in. There's obviously something connecting them."

Liz' smartphone beeped. She automatically looked at the screen. A new notification on her blog from "nobodybutme".

"Rursus," she cried out excitedly. "Let's go see Harding!"

As the others looked on, puzzled, she headed for the front door.

The plastic cups of coffee were piling up on the cluttered desk of Inspector Brown. They had made phenomenal progress in the investigation since his visit to Oneta House. He had combed through everything about the two victims' professional life: conferences, seminars, articles, etc. Still, he had not gone back far enough. But when he was ready to call it quits and had looked at their theses, everything had become clear! Lloyd Causton and Walter Diggins, at one time, had both studied the Eocene Epoch!

After a few phone calls, he had found a contact to whom he sent the composition of the water found in Diggins' lungs. The response was explicit: it apparently belonged to what an ocean during the Eocene would be like. Troubled and satisfied at the same time, he then called his informants who hung out around the "speaker's corners" in London. A strange group was preaching regularly in the parks at twilight, inciting the listeners to go back, to leave the world, to join the "Rursus", which would reestablish the broken balance.

That was when Brown saw the little troupe of Five-pointed Stars—well, its four members (Otto, Liz, Edward and Professor Kay)—show up. He had never believed in the story of the fifth member, the ghost of Pamela, in spite of all the respect he had for the journalist/alleged medium. For him, the group could just not bring itself to change its name, perhaps in memory of their friend who had been murdered years ago. It was that tragic event that had brought him in contact with the four. Pamela's murder remained unsolved.

"Inspector," Kay's voice faltered when he spoke loudly. "we've got news!"

"About the word Rursus, for example?" he asked innocently.

"How…" the professor was astonished.

"Intuition, that's all." He winked at Liz when their eyes met. She answered with a smile.

"We don't know yet what it's about, except for its Latin definition: backward," Edward replied. "On our way here, we did a quick search on the net but found nothing worthwhile."

"It's a cult that popped up in London recently. It apparently uses the old-school methods, handing out flyers and talking on street corners. Its message is to go back to times of purity, meaning to get rid of the human species."

"Which explains the signs from another time," Otto nodded.

"I dug into the past of our two victims and found out what connects them."

"The Paleocene?" Kay suggested, rubbing his gray goatee.

"The Eocene," the inspector specified, being surprised this time.

"Hee-hee, there are only books on parapsychology on my bookshelf," the old Lord chuckled as he held up a thick tome. "We crosschecked the clues you gave and Otto came up with the brilliant idea that Diggins and Causton died… somewhere else. *Sometime* else, I mean."

"I wouldn't go that far," Brown held back a scowl.

"My dear Harding, you wouldn't believe in Nessie if she were right in front of you," Liz teased.

Someone knocked and the door opened. A tall blonde man stood there in a shirt that was a little too tight.

"Sergeant Hodgson?" the inspector said.

"I did the research you asked for." He stopped and looked at the four civilians but his superior waved for him to continue. "In the last three months, four scientists have disappeared in the United Kingdom. First, the paleontologist Diggins in Cardiff; then, the geologists Ruby Partridge from Manchester; then, Duleep Jaykar from Glasgow; and finally, Lloyd Causton from Cambridge."

"Thanks, Hodgson."

"Oh and your informant called. The founder of Rursus is a man named Devon Finchley and he's at speaker's corner in Hyde Park right now."

Without a second thought, the inspector rushed out with the group on his heels, leaving the sergeant confused. The police station was a few miles from the park, so they all jumped into Brown's car. It only took them a few minutes to get there. The inspector had agreed to split so as not to alarm the suspect. In the wet grayness, only six people were listening to the speaker, trying to stay warm under their hoods.

"...the Great Break. It already happened but nobody remembers because Man didn't exist! Nature's given us warnings, but we're not paying attention! Why study the past if we get nothing out of it? See how Man has proliferated and corrupted this Earth!"

And it went on and on, the orator promoting a mass extinction that would be fatal to the species. The few spectators did not take long to clear out, disappearing into the night to forget about the nonsense. Otto, now soaked in his fitted suit, pretended to leave, followed by the professor. Liz hung onto Edward's arm and listened politely to the lightly-clothed man in his fifties, whose only real protection was the thick cloth he held over his head. When he had finished, his flushed face glistened in the light from the streetlamps. His dilated pupils made him look moronic, which was not helped by the huge necklace he wore: a bronze nautilus the size of a dinner plate.

Without a word, Inspector Brown also walked away behind some bushes. When the last couple finally left, the suspect stopped ranting and headed for the exit.

"You'll see, you bunch of fools!" Finchley fumed. "Humanity will disappear! The end has already begun! Bury your head in the ground, that's all you're good for."

The members of the Five-Pointed Star and the inspector came together from all different directions. They climbed into the car while the suspect hopped on a bike. They followed him, keeping the headlights off in the falling rain. It was easier than expected. When they saw Finchley lean his bike against a fence near the Tower of London, Brown parked on Water Lane.

As the guru was marching up Lower Thames Street, the group split up. Brown took Liz and Otto to go along the choppy Thames while the professor and Edward Bruce made a detour through Tower Place. Otto and Liz sprinted down Three Quays Walk and Brown went over Tower Millennium Pier. All three passed by a small, round, yellow brick building then came out on the esplanade by the drenched lawns along the fortress. They saw no trace of the guru. The inspector stomped around the vicinity looking for him.

When Kay and the lawyer joined them, as frustrated as the others, Brown could not help shouting out in rage, "But he can't just fly away!"

"Fly away, no," Edward squinted, "but bury himself maybe."

"What…"

"The Tower's Tunnel over there," he pointed to the yellow brick building. "In Victorian times, they used it for pedestrians to cross the Thames."

His companions followed him to the building that had lettering around it: London Hydraulic Power Company. The iron door was banging slightly in the wind so Edward did not hesitate to enter. Inside, there were so few light bulbs in the darkness that each of them turned on their phone before the group started down the circular stairs. A low rumbling was making the brick walls vibrate and it got stronger the farther they went. The smell of wet stone and sludge and ozone filled the space.

At the bottom of the stairs, Edward waved to the others to turn off their lights. In fact, a bluish glow shimmered in the distance and they could hear voices in the deafening hum. Brown gestured to the Five-Pointed Star to stay still and he started sneaking down the passage. Feeling his way along the cement walls, he was soon surrounded by big water pipes— now, he could hide behind them if someone came.

When the blue glow seeped down the tunnel like molasses, the inspector got scared. The light looked almost *solid;* at least, you could not see through it to the ground or walls or pipes or anything. It was as if it was *replacing* whatever was in its way. Brown struggled against his fear to keep going. At the moment when he put his foot on the pool of light, he felt a gentle warmth penetrate his body and the cuffs of his wet pants started steaming.

In disbelief, he realized that he was walking on white sand. He leaned over and picked up a seashell the size of his head to make sure he was not dreaming. The more the light spread down the tunnel, the more Brown felt like he was suffocating. He threw off his wet coat and his jacket and tie, hypnotized by the landscape taking shape around him: a stretch of sand bordered on one side by a forest of slender palm trees and on the other by a turquoise sea. In the middle of all this, a huge, black vortex opened up under the stoic eye of the Moon.

In places, parts of the tunnel remained—a bunch of cables hanging over here, a metal arch with rusted bolts over there. Brown saw too late the hooded figure swinging a stick at his head. He was not aware that they were dragging him to safety while Edward and the professor rushed onto the beach to be done with this madness.

A small crowd of disciples wearing khaki hoods had their backs turned. All of them were reaching out to the vortex and chanting in Latin. Behind them lay a dark-skinned man, lying unconscious on the ground. His shirt was stained with blood.

Professor Kay motioned to Otto and Edward to surround the cult. They were armed with what they could find—Otto a piece of driftwood, Kay a giant bone and Edward a big shell with sharp spikes.

It was only when Finchley moved that the three men noticed he was holding a woman tied up with a nautilus freshly carved in her forehead, bleeding profusely. Her screams were drowned out by the rumbling vortex as he pushed her closer to it.

"Let her go!" Otto yelled and ran at Finchley.

The guru turned his demented eyes on the butler. He pushed the woman away, bent down, picked up some sand and threw it in his face. Blinded, Otto swung wildly at the empty air before being overpowered by three disciples.

"Damn parasites!" Devon Finchley cried out, lowering his hood. "You're interfering in the course of events!"

"What have you done?" Kay groaned, unable to take his eyes off the vortex.

"I've restored things!" the fanatic spit out. "Rursus is here to send us back! Rursus is going to wipe out this wretched society! Rursus is going to suck up centuries of corruption and restore a world where Man has never befouled the Earth!"

"And where will you be in all this?" Edward's eyes glowed with rage.

"Our existence will not last long, but the world will finally be cleansed! Look at those so-called experts of the Eocene, that wimp Diggins and that imbecile Causton! They didn't survive even one day!"

"So that's why you kidnapped them?" the professor clenched his fists. "To see how long they could survive as experts in that distant epoch?"

The guru laughed uncontrollably.

"But you have no idea what you're doing!" Otto shouted while still being held prisoner.

"Rursus is nothing compared to the Plan," Finchley said coldly. "We've opened the breach onto the Eocene by using the ideal environment, there in the Thames riverbed. Did you know that the London clay is chock full of fossils and makes a perfect connection to the past? We've gone back almost forty-five million years. Yes, backward! And without knowing it, we've created a window onto an even older time. See that vortex? It'll go to the Origins, to when Life didn't exist. The Big Bang itself won't happen once we've found the way to enlarge it!"

"Twisted bastard! Stop this right now!" Edward was losing his self-control.

"Too late. The past is gobbling up the present. But what..."

Finchley did not finish because a white sphere hit him in the chest. Bright flashes crackled over his body and after a short convulsion he collapsed. With her hand clutching her necklace, Liz marched toward the hooded cult members. Bright rays of light were springing our between her fingers. Her expression was intense, strained, and she seemed about to pass out.

As she approached the vortex, a form materialized in front of everyone. It was a thin woman with rich, brown hair—Pamela.

Liz had summoned her and was maintaining the connection thanks to the crystal. Two other forms, more pale, the ghosts of Diggins and Causton, floated at her side.

Like a Valkyrie, Pamela swooped down over the remaining fanatics. The closer she was to the vortex, the more solid and colorful she became. Understanding how to get back some energy, the two dead scientists approached as well. Then, out of the blue, they pounced on a young man. His body rose up, contorted, faced the roaring vortex, and was sucked into the void. Only then did his companions react and start chanting more loudly, holding hands.

Causton and Diggins grabbed three other cult members and sent them to the other side. Pamela came over to help them fight the remaining fanatics—a young woman who was icily calm, raging twins and another woman with short, gray hair. But the chant they were doing formed a protective shield around them. Pamela got too close and received a shock, which sent her flying dangerously close to the vortex.

Finchley, who had been lying on the ground, jumped up and held his palms out towards Pamela's forehead. The ghost lost all her willpower and floated away near the terrifying mouth of the void, slowly being sucked in.

"An offering like this should speed up the end of the world!" the guru rejoiced. "Too bad I can't put my mark on her!"

"That's enough, Finchley!" a stocky man came out of nowhere and hit him over the head with a stick.

The professor and Edward were petrified, watching Pamela slip slowly but surely towards the vortex. After throwing the disciples into the depths of darkness, the spirits of Causton and Diggins were, alas, sucked in themselves. They disappeared in a green flash.

"We have to reverse everything!" the newcomer yelled in a panic. "It's me, 'nobodybutme'! I called on you to stop all this!"

"You should've thought of this before, right?" Liz panted, out of breath.

"We have to send Humanity into the past in order not to destroy all forms of life!"

"The crystal! We can use it as a bridge between worlds!" Liz shouted.

She dropped to the ground and started digging frantically in the sand. Otto was with her, taking off her necklace. The crystal was shining so brightly that it was hard to look at it. At her signal, the butler dropped the necklace into the hole.

There was a silent explosion that threw everyone back and a dark mist rose from the sand, from the forest and from the ocean. Furtive forms took shape and vanished right away. Neither animals nor plants they were more like primitive nightmares. The rumbling of pandemonium had stopped and was replaced by an almost terrifying silence.

The shadows thickened before rising into the sky, looming. They gathered together abruptly, a screaming, smoky whirlwind, before rushing headlong into the vortex. Another explosion went off and the twister swelled up dramatically, threatening to engulf the group of humans. Then it collapsed in on itself, shrank down and disappeared.

The whole scene had lasted a fraction of a second, but the spectators could not believe their eyes. Pamela was freed from the vortex now and conscious again. She faded from the sight of the others so that only Liz could see her.

Edward and Pamela had stared at each other the entire time. They were, therefore, the last ones to notice that the antediluvian landscape was gone, leaving behind the normal course of things: the Tower tunnel, dark and humid, dimly lit by old bulbs. The sound of hurried footsteps made them all jump. The disciple of Rursus who had switched sides was escaping down the tunnel. No one ran after him. Pamela smiled wearily at Liz before disappearing.

"She's gone, right?" the lawyer asked sadly.

"Yes, Edward," Liz patted his arm.

"I'm glad I got to see her." Tears welled up in his eyes and he looked away.

"Let's go home, I have a craving to feel rain on my face," the professor said cheerfully.

Otto and Edward pulled Finchley to his feet, still groggy, and pushed him down the tunnel. The two geologists had evaporated. After fifty yards of so, they came across Inspector Brown, sitting in the middle of the tunnel, in bad shape. His temple was badly cut over a bruised swelling. Liz helped him up and led him outside. Professor Kay, bringing up the rear, picked up the clothes that the inspector had peeled off earlier. The tropical warmth had already given way to the seasonal cold.

The four "active" members of the Five-Pointed Star stared at the inspector as if he were babbling nonsense.

"I think the blow to my head by our fleeing suspect made me hallucinate."

Wavering between fury and amusement, Liz chose the second option.

"And the witnesses in the area who saw the quays turn into an exotic beach were invited into your vision, of course," she teased with a malicious glint in her eye.

"Mass hallucination, my dear," he smiled back. "Fear and panic because of the tremors, no doubt. Which obviously caused a gas leak."

"How do you explain the deaths of Diggins and Causton?"

"The work of very creative fanatics."

"And the geologists found with the Rursus symbol carved into their skin? What do you think of them? How Mr. Jaykar was found in Sussex and Mrs. Partridge in Cornwall when they were with us just minutes before?"

"They have no memory of their kidnapping, unfortunately. And we all suffered the effects of the mysterious gas."

Liz opened her mouth to argue but she changed her mind. He would have laughed if she explained that the nautilus symbol was charged with supernatural power and that it bound them to our present time. That's why, when they died in the Eocene, the poor geologists were found in the present. And also why Jaykar and Partridge were found in different places. They had been sent back to where there were traces of that very distant past. But the journalist just gazed at the inspector without saying a word. She had no desire to argue with him.

Harding stood up to say goodbye to the team, "I'll see you at Finchley's hearing."

Inspector Brown lumbered out of Oneta House, still exhausted from his adventure in the London tunnels.

"What really destroyed the vortex, Liz?" Edward asked.

The journalist's sparkling eyes darkened. "Chthonian forces," she shivered. "I used the crystal to amplify them. An intuition… that paid off."

"And Pamela?"

"She's fine. Her energy will need some time to recuperate but it could've been worse."

Edward nodded and turned back to his cup of tea. Otto was talking with the professor about a book in the library. Liz went over to the big windows, opened the curtains and contemplated the trees in the garden. She rubbed her neck where she usually felt her necklace. It was lost forever, lost in a past age that she hoped never to see again. She would have to find a new crystal for her séances.

The sun had finally made its appearance and Liz let its comforting rays wash over her.

Prince Kabur and Lagrid by Luciano Bernasconi

Kabur is a Prince of Thule, one of the kingdoms of Hyperborea, which existed nearly a hundred million years ago, when the First Humanity inhabited the Earth. He is a brave warrior who wields the sacred spear of the Danaian "god" Lug—his ancestor—using it to defeat demons and evil wizards. This adventure takes place during his quest to find his beloved, the beautiful Lagrid, kidnapped by the sorcerer Selinor Psah...

Julien Heylbroeck: *A Wedding in Olyazabad*

Kabur had been riding for weeks without letting up. In the blazing sun, the deserted landscapes passed by, one after another, and chance encounters became rarer and rarer. The cracked, ochre ground crumbled under the hooves of his scrawny unicorn. For three days now, he had walked part of the way to give the poor, emaciated beast some relief.

As he approached the first slopes leading to the steep summits on the horizon, the proud prince allowed himself a rest and sat on a rock. In the shadow of an arch in ruins, built long ago by some forgotten race, he uncorked his flask and tried to quench his thirst. Alas! There were only a few drops of the good Foralume wine left. He savored them, appreciating the strong smell and taste of the heady vintage.

This reminded him of his stop-over in that proud city, its thick walls and especially its well-stocked taverns. That was where he had left Arianrod. They had gone their separate ways, she, the daughter of the grand master of the Fomores, to pursue her mysterious goals, and him still searching for the beautiful Lagrid, kidnapped by the filthy thanils. The stone bird-men had flown off with his fiancée to take her into Gondaxa, to Selinor Psah, the evil sorcerer-sultan of Arkhanal.

Since then, after crossing the great sea, Kabur had ridden to the southern lands, tirelessly, even when Kelios, probably to test him, fired his piercing rays at him. These dark thoughts gave him more energy and the young prince of Thule cut short his break, determined to reach the mountains by nightfall. His mount proved more stubborn. It had scraped up some scarce clumps of dry, bluish grass and was chewing it eagerly. But the two of them continued their ascent. Little by little, the heat gave way to cool air, then to the cold, as the prince made his way up the side of the mountain.

At a bend in the pass, as the cold, dry wind blew down from the snow-capped summits, he came upon a strangely shaped plateau. Ribbed with deep crevasses, the rocky area was bounded by steep slopes, sometimes crossed by a network of rocky bridges or vines, everything in a sorry state. Along the cliffs or on certain outcrops, there were some dwellings. Some were built along the precipices, dug directly into the rock. Together they formed a village of troglodytes but nobody was in sight.

A few small forts set up on the narrow peaks watched over the surrounding land with the peacefulness of stone relics that believe themselves immortal. In the middle of the fissured valley stood a huge ziggurat with many terraces and a temple or palace with thick walls on the top. This was probably the old dwelling of the lord of the place, Kabur thought. The pyramid with serrated sides seemed to be challenging him to come closer. The prince of Thule paid no mind. He went only where he could follow the traces of his beloved. He followed a weed-strewn path into the valley.

Everything about the place looked deserted, abandoned. A few torn banners with illegible designs fluttered in the air, here and there, marking the entrance to the realm that Kabur knew nothing about. A curious sight was this frozen landscape, still bearing the mark of conquering man. Man who does not hesitate to shape the earth to build its cities in even the most inhospitable lands. The warrior resumed his journey, warily, his hand firmly gripping the shaft of the Spear of Lug.

He passed the first village with its houses built into the steep rock face. On several levels connected by rope ladders now in shreds or by crude elevators hanging from rusted pulleys, the twisted, slanting alleys beaten by the winds rejected the prince of Thule's advances with cold and hostile gusts of wind. As if the intrusion of a stranger into these ruins desecrated the tortured rest of its vanished inhabitants.

The barbarian's unicorn snorted and stamped the ground, affected by the sinister environment. But Kabur had to cross this weird-looking pass to get up into the mountains. He yanked gently on the reins to urge the animal to take the first steps. The main road leaving the village led to a bridge, a long, narrow column of stone chipped around the edges. With no guardrail it spanned a deep chasm in which a silvery river wound its way far below. Obviously, the inhabitants of these villages did not suffer from vertigo, Kabur thought.

Night was falling and it would have been more prudent to stop and take shelter from the wind in one of these converted caves, but Kabur preferred to keep moving. A bad feeling told him not to stay on the cracked plateau any longer than necessary. And he had faced so many setbacks already that he had learned to follow his intuition. Noxious, sulfurous fumes drifted up from the cracks poisoning the air and sometimes creating thick and acrid clouds that stung his eyes and nose, making it hard to see around him.

Kabur put one foot on the bridge, then another. He tapped his toe, first lightly then more firmly. The bridge held. He could pass. He pulled the unicorn and it followed reluctantly, neighing. The animal's distress echoed off the cliffs and houses making it sounded louder. This again frightened the creature even more. The warrior patted its cheeks and whispered comforting words. Together they advanced across the narrow passage.

Suddenly, Kabur heard metal creaking and, after concentrating on his feet, he looked up. A few yards ahead, at the end of the bridge, a figure stood still, watching him. Dressed in a loose, black robe whose edges were decorated with nails and twisted metal pieces, patched in places, the face of the individual was hidden under a long hood. The sound probably came from him although it echoed behind Kabur.

No! It was not an echo!

The prince turned around to see a similar person standing on the other side of the bridge. This one was rattling a chain made of heavy, black links and weighted at the end by a shiny hook. The man in front was also preparing for a fight because he unsheathed a curved sword with sharp spikes on the back. Kabur squeezed his spear.

The unicorn felt the tension and wanted to turn around. Luckily, it did not bolt, but the warrior let it go nevertheless. There was just enough room for it to turn around and start galloping toward what the poor beast thought was safety. The man in front of it now swung his hook and threw it at the unicorn. Skewered in the neck, the animal cried out in pain but the noise was cut off when the figure yanked his weapon, gashing the animal's throat. It only took a few seconds for the unicorn to spill its blood and die.

Kabur, who hated wanton killing, swore to make the man pay for his impudence. But his attention was drawn to the one in front of him who was laughing—a dry, dismal laughter devoid of emotion—and taking off his hood.

Although the prince had encountered many creatures, he stumbled backward upon seeing the ravaged face of this individual. A metal grill was embedded in the skin in bands across its skull like an evil mask that hid even the eyes. All that could be seen in the mass of steel was a filthy hole—he could not even call it a mouth, whose twisted fangs dripped gray drool.

The man with the iron face let loose a guttural cry and ran towards Kabur, who was expecting as much and was in position, spear out front, but still glancing back at the other assailant, who was walking forward slowly, dangling his deadly chain.

Kabur blocked a swing of the sword and pushed it to the right, throwing his left elbow at the monster's throat. The strength of the blow made him fall back a few steps.

"Ha ha! Now you realize you should have let me pass," he said. "I am Kabur, prince of the royal blood of Lug and heir to the throne of Thule. I'm not some helpless peasant whom you can rob."

Logically, any normally built person would have had a broken his jaw but his enemy just clicked his teeth in rage. Then, Kabur heard a weapon whistling behind him, so he dropped to the ground and rolled. The hook flew over him, slicing off a few blond hairs, which floated in the stale air for a moment before twirling off into the shadows.

The attacker before him jumped forward and tried to cut off his head. Kabur swept the creature off its feet with a kick and it fell to the ground. But the demonic creature behind him was not finished. It came right up to Kabur and gashed his back with a clawed hand. The prince screamed briefly in pain and turned around, his back already soaked in blood.

"Coward! Striking your opponent in the back! You'll pay for this treachery!"

Too close to use his spear effectively, Kabur rained blows on his enemy with his fists and knees, swearing by Kronan that the wretch would regret being so craven. The creature was surprised by this assault and stumbled and fell. Kabur raised his spear and took aim at his chest to finish off his opponent.

"Die, vile demon!"

That was when the creature, with inhuman strength, threw its hook at an outcropping and used it to pull away from the lethal blow. It escaped, swinging over the void, hanging onto its chain, leaving behind a thunderous laugh.

Kabur did not have time to pull back and his spear struck the stone bridge. Since his strength was doubled by his rage, joined with the power of his weapon, the blow split the stone and the bridge started to tremble like a serpent mortally wounded by the magic spear.

The sword-wielding monster backed up cautiously, his weapon held up to prevent Kabur from advancing. The prince, his back still on fire, tried to reach the end of the bridge, but the stone cracked and tore apart, collapsing on both sides.

Kabur fell along with the wreckage into the abyss.

"He's coming around. His eyes are moving behind his eyelids."

"Hush, not so loud. The demons might still be on the prowl. We should never have helped him."

"Be quiet, you baby, the old man will know what to do. He's wise. We can trust him."

Woken up by the conversation Kabur opened an eye. A grimy face with a big scar was staring at him.

"By Kronan, where am I?" the prince of Thule asked.

He tried to get up, but the sudden movement rekindled the pain in his back. He brought his hand up and felt a thick bandage.

"You took care of me? Who are you? You should know that Kabur, prince of Thule, will generously reward you."

"Prince? Thule? You don't say... You're really Kabur?"

Another voice, a softer voice, a woman's voice, spoke up. "I should have known. Who else could have survived a fight against those demons?"

The young woman stepped forward. She had beautiful brown hair and a pale face whose cheeks were hollowed by hunger. She would have been beautiful and voluptuous before the time of famine.

The warrior looked over her depleted body. Wearing a tattered dress that exposed her protruding ribs, the woman shifted her rags as if she were surprised by the prince's intense gaze and was ashamed to be seen like this.

"Demons? Well, they certainly had monstrous faces," Kabur groaned, trying to stand up.

At first, he swayed back and forth, but became steadier as he walked across the room. He was in one of the stone dwellings. There were no windows; the room was lit only by a few candles; the smell of urine and sweat and soot tainted the stale air. Kabur needed to breathe. He was suffocating in such a closed space.

"By Kronan, I'll ask you again, where am I?"

The young woman felt his confusion and put a gentle hand on the glistening shoulder of the young, impetuous warrior.

"Stay calm, prince of Thule. You're safe here. We're hidden in the depths of the city. The demons don't come down here."

"Yes, but what is this god-forsaken place?"

"Welcome to Olyazabad, Kabur," the scarred man responded. "I'm Karlson Dairse, former chamberlain. And this is Jassalba," he pointed a stump at the woman, and Kabur realized then that his arm was missing from the elbow down. "And finally, there's Shukar Gotmat, an old civil servant."

The man motioned toward a frail individual in the background with bulging eyes and thin tufts of hair around his ears. Kabur noticed that all of them had their skin covered with sand, which made them look even more pitiful.

"As you see," Karlson went on, "we're living here like rats. At the bottom of the chasm, in the gullies, in the dark and forgotten tunnels dug by our mining ancestors. We're like rats, terrorized by prowling beasts ready to devour us if we make a mistake. We hide our scent and cover ourselves with dirt because, in hovels like this, it's hard to smell the roses of Ilshanyi, right? Oh, misery! May the Gods deliver us from this wretched life!"

Kabur shook Jassalba's hand tenderly, then pushed her away gently. He took a few steps, flexing his muscles and bending his joints to awaken his injured body. He started to feel warmer and hungrier.

He turned to the one-armed man and said:

"I don't want to abuse your hospitality, but would it be possible to tell me how I can get something to eat?"

The old man, blind and stooped over, shuffled over to him. A child was helping him, guiding him through the maze of stalagmites. All around this strange pair, the ground between the hills of hardened dust was covered with carpets and a little basic furniture sagging under the manuscripts and papyrus rolls. On one piece, like a pedestal, a round, red stone sat in a bronze cup and gave off a pleasant heat.

"Sit down near the fire stone, my friend. Welcome to Olyazabad... Oh, this city was once the most beautiful of all. The Jewel of the Mountains, they called it. Today, it's just demon territory. But I hear your belly growling. You know, we don't have much here, but we'll share our tubers with you. Because I now know that you are our liberator. I felt it coming in the air. Through the putrid clouds, I felt a fresh breeze blowing in, bearing hope."

"That's the old man who told us to save you," Jassalba explained.

The young woman invited him to sit next to her near the red stone. She took a bowl and handed it to him. It had a pungent smell, a little musty.

"It's our tuber soup. It doesn't fool hunger for long, but it's better than nothing."

Kabur tasted it. It was awful. Worse than the slop they gave to prisoners in Thule and that he had tasted as a youth on a dare from Gowin. He gulped down a few mouthfuls, more out of respect for his hosts than to calm his stomach, then he put the bowl down. The old man had started telling the history of the city:

"Only a few years ago, Olyazabad was a prosperous city, governed by Alashkar, a good and just lord. Located on the steps of the High Southern Mountains, the city had a population of thousands. Miners, sculptors, prospectors, many people lived off the riches buried in the heart of the mountains. The weather was once as sweet as honey. Children's laughter filled the streets. Then, one day, the son of Alashkar, a feisty young prince named Golshan, was coming back from the hunt with a weird catch. In his nets he had captured a beast-man. It only had one hand, like Karlson. When traveling south the creature's cart had lost a wheel, and it was stuck in a pass of freezing crags. An isolated spot, hard to reach, especially when you're loaded down like it was. The beast with a half-human, half-animal face, was transporting a heavy sarcophagus. When the king opened it, we all saw the spikes inside. A strange iron maiden, that's what the traveler was carrying..."

The old man drank from the bowl that the boy gave him, then continued in his sad, hoarse voice:

"Alashkar laughed at his prey. He proposed throwing the beast into the inner arena of the Ziggurat to entertain his people by making it fight their best warriors. But the beast made a deal to save its life. It offered to teach the king how to use the iron maiden in exchange for its freedom. It said it was not an ordinary instrument of torture. The king laughed at the pathetic offer and sent the beast-man away. Such a device was surely unworthy of a king and was worth nothing. But the old advisor, a crazy man by the name of Darbid, felt that the thing was brimming with magic. So, he advised the king to listen to the monster's proposition. After all, maybe it was a way to gain more power, piles of riches, and thus compete someday with Foralume and Lorgash and even mythical Thule..."

There was silence, disturbed only by the odd sizzling of the red stone. Kabur grunted, encouraging the old man to continue his story. He had recognized the beast-man as Nardek, an old caravan guide, turned into a monster by one of Shivar's Fingers, a cursed relic that the young prince had long ago thrown into the Murky Sea.

The elder coughed and continued:

"The monster explained to the king how to use the dreadful artifact. In fact, although we realized it too late, the gruesome sarcophagus was a door into the Abyss. Every man put inside, by the torture and suffering inflicted on him, summoned a demon, and the demon obeyed its summoner. The first demons invoked in this way terrified us, but the king controlled them. Alashkar quickly became greedy for these servants. He sacrificed six people. Six demons came out with their faces horribly deformed and scarred. They all obeyed the king and became a Praetorian guard, as frightening as it was devoted. Six, but not one more! Still wanting more, the king inflicted the iron maiden torture on a great number of his subjects. Blood flowed over the flagstones of the royal Ziggurat. It spilled down into the lower levels, painted the walls red and sticky. But it was no use. No more demons came out. In the meantime, the six hungry monsters demanded to be fed human flesh every day, and the king began serving up his own people to please them. The banquets at the palace were so heinous, so unholy, that I still shiver at the thought. My soul will never forget those crimes. Olyazabad, I'm afraid, just like my soul, became forever stained…"

The old man had a coughing fit that shook his whole bony body. He calmed down after a few mouthfuls of foul soup. Then between wheezing breaths he went on:

"Alashkar even sacrificed Golshan, his son, thinking that his own flesh and blood would satisfy the appetite of the evil coffin. But it didn't. The young man died screaming, 'Father, have mercy!' as he was pierced all over, but the king was deaf to his cries. That was when the chief demon, the one called Kordar, whispered to the king that if he gave his beautiful, sweet daughter, Kheirana, in marriage, the doors of the Abyss would open again, bringing forth a whole army at his service. The marriage to bind the two beings together forever was supposed to take place in the dark, during a total eclipse of the sun. The clever demon knew that one was coming soon…"

The pause he took was met with silence. No one dared to speak. The old man turned to Kabur and his dead eyes seemed to stare straight through him.

"My good prince, I am consumed with shame, but now I am but Darbid the Fool…" He choked back tears. "…Darbid the Accursed who caused the fall of the most beautiful city in the world."

Kabur straightened his clothes, grabbed the Spear of Lug, and marched toward the exit. Jessalba ran after him, pleading:

"Noble Kabur, it's madness! You are in no condition to fight!"

The proud prince of Thule turned around. In his eyes danced the cold glint of death; his blond hair, blown by the wind, fell in front of them. He brushed it away with his hand.

"Nobody will say that Kabur let such infamy continue. Darbid knows this. The eclipse is predicted for tomorrow. If the iron maiden opens and lets an army through, all of Hyperborea will be threatened, including my own Thule. I'm going to put an end to the bloody reign of Alashkar the Cruel, which is what he will be called from now on! And then, poor Kheirana won't have to be given in marriage to the demon. She will never be condemned to the sufferings of the Abyss. I will free her and your city at the same time. Soon, woman, Olyazabad will be alive again with laughing children and gossiping old crones drying meat."

The prince ripped off his bandages. His own scar no longer oozed infection from the demon's claws. Kabur left the little group there and headed for the pyramid.

The sun struggled to rise above the serrated summit to spread over the plateau in scattered pools of light, but its rays had more trouble fighting the demonic cold that had invaded this accursed place. Kabur's fever was gone and he shivered as he felt the icy breeze. The ziggurat seemed to challenge him again to dare venture inside. The palace was gigantic. Sitting on a rocky peak, taking up the entire summit, it was connected to the rest of the plateau by several bridges that formed the arms of a stony star. Some of them were broken clean off, others half collapsed. Kabur spotted one that was usable, probably the one used by the marauding demons to hunt down the last inhabitants of the city. He had to cross over hanging walkways and wind through the alleyways of deserted dwellings. Sometimes, he had to go up, or down, on rope ladders, or use the rooftops. He passed by a number of skeletons lying on the ground, or piled up like macabre pyramids, frail and obscene imitations of the building where the foul creatures from the abyss were holed up.

Finally, after hours of walking and climbing, Kabur reached the bridge. He ran across the arching stone holding the Spear of Lug. The ziggurat spread out before him. He walked along the walls looking for an entrance. After searching for ten minutes, he found a worm-eaten door. Using his shoulders, he forced it open and entered an inner courtyard.

A grinning demon was waiting for him, standing motionless in the middle an empty shallow pool. The monster's hands slipped out of its sleeves, each of them holding a curved blade. Hissing what was probably an insult in its serpent tongue, it charged, twirling its weapons.

The young prince jumped behind a pillar and brandished his spear. The demon swung at his side, cutting a notch in the column. Kabur rolled and ended up behind the creature. He waited for the demon to turn around and then buried the double blade of his spear into the monster's heart. The demon roared and stumbled backward. It pulled the spear out of the wound, only making it worse. It attacked again, but was losing blood and becoming clumsier and weaker. Kabur swung around, blocked a sword thrust, and, in the same movement, cut off the creature's head. It rolled over his feet while the body dropped to the ground, spraying a geyser of thick, black blood.

"One down, five left to wipe off the face of the Earth so they can go back to their Lords of the Abyss!"

The prince of Thule clambered up several levels. The stairs were narrow and the steps high. Soon his muscles were covered in sweat, but he did not slow down. He kept climbing toward Alashkar the Accursed, while the Moon, on its own journey, rose up against the Sun.

A demon suddenly jumped out in front of him, cursing:

"Runt, stop this madness or you will walk the realm of my masters and suffer a thousand deaths!"

"I prefer a thousand deaths to a single life as a coward," Kabur answered, as he lunged forward.

The creature carried no weapon, but its entire body was covered with iron spikes that were linked by a complex leather harness. The demon, therefore, wanted to get the warrior in hand-to-hand combat so it could grapple him in a lethal grip. It grabbed Kabur's wrist when he lunged, and slid his arm against him, badly scraping the prince's side.

Kabur got away with a wincing pain and more anger. As he struggled free, he hurt himself again.

"By Kronan!" he exclaimed, "you're formidable but you're no match for me!"

The demon replied with a laugh, rubbed its metal-streaked face and rushed at him. Kabur had taken note of the monster's agility and his fighting technique. He dropped his spear and decided to turn his enemy's tactics against it. Shaka, his old weapon-master, had once taught him the science of barehanded fighting. He slid to the right in order to dodge the demon's attack, then grabbed his wrist between two spikes. With a clever move, he threw the demon down hard against the ground. In his confusion, the creature impaled himself on his own spikes, and along with his blood, spit out curses. Then he died.

Kabur paid no attention to him, except to leap over his body and continue on his way. The Sun was starting to be partly hidden by the Moon—time was running out. The prince climbed up two more levels. The ziggurat was empty, like a silent tomb, troubled only by the echo of his footsteps that resonated along the bloodstained walls. The prince crossed a series of deserted rooms with dusty furniture and withered plants. The dirty tapestries looked like the demons had used them to wipe their mouths after their unholy feasts; they were piled up in corners, or barely hanging on the walls in tatters.

A demon armed with a scythe jumped in front of him, foaming at the mouth. The weapon, a long, bone handle with a curved blade stained with greenish fluid, swung just over the young prince, who barely had time to duck a second before. Right away, Kabur swung the Spear of Lug at the scythe, which flew into the air. The demon threw his fist at the prince who took the hit in order to get closer. The punch was hard and heavy, and Kabur's sight went blurry for a minute, but he had unsheathed his sword and stabbed the demon under his chin. The blade went straight through the monstrous head, finding a passage between the iron mesh that formed his mask,

115

and knocked out a few fangs. The creature fell next to his weapon, dead.

"Three more of these abominations left and Olyazabad will finally be free," Kabur said, moving on without looking back.

But he had underestimated the hellish creatures' bag of tricks. Vexed by their fellows demons' failures, a pair of them rushed to kill him. They were the same two creatures he had already met on the bridge. The demon with the hook was swinging it and the other was raising its misshapen sword. But this time, Kabur was ready.

"You again... Our previous encounter was interrupted. I wasn't finished showing you the extent of my skills," the prince of Thule roared, as he rushed forward.

He struck with his spear at one, then the other, keeping them at a distance by weaving through the sculpted stone benches that filled the huge room. The attack by the demon with the hook was more dangerous because he was an expert with his weapon, which gave him a long reach.

Kabur suddenly had an idea. He got in between the two demons and pretended to be tiring. He panted and lowered his guard for a moment. The creatures were in a hurry to finish him off and feast on his flesh, so they were oblivious to his trick. The one on the right threw the hook as the other leaped forward. At the last second, Kabur dropped to the ground. The hook went whistling by and slayed the sword-wielding demon. Totally surprised, he tried to pull back the hook, but he was too late. Kabur impaled him on his spear, whose bloodstained tip stuck out the back. The creature tried to curse, but the prince cut his throat before he had time to say a word. Nearby, the other demon, pinned by the hook, died as well, killed by the clumsy hand of his infernal partner.

"Silence, monster, it's time for you to return to the Abyss that spawned you! If I'm not mistaken, I still have to deal with your leader, Kordar. He's probably protecting the king. By Kronan, I have to hurry because soon the Sun will have disappeared. Then all the monsters will be able to celebrate the evil wedding in Olyazabad!"

The leader of the demons was indeed at King Alashkar's side. The sight at the top of the ziggurat would have made the bravest man tremble. But Kabur was much more than a mere man. The blood of his ancestors, the legendary Danaians, ran in his veins, and he felt no fear, just extreme disgust for the weakness of his kind.

The monarch who had sacrificed his people to feed the creatures from the Abyss was perched upon his throne. Fed by the toxic influence of communing with demons, his body had undergone a horrible change. His head was huge and deformed, held up by chains attached to the top of his blood-stained throne. His two bulging eyes barely supported his protruding forehead where oily, tumorous growths palpitated and leaked foul puss. His nose had vanished behind two quivering holes above a toothless mouth stuffed with a swollen tongue covered in warts. Alashkar's puny body could no longer move with such a bulky head. Bedridden, or rather throne-ridden, the king had watched his limbs shrivel into fetal position like some unnamable newborn.

"Ahh... There he is... The defiant... The impudent..." the king struggled to articulate, slobbering and wagging a pasty tongue that looked like a bloodless, sickly slug.

Kordar stepped forward. He was the biggest demon of all, and besides his iron face, whose barbs pierced the gray flesh, he wore horns sticking out of its skull. He grabbed the weapon off his back and hefted it with a smile. The huge war hammer was engraved with faces in agony. He paid no attention to the king, did not even look at him, as he walked slowly toward Kabur.

The prince of Thule, in turn, stepped forward, pointing his spear at the creature that was three heads taller than him. After a brief moment of sizing each other up, the two enemies attacked. One let loose profane howls while the other shouted the name of his god-ancestor.

117

When Kabur blocked the demon's attack, his spear vibrated under the mighty blow. But the prince held on and counterattacked, driving Kordar back, again and again, dealing swift, precise blows.

The demon lost ground and roared. The hammer broke the stone columns, dug deep grooves in the floor, and threw out dust and shards all over the throne room. Kabur ducked under a side swing that smashed into a wall, then he charged, his spear held out.

Kordar saw him coming and barely dodged the attack. That was when Kabur let the spear go flying and grabbed his sword. In the same movement, he hooked around the demon's right leg and used it to swing himself up on his foe's back. There, he grabbed his horns to keep steady.

Kordar tried to shake off the human, but Kabur held fast. He lifted his sword high and brought it down into the demon's neck. Both of them fell to the ground and landed a few feet from each other. As incredible as it might seem, Kordar stood up. He was bleeding profusely, black blood that ran down his muscular, tattooed body.

Kabur faced him—now, weaponless. The demon ran at him, lifting his hammer. The prince of Thule did not flinch before the sight. He took one step back as his blonde hair blew in the breeze kicked up by the attack. Then, he threw a punch, as hard as he could, into the demon's belly. Right after that, he kicked him in the knee, which bent the demon over. Kabur grabbed one of Kordar's horns, held tight, and pulled with all his strength, breaking it clean off. Then he shoved it into Kordar's gaping maw. The groans of the monster were stopped short by the lethal blow, and he fell to the ground, staring at Kabur with dead eyes.

Alashkar flailed his arms as he tried to squeeze out of the throne where he was stuck. His head bobbled, a disgusting mass of quivering flesh. As he struggled, his jowls shook and sent a shock wave to his triple chin, which in turn made his bent neck vibrate.

"No... ahh... mercy, gentle prince... I... I can give you my kingdom... You'll be my son if you... want..."

"I don't give a damn about your gifts, Alashkar, you wicked king. You'll be remembered as the butcher of your people. May hell devour you!"

"I... I... wasn't in control... It wasn't my fault... Please..." the deformed man pleaded as the spear touched his chest.

Kabur paused. He remembered that Kordar had indeed attacked him without paying any attention to the king.

"Then who is it? Who's behind all this?"

Suddenly, a loud sob came from behind the red velvet curtains. A gorgeous young woman with long golden hair stepped out of the shadows. Around twenty, the girl was lightly dressed in a flimsy robe that hid little of her graceful curves, and her gray-blue eyes sparkled.

"Curse upon you, prince of Thule! You killed my mate! Oh, curse on you," she spit out in a voice full of anger, scorn and despair.

Then she rushed at Kabur, trying to stab him with a dagger.

"Your... mate?" the prince said, astonished.

He fended her off easily.

"My father, that pompous idiot, thought he was worthy of the iron maiden, but he couldn't handle its power," she replied. "Me, I had respect for Nardek, and I listened to him. He told me so many things before leaving Olyazabad. He told me of the prophecy that said that I would become a great empress, reigning over all cities and kingdoms of the South. Yes! I accepted this union, which was the price I had to pay. And I was counting on leading the demons' armies and destroying any land that would resist my rule! Along with Kordar, my mate, I was going to rule the world. But now, it's over! And it's all your fault, Kabur! All I can do is die now! But I'll take you with me!"

With a shriek, Kheirana ran at Kabur, crying tears of rage and regret. So young and yet, already corrupted by the power of the Abyss!

"Curse you, Nardek, for befouling these pure souls!" Kabur exclaimed. "I will find you and make you pay, by Kronan!"

Gently, Kabur caught the young woman. She tried to stab him again, but he knocked the blade out of her hand. Then, he grabbed her forearm and pushed her away hard.

Kheirana collapsed in tears, her robe forming a golden ring around her. She did not get up, but buried herself in sobs. Clenching his teeth in anger, Kabur picked up his spear and finished off the king, who was just waiting for death as he stared at his daughter.

Kabur then found the iron maiden behind the curtain. The accursed artifact whispered dreams of terrible, bloody dominion and unfathomable power, even to him. The prince brushed away the evil thoughts and raised the Spear of Lug. He let loose his anger with a few strong thrusts that destroyed the iron maiden forever.

The young woman watched him without moving or speaking, utterly lost in her despair.

Kabur ignored her and left the palace.

Once he was in the pass around the frozen Needles, Kabur turned around. He took a minute to enjoy the spectacular view of the cracked city. A ray of sunlight broke free of the lunar shadow and pierced the clouds. Its timid glow bathed the entrance of one of the troglodyte dwellings. In the doorway stood a dark-haired young woman, tiny at this distance, waving her hand to say a grateful farewell.

Jeff Sullivan by Luciano Bernasconi

Jeff Sullivan belongs to a long line of heroes, whose founding father, the Gaul warrior Gallix, received his powers from the Fomore "god," Levan (hence their family name, meaning the "Soul of Levan). Jeff Sullivan, aka the Man of Brass, is also a founding member and the leader of the Hexagon Group, a powerful team of superheroes that includes the Dark Flyer, Black Lys, and others. This adventure takes place before his sacrifice on the Moon during their battle against the Strangers and the Necromancer...

Romain d'Huissier: *The Incomplete God*

Like every night for a week now Stephen Hamilton could not close his eyes. As soon as his head hit the pillow, his mind would constantly go back over the theories and equations he was working on at Columbia University, where he taught astrophysics.

With his closest collaborators, he was working on unifying the four great forces of creation—gravity, weak interaction, strong interaction and electromagnetism—into one, a single equation to explain the secrets of the universe. And he had never been closer to his goal. He felt it in every cell of his body: the end was in sight. Every time he was about to fall asleep, a vision of the big white board on which he slowly but methodically, as his thoughts progressed, wrote down the long formula of the unification of forces, filled up his mind and chased away all his fatigue.

With a sigh, Professor Hamilton got up out of bed, being careful not to wake up his wife. He put on his glasses, dressed silently, and left the house.

After getting behind the wheel and starting his car, he headed for New York, leaving behind him the peaceful little town in New Jersey where he had lived for fifteen years. It only took an hour to get to his laboratory. He barely even said hello to the guard, just flashing his badge as he drove in, before sitting in front of the big board that refused to leave him in peace.

The white surface was covered with symbols and numbers and traces of small, crowded writing. Common mortals would see nothing here but a confused mathematical gibberish, but Professor Hamilton could decipher the long equation easily, moving his lips without making a sound, lost in thought. Once he got to the place where the formula looked unfinished, he grabbed a felt pen and started filling it in.

The squeaky sound of his labor filled the dark silence of the building with a nagging whine.

It was a beautiful, sunny morning and Jeffrey Sullivan was not sorry he had taken the day off to go to the conference where his friend Dominik Nero was speaking at Columbia University.

At this time, the speaker was busy shuffling his note cards while fumbling with his tie. A young, dark-haired man with impeccable taste, Dominik Nero ran a multinational corporation specialized in high tech: NeroTek. He was a well-known engineer and distinguished scientist, so it was not uncommon for him to be invited to speak at various conferences.

Seeing his friend having trouble, Jeff Sullivan went to help him with his tie. Jeff was taller, better-built and older, but also as blonde as his friend was dark.

"Calm down," he advised. "You just have to present the results of your work. It's not like you have to save the world from an alien invasion."

"Yeah, but at times like this, I'd rather face the Necromancer than the public."

Dominik Nero and Jeff Sullivan were, in fact, more than simple civilians—they were superheroes, members of the world famous Hexagon Group. With his moniker of the Man of Brass, Jeff was the leader, while Dominik was known as the Dark Flyer when he donned his high-tech armor. They had fought many battles together and with other members of the team.

"I'm telling you!" Dominik went on. "If I have to deal once more with fresh young students eager for my knowledge... But today, most of the audience will be from the military... My results on neuromechanic interfaces are very interesting to the US army."

"Of course," Jeff agreed. "But you've protected your patents and your father made NeroTek almost impregnable before he left it to you. Your invention will be a great benefit and hope for the disabled, and this kind of conference will get your work recognized."

Dominik sighed. "You're right, as always. Anyway, it's not as if I can pull a runner now. Go on and get a seat in the amphitheater. I'll be right there."

Jeff wished Dominik luck and left the small room next to the stage to sit at the top of the half-circle. He took a minute to look around. Just like his friend had said, there were a bunch of military men dressed in civilian clothes, standing out like a sore thumb by their posture. There were probably even one or two agents from CLASH. The students and visitors like him made up only a small portion of the audience, and given their attitude, the kids were just trying to skip out on a class that would be more boring. However, Jeff did notice a number of pretty college girls—Dominik's reputation as a billionaire playboy was widespread, he thought smiling to himself.

At last, the young CEO of NeroTek made his entrance. A scattering of applause welcomed him and Dominik bowed despite the lukewarm welcome—he could never help giving a show. This slightly outrageous behavior made the young students snicker, which was probably his goal. Then, turning serious, he stood in front of the microphone and started his talk, projecting complex diagrams in three dimensions on the screen behind him.

Jeff leaned back in his seat, ready to endure almost two hours of incomprehensible jargon. The things one does to support a friend...

Jeff Sullivan was shaken out of his drowsiness by a deafening noise, like a nearby explosion. Everyone in the theater jumped to their feet and the military men put their hand under their jackets, uncertain what they should do next. Dominik Nero had stopped talking and some anguished cries rose from the audience.

In a few bounds, Jeff rushed to the emergency exit and left the building. He was above the semi-circle on a metal staircase that zigzagged to the ground. As he had expected, it was an explosion that had shaken the building—and the source was very close, on the campus. Thick smoke was pouring out of a building away from the classrooms, probably a laboratory.

"Can you see what it is?" Dominik had been right behind his partner while the rest of the amphitheater had run outside through the regular exits.

"No, not from here. Maybe an accident...?"

Another series of explosions, less noisy, interrupted the Hexagon leader. Debris were thrown into the air and shouts of panic rang out everywhere.

"Invalid hypothesis," Dominik sighed. "A terrorist attack is more likely. CRIMEN perhaps?"

"I'll go take a look. It looks to me like a job for the Man of Brass."

Jeff Sullivan ripped open his shirt revealing a muscular chest under a golden uniform. In a few seconds, he had got rid of his civilian clothes and become the Man of Brass, one of the most powerful and most revered superheroes in the world. His noble bearing and peaceful demeanor immediately reminded Dominik why Jeff had been the undisputed leader of their group for so many years.

"And what should I do?" the young billionaire asked. "I didn't bring my armor with me."

"No need to put yourself in danger until we know more. Go help evacuate the people and try to find a CLASH agent."

"Got it, boss!"

Dominik ran down the stairs and into the crowd of onlookers to offer his help to the campus police.

Jeff breathed deeply and let his mighty power flow through him: the Soul of Levan. This energy source, handed down through his lineage since Antiquity, filled every cell with its extraordinary power, giving him the ability to control his own density. He could thus render his body as hard as titanium, or as light as air.

Rising into the air like a golden demi-god, Jeff headed for the epicenter of the explosion. At this altitude, it was easy for him to get a global view of the situation: a research building had been gutted by the explosion, and a trail of destruction extended into the maze of the university.

Jeff dove to the ground and right into the scattered debris. He used his superhuman strength to clear off the heaviest blocks of cement and look for survivors. When first aid workers came running to take care of the wounded, who were climbing out of the rubble after a few minutes, he was finally able to secure the ruins of the lab. It was then that he noticed that the walls had collapsed in, rather than being blown out, as if the disaster was due to an implosion and not an explosion. Puzzled by this, Jeff went in search of ground zero and found a simple office, one quite large, with all the furniture in pieces. Under the mangled remains of a big board, he found another survivor, whom he pulled out to hand over to the rescue workers.

Once he was sure that all the injured were safe, Jeff decided to track down whoever—if indeed it was a who—had caused the catastrophe, along with any accomplices.

The responsible party was easy enough to find. Flying over the trail of debris, the Man of Brass saw him sitting on the lawn at the end of the stream of destruction that his simple presence seemed to have caused. He was surrounded by police who did not look comfortable, but were not aggressive either.

Jeff landed between them and the police automatically relaxed when they saw the superhero. On closer inspection, Jeff could see that the being he had to deal with was not human. Even though it had a roughly human shape, it was ten feet-tall and its body looked like a map of the cosmos on which the stars and planets had been replaced by mathematical symbols and shifting numbers. The being had no face, but its head was tilted as if it were thinking—if that were possible.

Jeff was one of the most experienced superhumans in the world, but he had never seen anything like this entity. Maybe it was extraterrestrial, as lost and confused as the police surrounding it. Uncertain of anything, he decided to take a diplomatic approach.

"Greetings," he said, approaching with his palms open in front of him. "Nobody wants to hurt you. If you understand me, give me a sign."

The being turned its "face" toward Jeff and seemed to examine him closely. This made the Man of Brass feel uncomfortable and he cleared his throat waiting for a response. What he got was not what he was expecting. The creature just raised its hand and Jeff felt a shock wave hit him hard. His breath was knocked out and he was thrown against a wall so violently that he was dizzy for a few seconds. Although his ears were buzzing, he heard shots fired and shouting. When his head cleared, he saw the police had been struck in the same way as him.

"I should've expected that," the superhero muttered.

Tensing his muscles, Jeff rocketed toward the being, grabbed him up and shot into the sky, hoping to avoid any more collateral damage. The creature let him do it at first, but then, suddenly, Jeff felt himself becoming heavier and heavier... exponentially. Despite his strength, he started giving way under the weight, sinking farther and faster to the ground. The two interlocked figures finally crashed and left a crater right in the middle of the campus, which was fortunately deserted.

With his arms sore now, Jeff jumped back from the creature. Obviously, it had great power, especially this ability to control gravity, which it had used to strike him with a shock wave.

Jeff punched the creature as hard as he could as it was getting up. It was a waste of time. He felt like he was hitting a steel wall. Retaliation came swiftly: an electric aura formed around the creature and then it shot out at the superhero. A cry of pain got stuck in Jeff's throat as he took off into the air to escape another attack and take some time to think.

His opponent had an extensive arsenal and considerable firepower. Jeff had rarely been hit so hard—the last time was by his brother, the criminal Fred "Blackie" Sullivan. So, he decided to throw everything he had into the fight. Letting the Soul of Levan flow through his body, the Man of Brass made himself as dense as possible until he became as hard as diamond. Then, he bore down on the creature. The collision was frightening and made the crater even bigger as if an earthquake had hit the Columbia campus—and the rest of Manhattan.

This time the creature was shaken up. Jeff had put all his energy into the strike and had hit him hard enough to flatten a mountain. And he did not stop: using this brief surprise advantage, he rained down a series of blows on the entity, driving it back, step by step. Every punch hurt his fists and the noise of the battle made his ears bleed. He tried not to think of the damage he was doing to his surroundings—he had to trust his teammate Dominik Nero to evacuate the civilians.

Using so much power was exhausting, even for a superhuman as experienced as Jeff Sullivan. But he had to put this creature down, no matter what, because he would have no second chance. For the moment, the cosmic giant looked dazed, taking every blow without defending itself. But it was impossible to read its expressions and therefore to really know what it was feeling...

All of a sudden, an aura of emerald green energy started forming around the entity. When Jeff's fist hit it, his skin was burned by it and he had to grit his teeth as he pulled back—his hand was covered with smoking blisters even though his entire body was tougher than the hardest alloy on earth. Distracted by the pain and worn out by the constant effort, Jeff relaxed his power and stumbled backward.

The creature rose up before him, looking stronger than ever. It pointed a finger and a ray shot out of it: a projection of radioactive energy that engulfed Jeff in a blinding explosion. When the light faded, the Man of Brass was on the ground, his armor ripped in several spots. He was fighting to stay conscious. The pain distorted his face, but the determination was still there. The entity came closer, unscathed despite the beating it had just suffered. Jeff got up on one elbow and gathered the last of his strength to try to take off, to get away and catch his breath. Too late: his enemy was on him, raising a menacing hand whose palm was already glowing green...

Suddenly, a sizzling ray hit the creature in the chest and it backed up. Several other lasers hit their target and, all together, they formed a transparent sphere that imprisoned the creature and put it into a kind of coma, leaving it paralyzed and as still as a statue. Some CLASH agents came running up in their usual blue uniforms and helped Jeff to his feet.

Dominik Nero was there to ask his friend about his condition.

"You caught hell but you stuck it out."

"Barely," Jeff replied. "I need a minute to regroup."

A quick glance told the superhero that the creature was being held at bay by the agents armed with multi-frequency laser rifles. Ten or so of them surrounded their target and kept firing to keep it still.

"How'd you figure out how to neutralize it?" Jeff asked.

"He did it."

Dominik pointed to a guy talking with the CLASH officer in charge of the mission.

"He desperately followed around the rescue teams trying to talk to Captain Barson there."

Despite his arm in a sling and the thick bandage on his forehead, the man was easily recognized as the victim Jeff had pulled from the rubble at the epicenter of the explosion. He and Dominik went and interrupted the heated discussion between the survivor and the officer.

"Mr. Sullivan, I'm Captain Nathan Barson of CLASH," the officer with graying hair introduced himself. "Luckily, I was around and could put together a unit ASAP to help you."

"Thanks, Captain. Right now, I'm curious to know how you stopped the creature."

The injured man spoke up: "It's me, uh, well, I gave them the answer... Mr. Sullivan, I'm very honored to meet you... uh, yeah, sorry, it's not the time for that. I'm Stephen Hamilton, a professor here..."

"OK, go on and explain everything from the start," Jeff smiled and shook the professor's hand.

He let out a long breath and explained: "Yes, of course. In truth, this... being is a conglomeration of the four fundamental forces of the universe. You know, gravity, electromagnetism..."

"We know the theory, professor," Dominik cut in. "Get to the point."

"Well, uh, yes, OK.... I just advised the agents to adjust their rifles to shoot random frequencies to disturb the interconnection of forces that make up the creature."

"I'm sure there's a 'but' coming," Dominik muttered.

"But it's a temporary solution at best," the professor admitted. "The creature manipulates the forces that make the very fabric of our reality. It will quickly analyze what's happening and adapt itself..."

Jeff Sullivan took a minute to think. If the professor was telling the truth, then this being was a god—or as close to one as one could get.

"But how do you know so much about it?" he finally asked.

Professor Hamilton gulped and lowered his eyes before answering in a whisper, "Because... I, er, created it."

Then he explained the goal of his work, his recent obsession that got him working day and night on a formula to unify the forces, and finally of his strange epiphany the night before. The last thing he remembered before the explosion in his lab was confused, but he recalled having put the final touches on the equation after an all-nighter, and then the creature had materialized in front of him before starting on its path of destruction.

When his story came to an end, everyone was silent. Jeff looked at the creature being held prisoner in the distortion field... but for how much longer? If it really was an incarnation of the fundamental forces of the cosmos, its power was far greater than the best superhero on earth. How could they beat it?

"Should I call Hexagon?" Dominik pulled Jeff out of his reflections.

"No. We can't fight a creature like this in the middle of New York. You're the scientist; you've got to find a solution—and fast."

For once, Dominik stayed serious. Rubbing his chin distractedly, he studied the creature whose body was jumping with countless sparks as the CLASH lasers kept firing. His keen mind ran through a bunch of options, but his knowledge of physics told him that they could not overcome an entity who freely manipulated the four fundamental forces.

"Yes, of course!" he exclaimed. "It doesn't add up. Professor Hamilton, you said this being is, in a way, an incarnation of the unifying equation of the fundamental forces?"

"Well, yes, pretty much. At least, that's the only explanation I could find."

"But such a creature would be a form of cosmic life, transcending matter and mind, don't you think? Above all, it'd be an omnipotent force, the closest thing to God we could imagine."

"No doubt," the professor agreed. "But I don't see where you're going."

"It's simple," Dominik explained. "Jeff managed to go a few rounds with it. And our CLASH rescue team here is holding it prisoner with a pretty basic trick. If this... Living Equation is really what you imagine it to be, then no one and nothing would be able to stop it... and I doubt it would choose this shape to manifest itself."

"Yes," Jeff jumped in. "If I follow you, this creature might be very strong, but it's not invincible. So we have to ask: what do we do to keep it from causing more destruction?"

"No idea," Dominik admitted. "But I know someone who can help—Professor Quanter. He's at a symposium in Boston today. I can be there in less than half an hour with the Hexajet."

Quanter was, without a doubt, the brightest mind on Earth, a scientist whose brain worked as fast and precise as a computer. If any man could understand the Equation and defeat it, it was him

"Excellent idea," Jeff agreed. "Here's the plan: I'll stay here in case the Equation, as you call it, breaks free. You call Quanter to warn him and bring him back as soon as possible. Brief him on the way. And you, Professor Hamilton, go back to what's left of your lab and try to rewrite your formula—Quanter will need all the help we can give him."

"Aye aye, boss!"

Dominik saluted military-style, but the little joke could not hide the admiration he felt for Jeff taking control of the situation like the great leader he always was.

Dominik Nero had left New York almost an hour ago and Jeff Sullivan had recovered from his wounds, thanks to the supernatural energy given to him by the Soul of Levan, but he still was not in the best of shape. Reinforcements from CLASH had arrived in the meantime, but the Man of Brass knew that they would be of little use if the Equation adapted to the trap holding it down.

Moreover, the creature was lifting its head... slowly. Despite having no face, and therefore no facial expressions, Jeff knew that it had found a solution. He took a deep breath and turned to Barson.

"Captain, get your men together and make sure the campus has been evacuated. Form a second line of defense in case I fall."

The CLASH agent looked at the superhero with admiration and just nodded before barking orders to his men.

Jeff went back to the Equation, whose erratic movements were becoming more fluid. His body started glowing and the light began deflecting the lasers. Suddenly, in a flash, the prison's ball of energy disappeared. Obeying their officer in charge, the CLASH agents retreated, leaving the superhero alone to face the liberated entity.

"Second round," Jeff mumbled before rushing forward.

The frontal approach had little chance of succeeding, but this time Jeff was mostly trying to gain time. The creature held out its arms and his hands locked with the Hexagon leader's. They braced themselves. The Equation towered over the Man of Brass, but the superhero held his own. He felt the creature sending out strong gravitational discharges to weaken him, but he kept adjusting his own density to compensate for it—a Herculean effort that put his mind through hell because of the concentration it required.

Calling up his hand-to-hand combat training, Jeff used a shock wave to throw his opponent. He fell back with a foot on the creature's stomach and sent him flying over his head. He jumped to his feet and took off from the ground. Once above the entity, who had been thrown through a wall and destroyed it, the Man of Brass plunged on it with all his heavy mass, a tactic that had had a little success before and that made the ground quake for miles around.

The superhero landed like a bomb, burying the Equation in the ground. He took off again right away, but not without picking up some rubble. When the Equation crawled out of the hole, Jeff threw everything he was carrying at it as hard as he could. Once again, the impact caused the building to shake and a thick cloud of dust covered the ground for an instant.

Jeff caught his breath while sizing up the scene, knowing full well that his antagonist had suffered little damage, if any. In fact, its answer was swift, in the form of bright blue energy beams that shot into the sky. Jeff dodged the attack, but realized too late that it was only a diversion: the Equation came flying out of the dust cloud at lightning speed and grabbed him by the throat, dragging him higher and higher.

At a certain point, the creature threw him down and bombarded him with gravitational waves to hasten the drop. Unable to fly under the crushing weight, Jeff watched the earth coming to meet him—fast, much too fast.

The impact was devastating. A huge crack literally split the Columbia campus in two while the sound wave broke all the windows for miles around. By some miracle Jeff did not pass out—the pain tearing through all his muscles denied him the generous gift of unconsciousness. But he was out of the fight. He had done his best, but even he was powerless against the Equation.

The creature landed nearby and lumbered toward him. When it was looming right over him, Jeff felt a strong sensation of *déjà vu*. He thought of his wife and daughter, awaiting the final blow.

But once again, fortune smiled on him. Some mathematical symbols materialized like a hologram right in front of the Equation. The creature stopped moving and raised its head and looked for the source of the apparition. Jeff got up on one elbow and did the same, even with the veil of blood blurring his field of vision.

A man was standing nearby, tapping casually on a virtual 3-D keyboard. Jeff recognized Professor Quanter and Dominik Nero next to him, this time dressed in his Dark Flyer armor. There were also Captain Barson and Stephen Hamilton. For a moment, the Equation studied the "message" that Quanter was sending, then some symbols floated off its black skin to form an answer. This time, it was Quanter who scrutinized the dancing formula. He frowned, then smiled, and started typing on the keyboard again. He and the entity seemed to be engaging in a mathematical conversation made of abstract concepts.

The Dark Flyer came to help the Man of Brass get up. Jeff leaned on his friend and grimaced in pain. The two superheroes stepped cautiously away from the Equation and went to join Quanter and the others. After one last message, the eminent scientist turned to Jeff.

"Well well, old friend," he smiled at the swollen face, "I've seen you looking better."

"And they say my sense of humor is sometimes in bad taste," Dominik muttered.

Still a little shaky Jeff shook Quanter's hand—more thankful than he would ever admit.

"Professor, I'm glad to see you. Especially right now. We believe you're the only one who can fix this crisis."

"My, my, the problem was well worth interrupting a conference that was nevertheless quite interesting. Just think of it, the concept of incarnated astrophysics! And beating the daylights out of a superhero to boot!"

Not far from them, the Equation was standing still, but its "face" was turned to the small group, making everyone , except Quanter, feel uncomfortable.

Captain Barson demanded: "Explain this. How are you talking to this thing and what did you say to calm it down?"

Before answering, Quanter sent another message to the Equation.

"Excuse me, I'm trying to copy our conversation. I'll put my virtual keyboard into vocal mode so it'll directly translate what we say."

After a few taps, the scientist finally turned to the group, which was hanging on his every word—Quanter really knew how to play it up.

"OK, this entity that's now listening to us is an unfinished singularity. It's a mathematical concept that should have transcended itself and merged with the universe, but it became self-conscious during the process because of an error."

"An error!" Professor Hamilton was surprised. "But I thought I solved the mystery, found the formula…"

"Sorry but no, dear colleague," Quanter replied. "On examining the remains of your board saved from the disaster, I noticed some minor errors, infinitesimal ones. Sometimes simply estimations, but they were enough to keep our new friend from reaching its cosmic plenitude. If it's any consolation, keep in mind that your thinking was brilliant. For the moment, you are the closest man to the secrets of the universe."

"Too bad I was working in such a trance that I remember almost nothing, and the little I can isn't enough to reconstruct the enigma."

A long silence followed while everyone thought of the consequences of this revelation.

"But then, what are we going to do with the Equation?" Jeff finally asked.

"The answer is obvious!" Captain Barson said. "A creature like this can't be walking around. Just look at the damage it's done! CLASH will get rid of it, put it away somewhere safe where it can't hurt anyone."

Quanter smirked at this military tirade. "Really, Captain! Do you think your organization can hold the Equation against its will? Plus, this being has no intention of hurting anyone. Just materializing in our reality caused the first explosion, when it absorbed the scattered atoms to forge a physical body. Lost and confused, our friend went to explore its new environment, but such a concentration of raw power was enough, simply being there, to unleash various catastrophes, especially since it couldn't control its powers."

"But look at what your little friend did to Sullivan!" the skeptical officer pointed out.

"Oh that... The Equation obviously felt some kind of threat. Since we have no idea how it perceives things, it's possible that it saw through Jeff's flesh and blood and directly into his energy matrix, the famous 'Soul of Levan,' which looked dangerous to it."

"No big deal," Jeff said. "Given the circumstances of its arrival in our world, I can understand that there was a... let's call it, a misunderstanding."

"The question remains," the Dark Flyer said. "I can't imagine what a supervillain would do if they got a hold of the Equation somehow..."

Without responding, Quanter turned to the mathematical entity and sent it several short messages. It took time to analyze everything, and then answered, again making numbers and symbols float off its body.

"What the devil are you talking about?" Professor Hamilton was still fascinated by "his" creation.

"I'm explaining, in terms quite complex but exhaustive, its underlying nature and why it's imperfect. And it asked me how to fix the incompleteness it feels."

"And what are you going to say?"

Quanter shrugged. "I have no idea. Maybe I'll keep it with me and spend all my time trying to 'fix' it so it can finally fulfill itself…"

"I have a better idea," Jeff interjected.

He turned to the creature, put a hand on his chest and pointed to the sky. "Go back to where you came from," the superhero said. "Explore the universe and learn about yourself. And I hope that, if you ever come back, we can truly consider you a friend."

The Equation stared at Jeff for a moment, then looked up. It raised a hand to say thank you… and maybe sorry. Then it rose into the air, slowly at first, then faster and faster, and finally disappeared into the atmosphere as the group watched on.

"Well done, Sullivan," Quanter said with sincere admiration. "This being does indeed belong to the cosmos, so it's only appropriate that it should return there. I hope it finds itself out there."

Barson still sounded unhappy, "I'm not sure my superiors are going to like this."

"Come on, Captain," Dominik spoke good-heartedly, "I'm sure you can write a report that will focus on the bright side of things. And for inspiration, I'm inviting you and all your men to the best restaurant in Manhattan."

This offer did brighten everyone's mood. But before going to enjoy themselves, they all took a minute to reflect on the fascinating encounter they had just had.

Very far from Earth, on the edge of the universe...

In the astral void, the Equation was drifting lazily. It felt the solar winds against its skin; it heard the song of molecules; it saw colors exploding over the visible spectrum. Around it seething creation pulsed, even though the closest living being was hundreds of light years away.

It did not feel alone, however. It knew that it had a friend... somewhere... far away... Jeff Sullivan, the Man of Brass.

Ozark by Alfredo Macall

*Russell Red Horse, aka Ozark, is a young Lakota warrior who
inherited the magical powers of his teacher, the wise shaman
Wa-Tan-Peh. With the help of various allies, Ozark and his
magical horse Mustang, the embodiment of the Lakota spirit,
fight various supernatural creatures that threaten the Earth...*

Jean-Marc Lainé: *The Waste Land*

A gust of wind chased away the dead leaves. The rustling
fibers flew off as if a panting giant was running through the
abandoned garden. The grayness of an early autumn seemed to
have already invaded the scrawny groves and ragged weeds
that surrounded the house and ran toward the cliff. Shades of
dreary green and gray, dull grass; almost dirty, flowers aban-
doning their withered petals to the whistling winds; everything
portrayed an inexpressible but tangible sadness. The biting
cold breeze from the ocean swayed a few bare branches and
kicked up a small whirlwind of brown leaves fallen too soon.
In the distance, the surf grumbled its eternal dissatisfaction, a
constant reminder of the ocean's rebuke.

The shaman contemplated the front of the house.

He had come on the road, around the back of the city and
along a sidewalk that led to the rocky point before disappearing into the dunes. He had had no trouble finding the house. It
was the last, the farthest, the most secluded building. It was
also the windiest. It was the one hiding in the thickest shadows. It was the darkest.

For a moment, the shaman was lost in thoughts looking
at the garden, turned into an ugly, wild land with its withered
flowers and leafless trees, where sad birds never sang.

He had pushed open the gate and walked around the
house. He had taken a few steps on the oily grass, glanced out
over the boundlessness of the cold, stormy ocean. Since morn-

ing, he had been expecting rain, but the gray sky would not turn to drizzling. Nothing was going to wash away the infinite sadness that tarnished the place.

The shaman took one last look at the garden, the neglected groves and the barren trees, then he approached the French windows on the side of the house. He walked over the large paving stones upon which no one trod anymore to go and dream of the distant horizons beyond the seas, and that moss and humidity had covered with a downy, greenish lace.

The shaman was about to knock on the glass door, but hesitated. There, standing on the stained gray stones that had lost their original shine to the dreary passage of time, by the raging rains and moaning winds, he thought again of the man who was living in this house with dusty windows and a weed-infested mailbox.

This man had written some great books, the shaman acknowledged to himself—great books on magic, the pages of which spoke clearly about what he knew of things that the common mortal did not know. The shaman, like many magicians, had devoured his works, which were a reference for the neophytes, as well as the fans, the charlatans, the carnival entertainers, and even for the true sages, the initiated, who knew the arcane secrets that underpinned the world. There were books to make one dream, distrusted only by the most rigid and stern, but that brought bright laughter to whoever was most in need and carried them away to inaccessible spheres.

The man who had written these books knew how not to be taken seriously, except by sorcerers and magicians whom he depicted as a colorful and industrious lot. The magic of his books was simply to hatch in the hearts of his readers a warm and familiar, friendly and intimate, idea of what magic was. Without ever defining or explaining it, he made it tangible. Nice and honest.

His books sold extremely well. A magic success, as the critics liked to joke.

The royalties had made the man rich, and yet for two years, he had not written a single word. For two years, he had been living here, in the midst of dry trees, dead flowers and silence. For two years, death had taken over his house.

Ozark knocked on the door.

The sound echoed like a toll bell, hanging for a moment in a blast of wind, then vanishing into silence again. The shaman waited a short time, that still felt like an eternity, before he heard a noise. Through the dirty window, he could see a figure approaching. The door slid open slowly and the writer's face peeked out.

He was in his forties, tired, sad and febrile, like a librarian with red eyes that might have spent long days bent over a hopelessly undecipherable manuscript. The writer looked at the shaman with his weary eyes in which there was a mix of a cynical understanding of the world and that spark of surprise when discovering something totally unexpected.

The writer pushed the door open, stepped aside, and with a joyless smile invited the Lakota sorcerer into his home.

The shaman stepped into the house. The wind from the open sea cleared out, but only for an instant, the musty smell of dust and ink that had settled on all the furniture.

The writer looked at his guest. Ozark was a head taller than him and his rough cloth coat and flannel shirt hid the shoulders of a wrestler. The man of letters was surprised to have to look up to address his visitor. For a moment, his heart skipped a beat and his body felt the cold grip of fear. Then he sighed and, like everything else, the fear did not matter to him.

"I kind of figured you'd end up coming here, Ozark. I know you. I wrote a book about you."

The shaman looked at the writer with a sweet smile full of understanding.

"I know. I really liked what you said about Native American magic."

An uncomfortable silence followed. The two men walked away from the French doors. Ozark followed the writer down a long, dark hallway, scattered with papers and boxes. There was some spare change and a key ring sitting in an ashtray, waiting for someone to remember them. A Maglite stood

next to an empty vase. Dried up pens lay on a table next to un-
paid bills; one of them rolled off. As he went by, Ozark ran a
finger over a table top and left a deep groove in the dust.

In the middle of the hallway, some stairs led to an empty
bedrooms upstairs. The steps were cluttered with books and
mail. Some of the tomes were still in their boxes, along with
press releases that nobody had looked at. Ozark recognized the
name on one of the covers: *Wilburn.*

"I'm surprised to see you dressed... like everyone else."

The writer did not turn around. His eyes were sad and his
lids half-closed when he spoke to his startled guest, as if he
were speaking to an old ghost he would regularly encounter in
the stale air of his empty house. Without waiting for the sorcerer to answer, he said:

"I'd expected you to come on your flying horse. Life is
monotonous on the coast. That would've been a colorful sight.
Something unusual to get people talking."

At first, Ozark believed he was being ironic, but the feeling vanished before the writer had finished speaking.

"It wasn't the proper circumstance. This is just a friendly
call..."

"Friendly? Seriously?"

The sorcerer heard a gasp of righteous anger being
choked back by the writer.

The two men entered a big, messy room that was full of
memories, ideas and projects, lying dormant on stacks of paper. The writer's desk was covered with magazines, files spill-
ing out newspaper clippings, books with worn-out covers and
bristling with post-its that had faded in the sunlight. The pale
curtains were wide open. Odd pens and pencils had rolled over
the Moroccan leather, or on the window ledge, and gotten
stuck between books or long-forgotten mugs. The computer
screen was black and dust had started throwing a gray veil
over it. On one corner of the table, there was a photograph of a
young, brown-haired woman and a smiling girl sitting in a polished frame. Someone had pushed the rest of the books to

make room for it. There was no dust on the frame; this memory of bygone days was cared for.

Ozark sat in silence, thinking. The man looked at him, probably for the first time. His eyes bored into the shaman as deeply as they could, with fierce cruelty tainted by curiosity, the kind that accompanies making new acquaintances, or reuniting with old old ones.

The sorcerer and the writer looked at each other.

Ozark noticed an old Remington typewriter sitting on a nightstand, stuck in a dark corner where the light could never reach it. Next to it, on a mini-bar, were some open bottles of whiskey, bearing witness to long-forgotten inspiration.

Ozark knew that the writer would not offer him a drink.

"I very much... appreciated your books," he said. "All magicians like them."

The sorcerer trained his penetrating gaze on the writer. But the silence only got heavier.

With a flick of his wrist, Ozark pointed at the typewriter sleeping in its shell.

"You're not writing anymore," he observed.

The writer sighed. He looked down at his shoes for a long time, lost in the maze of shadows that the dry trees, shaken by the sea winds, cast on the worn floorboards. A long moment passed; he stooped, crushed, wiped out. Then he raised his head. His eyes were pale and sad, wearied by the seasons and faded by the salt of too many tears. His disheveled hair and stubbled chin were the very picture of despair and self-denial.

"I..."

The words would not come out of his mouth. He did not know what to say. Or how to say it. Maybe he realized that there was nothing to say.

His hands shook terribly, quivering in the air like nervous spiders. When he put his palms on his knees, his fingers beat a chaotic rhythm, a frenzied dance, an incomprehensible Morse code without rhyme or reason.

"I... It's gone... Gone forever... It's empty, it's black... I can't..."

Ozark listened without saying a word.

"I can't... write anymore."

The sorcerer reached out and gingerly picked up a few sheets from the top of a dusty pile.

"When... How long has it been?"

Some newspaper clippings were sticking out of a folder, cut with a trembling, nervous hand. A headline about a tragic car accident involving a local family two years ago. Everyone still remembered it.

"An accident. The car went over the guardrail."

The local press had spread the news. The photo of the young, brown-haired woman and the smiling girl had made the front pages. The neighbors had found out about it in the morning edition. They had come to express their condolences, offer to help, if there was anything they could do...

"The papers talked about it. It was on Independence Day."

The writer had cut out all the articles he could find, two years ago, and put them in a folder to paste them into a scrapbook later. But he had never even opened the scrapbook and had closed the folder on the images of vanished joy and the metal carcass.

"They died instantly."

One of the articles had profiled the Wilburn family. The writer father, the editor mother, working for a big New York publisher, and their young daughter, a happy, friendly child, loved by all her schoolmates. A short item had summarized the career of Lawrence Wilburn, a successful writer and respected essayist, discreet, hard working, humble, a good neighbor and a respected citizen in a town that was proud to call him its own.

"For two years, you haven't written anything..."

The writer's face collapsed under the weight of sorrow. The painful memory, the bitter agony that had never left him, wrinkled his features; an invisible hand crumpled the already worn-out portrait of the successful writer. He buried his face in his hands to hide his grief.

Sobs racked his throat. Tears ran between his fingers and moistened his hands in waves of uncontrollable sorrow. The writer had no words to express his mourning and shout out his suffering. Words, his tools of choice, his faithful companions that had never abandoned him over the long road that had led to all his books, now had left him alone to face the inexpressible.

Helpless, the writer wept.

Ozark stood with his back to the window. The sun was setting on his shoulders as he watched the despairing writer, stooped and sluggish. His eyes sparkled in the shadows, but his face remained indecipherable in the darkness.

"How long have you been holding back your tears?"

The shaman did not need to put his hand on Wilburn's shoulder. He did not need to lean over him. He did not need to get any closer. He just had to talk.

"You, too, are a magician—after a fashion."

The writer stood up and went over to the photo sitting alone on the corner of the desk.

"Your spells are made up of syntax and vocabulary, your powers are poetry, and as a magician, your influence on the world around you is powerful and far reaching."

Lawrence Wilburn picked up the picture frame and stared at his dead wife and daughter. He started crying again. A tear fell on the glass.

"For two years, you have been wasting away and the world around you is dying. The flowers in the garden are withering. The birds go elsewhere to sing, farther and farther away. The land is barren. And the damage is slowly spreading. Sadness is taking over the world."

Wilburn raised his head. He looked around at the cluttered desk that had lain dormant for two years. Without turning around, he felt Ozark's eyes weigh on him, the eyes of the shaman full of confidence.

He did not need Ozark to put his hand on his shoulder. He did not need Ozark to come closer. He just needed him to listen.

"But today your tears are going to clean all this up, I'm certain of it."

Ozark opened the window. The sea wind rushed in, quietly rumbling among the furniture. The faded curtains waved as if endowed with a new life. The sheets of paper hummed and murmured like whispering conspirators.

"Cry, my friend, cry."

Ozark crossed the room and headed down the dark hallway, leaving the writer alone in his office being washed with a new breath of life. A few sheets whirled up in a gust of wind and fell at his feet in a jumble of ink-darkened pages mixed with blank paper. Words from the past joined promises of writing to come, a life's work to be put back in order, to be completed.

Ozark left through the French doors and crossed the garden.

"When a person expresses himself, it's a door that opens for everyone."

Ozark put his hands in his coat and breathed deeply, a big smile on his face. He looked at the branches of the chestnut tree. A bud was springing out.

Ozark turned around. Lawrence Wilburn was standing in the doorway. The writer returned his smile. His face was calm and gentle. He looked rested, despite the traces of tears on his cheeks.

"You know that, Lawrence. All shamans know it."

Ozark stepped off the heavy flagstones and walked on the grass. The wind carried away the dead leaves and the last spots of gray were swept off the greenery.

In a corner of the garden a grove was in bloom again, flower stems standing up, still shy but showing some color under the sun.

On one branch, a bird alit. A little higher up, another sparrow was already perched. They started chirping, chanting a polyphony that they were in no hurry to end.

Ozark turned around one last time.

"I'm looking forward to your next book."

Sibilla by Stéphane Roux

Sibilla is a descendent of Elena Drago, the sister of 16th century Captain Dragut, raised by Cagliostro, one of the Twelve Immortals of Atlantis. The present-day Elena was raised by her mother to assume the mantle of Heir of Cagliostro in order to fight evil. She works at home, writing a popular column about the occult (which she signs "Sibilla") for the Milan-based magazine Flash...

Jean-Marc & Randy Lofficier: *Sibilla in Tribeca*

In the secret circles of Manhattan real estate, it was known that the penthouse at 58B Warren Street was haunted. For me, it just had "character."

I'm Marty Trumbull, real estate agent, owner of Empire State Realty, the best agency in Tribeca. Well, let's say, in the top fifty.

58B Warren Street was a beautiful red brick building built in the '60s—that is, the 1860s—with big windows overlooking a street full of nice shops. A dream property for a couple of famous artists or some young Wolves of Wall Street.

The only snag was that the penthouse had so much "character" that half a dozen tenants had disappeared without a trace, two had to be committed, one had undergone a conversion and become a priest, and the last one had bashed in his wife's head with an ashtray.

"Character," like I said. In spades.

The rental had been listed with all the neighborhood agencies, starting with the most prestigious, before ending up at mine, which was a natural selection process with which I was intimately familiar.

After the third disappearance, my lawyer, Marv, had strongly suggested that I add the words "may be subject to hauntings and other paranormal phenomena" to the Notice of Disclosure that I had to hand over to potential tenants. The laws of the state of New York don't take that stuff lightly.

I had done a little investigation, and come to the conclusion that Marv was right. The building had belonged to a certain Benjamin Darkstone, an idiot obsessed with the occult who had reportedly spent thirty years of his life locked in his penthouse, meditating over an old skull he had unearthed from God knows where.

Then, about five years ago, Darkstone died, or disappeared. Nobody knew exactly what had happened to him. As often happens, his heirs, or in this case the city of New York, had turned the building into condominiums, which had quickly found buyers and/or tenants, including the penthouse with its smashing view of the surrounding rooftops.

But, as it turned out, the penthouse was haunted... Sorry, Marv, "was subject to hauntings and other paranormal phenomena."

The tenants didn't last and, from one agency to another, the listing had ended up on my books. The board of the building, represented by one Millicent Mulberry, a former tax auditor, had made it clear to me that they had hesitated between me and a potted geranium, and the geranium had only gotten two votes fewer than I did.

After the ten failures mentioned above, I kind of wished they'd picked the geranium.

And that's when Sibilla entered the story.

Reflecting on it, it wasn't very surprising that she'd heard about the case. She wrote a popular column about the supernatural in *Flash* magazine. Ghosts, vampires and werewolves were her daily bread, if I can put it that way.

She arrived at the agency just before closing, beautiful and radiant like a movie star. His auburn hair fell in elegant waves on a jacket cut by a great couturier.

I immediately put on my most sincere smile, the one that aims to convince the customer that we've been old friends since kindergarten, and were merely separated by a cruel fate.

"Are you the agent for the 58B Warren Street penthouse?" she inquired in a sing-song voice with a hint of Italian accent.

My jaw dropped. This was the last type of person whom I thought could be interested in the haunted penthouse. Of course, I didn't know who she was—yet.

"You wanna see it?" I asked. "It's a little late though; it would be a shame for you not to see it in broad daylight..." ("Like Dracula's grave," I added to myself.)

"No, I don't want to visit, I wish to spend the night there."

Seeing my stupefied expression, she pulled a letter out of her Gucci bag and shoved it under my nose.

"I have obtained permission from the board. Here is a letter from Ms. Mulberry..."

"No need, I believe you. You know the place?"

"Perfectly."

"Then here are the keys," I said, handing her a set immediately. "Let's talk again at, say, 10 a.m. tomorrow morning, here... Is that good for you?"

"*Molto bene*, Signore Trumbull. *Arrivederci!*"

She left, leaving behind her a slight scent of heliotrope.

The rest of the story, I learned from Sibilla the next day; I'm going to tell it to you like she told it to me.

Sibilla had learned about the haunting of Warren Street from a photographer friend of hers named Dave Kaplan, who had reported on the transformation of the neighborhood and had heard about it.

She had first thought it was either a fraudulent case, or not all that interesting. It was the murder of the wife of the tenth tenant that got her to take another look at it. Like me, it hadn't taken her long to identify the building's former owner: Benjamin Darkstone. But unlike me, this discovery had triggered all kinds of alarm, because in her world, Darkstone had been a feared and renowned warlock. She didn't tell me much more about him, and frankly, I didn't want to know more.

A brief visit to the building had confirmed her fears: there were supernatural forces at work, the nature of which was beyond mere mortal comprehension.

I thought Sibilla was just a hard-working journalist who had carved out a niche for herself at the crossroads of *Dear Abby* and *X-Files*, like, what to do if you find a vampire in your kitchen. I was wrong. So wrong.

I still don't know who Sibilla really is. Certainly, it's easy to learn her true identity: Elena Drago. Those who claim to know these things tell me that, in some circles, she is known as the "Heir of Cagliostro." But those who *really* know these things remain stubbornly silent. And they're right. My former tenants can testify that this kind of knowledge is rarely beneficial to those concerned.

The door didn't squeak when Sibilla entered the penthouse. Knowing the reputation of the place, I made sure all the hinges were kept well oiled!

It's never really dark in Manhattan; having left the blinds open, the ambient light of the city bathed the penthouse in a shroud of comfortable darkness.

Sibilla swept the surrounding space with her right hand—the one with the Ring of Cagliostro on her middle finger. Her preternatural senses warned her that she was not alone; yet none of the known signs of poltergeist infestation were present, otherwise the Ring would have reacted.

She'd shaken her head, like she was chasing off a persistent insect, and crossed the large living room. But as she stepped forward, she felt like she was moving through liquid, one less dense than water, but whose invisible and intangible presence was none the less real.

She murmured an incantation and, all of a sudden, she felt the oppressive sensation dissipate. She was again able to move at will.

The penthouse consisted of two bedrooms, two baths, and a modern, fully equipped kitchen. Sibilla visited each of the rooms. She said she thought they were tastefully decorated with a few low tables, some judiciously placed armchairs, and flower vases, etc. She didn't notice anything unusual—at first.

When she entered the kitchen, she had a nasty surprise: a large knife came off the wall and flew through the air towards her at great speed. Would it have stabbed her in the face? We'll never know because Sibilla made some kind of weird gesture (I don't know anything more than what I'm telling you) and the blade flew off to plant itself into the door.

Two other blades did the same thing and suffered the same fate,

Raising her arms, Sibilla then uttered an incantation—something powerful, I guess, 'cause it made the kitchen vibrate, then fall apart, and shattered all the windows. I know this to be true, because the tenants from the floor just below sent me a registered letter a few days later to demand that their own broken windows be replaced at the building's expense.

Having, er, "cleaned up" the kitchen, Sibilla returned to the living room. When she arrived at the center of the room, she shook her head and said, simply:

"So?"

Suddenly, a violent wind, with the force of a tornado, invaded the room. Its origin—so to speak—was a tiny black hole, no bigger than a pinhead, suspended in the air about three feet away from Sibilla.

In a matter of seconds, paintings, coffee tables, flowers, vases, armchairs and tchotchkes were sucked up by the tornado, then compressed and swallowed by the "hole." So much for the tasteful decoration!

There was nothing that Sibilla could cling to in order to avoid a deadly fate. Already her leather coat had been swept away. Clenching her teeth, she tried to move in the opposite direction of the tornado, her arms outstretched, like the mime Marceau pretending to push against an invisible wall.

Then, she screamed another incantation and the tornado disappeared, just as quickly as it'd arrived.

Smoothing her hair, Sibilla went to the "black hole" and plunged the tip of her index finger into it, then she pulled it back out and tasted the end of it.

"You don't scare me anymore," she said, "and I think I'm quite capable of thwarting all your tricks. Don't you think it's time for us to talk?"

A "face" then appeared in the center of the room. I use the word "face" broadly, because, according to Sibilla, there was nothing human about it. It was a triangular shape with six eyes, two located at each point of the triangle, with a slimy opening in the center.

"You have nothing to do in this space-time," said Sibilla. "You have caused enough pain here. Be grateful that I do not choose to exercise just revenge against you. All I ask you to do is leave—and swear on all that is sacred to you never to return."

According to Sibilla, the "thing" tried to negotiate, but as she explained to me the next day, since she now knew the name of the thing having "tasted" it, she had acquired power over it. How she managed that trick by merely putting her finger into that pinhole and licking it, I would never know. But all trades have their little secrets.

In the end, the "thing" had no choice but to give in and obey Sibilla's injunction, which sent it back to the the subspace from which it would never have come, had not Benjamin Darkstone, by mistake or mischief, released it with the help of his ancient cursed skull.

Once it was gone, Sibilla was left alone on the flagstone floor, which was the other side of the ceiling of the floor just below it.

Because the "thing" had been the entire penthouse of 58B Warren Street, which now no longer existed!

The idea that I had walked inside this unspeakable "thing" several times made me feel nauseous! But now, Sibilla had restored the natural order of things.

As for me, as the agent for the board of the building, I still had an equally formidable opponent to face: City Hall who wanted answers about what had happened to an entire floor of an "historical building" in Tribeca.

The "thing" might have been preferable after all!

The original Dark Flyer by Alfredo Macall

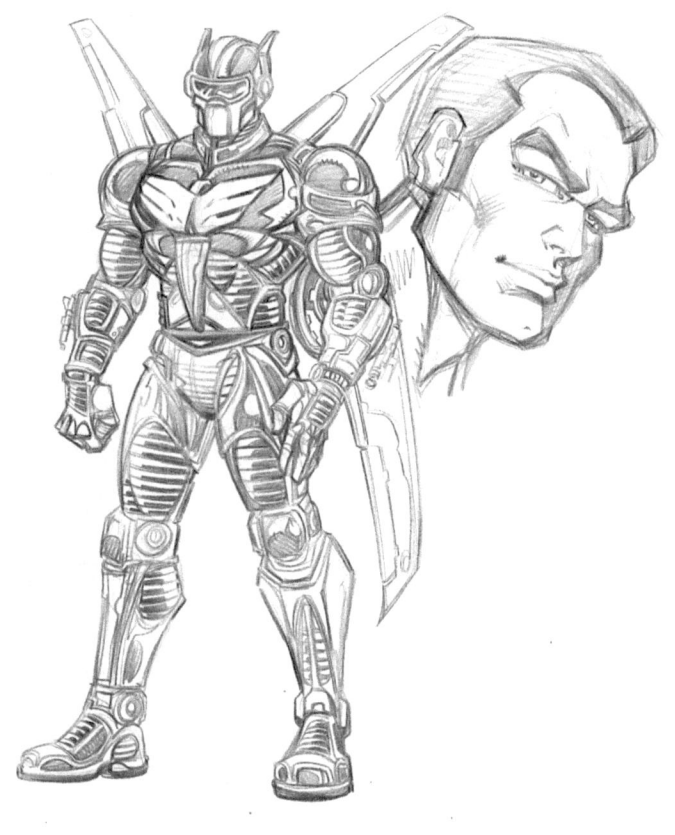

The second Dark Flyer by Alfredo Macall

Billionaire industrialist Cletus Nero, the owner and founder of aerospace giant NeroTek, took the identity of the Dark Flyer in order to avenge the death of his wife. He used his company's various inventions to fight the evil crime cartel Phantom, and became one of the founding members of the Hexagon Group. After he retired, his son Dominik inherited both his job as the CEO of NeroTek, and his superhero career as the second Dark Flyer...

Ghislain Morel: *C.O.L.M.*

For Chloé

Mumbai, 4:00 a.m.

The vehicle was racing down the highway at full speed and did not stop at the tollgate, barreling straight through the barrier. A silhouette of flame and gold was flying over the road until it caught up to the armored truck that was speeding onto the Bandra-Worli Sea Link bridge that skirted around Mumbai.

At that time of the night, the lanes were empty. The flying man rolled gracefully over the huge SUV and came down on the right side. The passenger window opened, showing a dark-skinned man wearing sunglasses and armed with a large-caliber machine gun. It took him a second to aim at the Indian superhero, and then fire continuously at the amazing golden armor being propelled by two bright jets of plasma.

Professor Rarchek Shankry had perfect control over his armor and knew everything it could do. Rather than dodge the bullets, he shot a cone of burning plasma out of his glove that instantly vaporized the metal and blinded the shooter.

Since the thug had to cover his eyes, the sparkling figure known to the world as Agni flew at the truck and grabbed the rear passenger door, which he tore off with a burst of his reactors. When another round was fired at him, Agni used the armored door as a shield, which he then threw into the sea when the gunfire stopped.

The driver knew that the only way to complete their mission was to escape, so he started swerving dangerously on the bridge to get away from the flying superhero.

Now that he could see into the truck, the armored scientist waited for it to get close to the guardrail, then he shot out at the thug sitting in the backseat. The guy sprayed him with bullets from an Israeli automatic pistol, but they did no damage to the golden armor.

Agni grabbed the fat but muscular man and, with a flick of his wrist, threw him out of the SUV. He suffered the same fate as the door a few seconds earlier.

On the seat was a small figure balled up in terror, frightened by the gunfire, the sound of mangled metal and the shouts of his kidnappers.

Agni shot two plasma rays at the tires, just hot enough to melt the rubber. The truck abruptly sank down and spun around. When the opposite door swung around in front of him, he tore it off, too, and tossed it away. Then, he flew straight through the backseat, carrying the child away in his arms.

The Indian "god of fire" soared up. At five hundred yards over the bridge, he looked at the controls on his armor, selected a flight path and shot off into the night.

After a few miles, he descended slowly to fly a few feet over the ocean.

"Don't worry, kid, I came to rescue you," he said. "I can't bring you back to your parents because they're in danger, too, and it's important to keep you safe. So, I'm bringing you to a friend of mine. He's very nice and he'll take care of you. You'll see, he's got a lot of fun toys."

The child in his arms was still trembling despite the heat given off by the armor. However, being worn out, he fell asleep during the weird flight that was taking him to safety.

It took a few hours to reach the island where the billionaire lived in semi-retirement. It was early dawn when the golden figure arrived and lowered his two plasma jets onto the pier. Cletus Nero, the superhero formerly known as the Dark Flyer, came in person to welcome the newcomer. Even if he was retired, his vacation home was still one of the most secure locations on the planet and its defense systems had warned him of the approach of a strange flying object. He immediately recognized his old friend. Both of them had worked in aeronautics and had met several times in their civilian identities. They had also fought crime together as their alter egos. Their respective intellects had recognized in each other the genius behind their tech.

The billionaire was intrigued by the child in Agni's arms.

"Greetings, noble keeper of this island, I have come to ask for asylum for this child who is under my protection."

"Good morning to you who, like the sun, arrives at dawn. Who is this boy?"

"His name is Ricky and he must remain hidden until his parents can share all their information about the Vega Cartel. Phenix is protecting them, but the boy was kidnapped to put pressure on them. I managed to rescue him, but the enemy will stop at nothing. I kept a low profile and hope I wasn't detected. You shouldn't have any problems, but you should stay alert nevertheless. Are you prepared to defend him if anything happens?"

"Don't worry. My security systems are extremely effective. If anyone dares to attack us now, they will have picked the worst time, because I've organized a little family reunion..."

Even though the island had its own landing strip, the new jet from NeroTek did not really need one. Its pilot slowed down and drifted over the ocean until he was hovering over a space in front of a large hangar, then he dropped down vertically. A door opened under the cockpit and a hinged arm lowered the pilot's seat to the ground.

The master of the island came up with his hands in the pockets of his linen suit.

"Did you have a good flight, son?"

"Super! I was able to test this new jet that we built for CLASH. It's an unarmed version, so it's lighter and I beat all speed records."

"Come inside. You can tell me everything, but I want you to forget about work and relax."

"That's the reason I came. The solitude here will do me some good. I'll get my bags and be right behind you."

The rear hatch opened slowly and a self-propelled cart came out. It waited a few seconds before falling in behind the two heroes.

"Dominik, I must warn you," said Cletus. "I have a last-minute guest. An old friend entrusted me with the care of a child being threatened by a criminal organization."

The new Dark Flyer furrowed his brow,

"Is it serious? Are you in danger?"

"I don't think so. It's unlikely that they will find this place. But if they do, there are two of us, plus all of the island's defenses to protect us."

As the two men headed for the huge mansion, they saw the boy coming out in his pajamas, obviously lost. He froze when he saw them, and, for a few seconds, his face twisted in fear.

"Ricky? Is that right? Don't be scared," said Cletus. "Don't you remember me? I'm the one who took you to your room last night. Let me introduce you to my son, Dominik."

"Please to meet you, Ricky," said Dominik.

The boy looked around awkwardly.

"I woke up and I was alone. I didn't know what to do. So I left to see if anybody was home."

"Not a problem, Ricky. There's no one else on this island except us and a few locals who help me with the housework. Almost everything is automated. You'll see, when you learn how to use the house, you'll think it's a blast. It's almost as if it were alive. I guess you must be hungry, no? Let's go get some breakfast. Follow me."

The three of them headed for the porch. They were barely inside when the boy started crying. Dominik picked him up.

"Come on, kid, what's wrong?"

Between sobs, the child managed to stutter:

"I feel all alone. I want to see my parents. I don't know anybody here. There's nothing to play with. I can't stop thinking about the horrible men who tried to kidnap me. And I don't even have my teddy bear!"

"Don't worry," said Dominik. "You're with us now, and we won't leave you alone. What do you say we go for a swim after breakfast? In the pool or, if you prefer, we can go to the beach. And there should be some of my old toys left in the house somewhere. You can play with them all you want."

The young billionaire felt really bad for the boy. He remembered his own lonely childhood after his mother's disappearance and his father's coldness. He was not about to let this kid suffer what he had experienced in the past.

All of a sudden Dominik's eyes flashed mischievously.

"Do you like stuffed animals? Because I think that I have exactly the right toy for you in my lab."

A bright smile lit up the child's face as Dominik walked away, pulling out his phone, connected to the NeroTek satellite network.

"Sweet? Hello! It's Dominik. No, everything's fine, don't worry. I just need you to make an urgent delivery for me, something I left in my lab, along with what I'll need to finish it. I'll send you the list. Can you do it right away? Find a plane and send the stuff... What? In three hours? Great! Thanks again, love. I'll call you tonight."

On the screen of a laptop sitting on an old, metal desk in the corner of an abandoned warehouse, the face of Vega—the South American leader of an international crime cartel—popped up.

"There's no excuse for losing the kid!" he said. "All my attempts to terminate the parents have failed. This damned Phenix had them completely off the map! All we've got left is the kid to leverage so they keep their mouths shut. He's got to be somewhere."

"Boss, I got some information from the Shiva Cartel. I had to cash in some favors and even promise a few more, but I found that Agni took him. I should be able to trace his thermal signature with our own satellite."

"Put everything you've got into it. I'm sending you Taos and Rico to take care of any other superheroes that might get in the way."

"Got it, boss! I'll keep you posted whenever I get news."

In his office in Miami, Vega slammed the screen down. He grabbed a crystal paperweight off his desk and hurled it against the wall, shattering it to smithereens. Then he leaned back in his chair and breathed deeply, closing his eyes to tame the anger that was gnawing away at him.

Cletus Nero was lying on a lounge chair, keeping a discreet eye on Ricky, who was playing in the sand with a plastic pail and a shovel they had found in a storage room.

He was a little sorry his son could not be with them, but Dominik was busy in the workshop with a mysterious crate that a plane from NeroTek's HQ had delivered in record time—less than three hours after his phone call.

The child still looked a little sad, but the sand and the ocean seemed to be a good distraction for him.

"Mr. Nero? I'm a little bored of the beach," said Ricky. "Can we go back to the house?"

"Sure. I've had enough sun for today myself. Let's go and see if Dominik has finished his project."

The retired billionaire took the child's hand and they walked slowly back toward the house. They showered off the sand in the yard and put on clean clothes. Sweet, Dominik's assistant, had added to the shipment some shorts, t-shirts and underwear for the child, as well as some essentials for the house. Ricky picked out a jersey with the colors of the Hexagon Group and electric blue short pants.

Afterward, they went into the kitchen and Cletus poured two glasses of freshly pressed fruit juice and got a plate of cookies from the cupboard. Then, they went to see Dominik, who grabbed a cookie without asking, and talked with his mouth full.

"It's great you're back! I've just finished. OK, it's a very advanced project of mine, and I wasn't sure about its final appearance. I owe it to you, Ricky; you've inspired me. When you're done eating, wash your hands and meet me in the living room."

The boy got excited. He swallowed the cookies and gulped down the juice in record time. Cletus watched on, amused, and emptied his own glass to keep up with the boy.

When they got to the living room, a present was waiting, about twenty inches high, wrapped in silver paper with a red ribbon.

"Is it for me?" asked the boy.

"Yes, Ricky, I hope you'll like it."

The boy jumped on the package and tore off the shiny wrapping paper so he could open it and see what was inside.

He took out a little brown teddy bear, around twelve inches high, with a white button nose and paws. The bear was wearing a green leprechaun hat and it had a clover printed on its belly and on the bottom of its feet. In its arms it also held a cloth clover with the words "I love Ireland" printed on it.

Cletus looked startled.

"This bear reminds me of something..." he said.

"Sure does! You gave one just like it to me when I was Ricky's age, when you came back from a business trip to Ireland."

"Can I keep it?" asked the boy.

"Of course, Ricky. His name's Colm. At least, that's what my dad told me."

"Hmm, I remember now," said Cletus. "In fact, I bought it in a souvenir shop just before flying back because I thought you'd like it. I called it Colm because of to the Irish actor, Colm Meaney, who was in *The Commitments*. I was afraid you'd give it one of those ridiculous, annoying names that you always gave to your toys, like Gugus, Yuck, or John John."

Dominik looked at his father with an ironic smile, then turned to the boy:

"Do you like it, Ricky?"

"I love it. It's really cute!"

"Great. Now listen to me. It's an experimental toy. It's made of very tough material, so you can take it anywhere. With any other bear, I wouldn't want you to take it to the beach, for example. But with Colm, you can play in the sand and even take it in the water with you. If it gets dirty, just run it under water. And always keep it with you, OK?"

"'Kay. It's so cool!"

Ricky went to his room with the teddy bear.

"Why did it take you so long to put a teddy bear together?" asked Cletus, suspicious.

"Because, as you suspect, it's not just a teddy bear. I just gave that kid twelve inches of NeroTek's most advanced technology—even more advanced than my own armor! Now, the kid's got nothing to fear."

On a runway in the middle of the jungle, an old, American army helicopter let off its two passengers. Not far away, a group of ten mercenaries was waiting near what looked like a flying assault vehicle from CLASH with its crates of weapons.

Mahyar, who was Vega's man in charge of the operation, welcomed the two newcomers: a gorgeous woman with long, black hair dressed in a skintight suit and a military jacket that showed off her perfect figure; and a giant dressed in camouflage pants and a military jacket that looked too small for him.

His muscles bulged and there were were big metal rings with huge bolts that came out of his back on both sides of his spine. Metal plates covered his shoulders and chest under the camouflage tank top. His bald head had burn scars. Another weird metal brace imprisoned his neck.

"Did you have a good trip?" asked Mahyar.

"As far as it could be in so short of time and with the available vehicles, yes, thanks," answered the woman. "Let's not waste time, where do we stand?"

Rico said nothing while Taos, Vega's personal body-guard, took care of the small talk.

"We have everything we need," replied Mahyar. "I recruited the best mercs I could find on the Asian market. They're all ex-military and most of them are experts in martial arts. They've been briefed on the mission: they'll take care the security and the staff, and grab the kid while you deal with the superpowered opposition. We've also sent a fast yacht over there as a backup escape in case that CLASH aircraft we bought on the black market after their tussle with Starlock gets damaged. We can reach the target in four hours if it performs as advertised."

"Good. When everything's ready, tell your men to get some rest. We'll leave at 8 p.m. sharp so we can attack at midnight."

"Yes, Miss!"

The giant started to grin and groan in satisfaction.

"About time."

"Don't worry, Rico," said Taos. "You'll be able to test your cybernetic improvements, but are you strong enough to beat a hero like Agni?"

The giant lit a cigar with his Zippo lighter, which he snapped shut. Another smile, nastier this time, crossed his face.

"I never believed in gods," he said.

The vacation had officially started on the Nero island. Father and son had time to talk, whether it was at the beach where they took Ricky, who was starting to smile again, or during their walks around the tropical paradise. All day long

Ricky dragged his teddy bear around, which pleased Dominik immensely.

Cletus asked his son:

"Tell me, you stuffed the toy full of sensors, didn't you?"

"You could say that. Let's just say I feel better if he keeps it by his side."

Every meal was a feast, and the young boy had almost anything he wanted thanks to the incredible technology in the house, connected to the highest speed electronic information network on the planet. He watched movies, cartoons, and played video games on the sofa with his bear, which was very eager to make comments about all the moves of the virtual characters. The two adults let Ricky enjoy himself, hoping it would chase his blues away.

After dinner, they allowed him to watch one last cartoon before getting ready for bed. Dominik brought Ricky to his bedroom and tucked him into bed. Every moment reminded him of his own difficult childhood, the sadness of losing his mother, and his father's being in too much pain to take adequate care of him. He was glad to be here for Ricky and hoped that his presence would help, that the boy would feel a little less lonely than he had at that age.

After tucking in the boy, Dominik handed him his teddy bear. Ricky hugged it under the covers with only his head showing.

"Good night, Dominik," he said.

"Good night, Ricky. Sleep well, tomorrow's going to be a busy day... full of activities. Maybe we'll take of one of my father's planes to go and check the other island. Would you like that?"

"Maybe... I don't know, I'm a little scared of flying."

"I understand. We can also tour it in a boat. OK, close your eyes now and go to sleep. I'll see you in the morning."

"See you in the morning, Dominik."

The new Dark Flyer turned off the light and closed the door. Then he tiptoed back to the living room.

"Not too much trouble getting him to bed?" asked Cletus.

"Not at all. I think the day wore him out."

"Good. Me, too, I'm exhausted. I was expecting a quieter vacation."

"We're alone now."

"You're right. We can relax now. I have an excellent, old rum. I think you'll like it."

"That sounds like a rather fine idea."

The two men sank into leather couches, holding their drinks and talking about their lives. Cletus told his son about his latest trips and lovingly described his armada of vehicles. Dominik gave a spirited account of his last adventures with the Hexagon group. It was a pleasant evening, but just before midnight, Cletus became alert as he stared at an old maritime map framed on the wall.

It took a minute for Dominik to notice his father's distraction.

"Is there something wrong, father? Is it crooked? Should I straighten it out?"

"No, there's nothing wrong with the frame. As a matter of fact, that map is a screen using electronic color ink. It's an interactive map of the island and the ocean around it. I made it look like an old Spanish map I once bought at an auction because it looked less obvious. You have to look at it closely to see that certain things on it are not standing still... Which is concerning. This morning, I spotted a yacht that's been cruising all day in the same direction... going towards our island, which is quite unusual..."

Dominik approached the map and could see what his father was talking about. He was very impressed. The drawing really looked like it was made on parchment, but certain dots on it were, in fact, moving. While he was admiring the details up close, the map suddenly started blinking red and he instinctively jumped back.

"Whoa! What happened?"

Cletus jumped up at the same time.

169

"Intruders in our air-sea space. Given the speed and altitude, it's not a civil aircraft."

"Trouble on the horizon. You think it has to do with Ricky?"

"I'm afraid so. I think it's time to get ready. I'll put on my suit and take off with my jet."

"Too bad I didn't bring a weaponized prototype of our new aircraft. You would have had a ball with it."

"Don't worry. The ones I keep here may look obsolete, but I keep updating them with our latest tech. My old F-15 is better armed and protected than most of the modern fighters."

"And I'll I put on my armor. It's in my bedroom."

The two superheroes gave each other one last nod and split up to prepare themselves for action.

The stolen CLASH plane slowed down abruptly when it entered the island's airspace. Only a few lights in Nero's mansion were signs that anyone inhabited the tropical island.

"No need for reconnaissance," said Taos. "We get as close as possible to the house and then get off!"

"OK, Miss," dais Mahyar. "Watch out! Missiles approaching! I have to make another round!"

The sudden acceleration threw half the mercenaries to the ground while the jet veered off toward the ocean at full speed followed by a swarm of ground-to-air missiles.

"Defensive measures taken! Anti-missiles launched!"

A dozen balls of fire exploded in the night air, creating an infernal noise and lighting up the landscape for a few seconds.

Taos pointed to the beach where the island's residents had spent the day.

"There! Put us down there to unload the first contingent. Then take off and leave me on the other side of the building above the jungle."

"I don't know if there'll be enough space to land…"

"We'll use cables if necessary, but I don't want to put all our eggs in the same basket."

The pilot landed the jet on the beach with great skill. When it touched down, the cargo bay was already open and the first group of mercenaries got out fast. The flying vehicle then took off quickly, forcing the last two soldiers to jump onto the sand.

"Flying object detected!"

"What? Where did it come from?"

"I don't know. It just appeared over the house. It's circling to gain speed. Classification: F-15 fighter. No sign of country identification."

"It's the original Dark Flyer! Launch a missile to keep him busy and take me to the second landing point."

"Target locked, self-guided missiles launched!"

The jet soared off, throwing the rest of its passengers off-balance. It sped over the house and the grounds in a flash. When it got over the tropical forest, it stopped and slowly dropped into the canopy. The rear hatch opened again and the mercenaries threw out their cables to start the descent.

When Taos jumped out, she saw the black F-15 speeding toward their plane, firing its machine guns. Some of the bullets ricocheted off the armor, showering the soldiers with shrapnel. One mercenary howled in pain and dropped off his cable.

The pilot activated his weapons but too late. The Dark Flyer had just sped off in a maneuver that was theoretically impossible for that kind of jet. He slowed down quickly, rolled over on a wing, and got in direct line with the enemy aircraft. Then he fired up his autocannons into the turbines.

As the engines exploded, Taos had just enough time to yell one word at her men: "Jump!"

The first group got off the beach in a hurry and crossed the yard around the house. As they approached, big armored blinds sealed shut all the doors and windows, transforming the pretty vacation house into a bunker. Bright spotlights lit up the area.

The cybernetic mercenary, Rico, motioned to his troops to split up along the front of the house and find a way in. Then two soldiers were thrown into the air by an explosion!

The cyborg looked up to see his enemy hovering over the front porch: a man inside an armored device: the new Dark Flyer! Two wings with jet engines framed his human form, making him into a hybrid of man and fighter jet.

The mechanized brute roared in anger and grabbed a minigun off his back. The rotary cannon started spitting explosives bullets at the young Dark Flyer.

Dominik shot up quickly, letting the lethal rain pass harmlessly beneath his feet. He answered instantly with two more missiles aimed at the giant. But the cyborg was now on his guard and exploded them both with his minigun. In the same movement, he kept showering the night sky with bullets in an effort to hit his target.

The new Dark Flyer decided to save the hardest for last. For a second, he thought of flooding the park with sleeping gas, but he suspected that the facemasks the soldiers wore came with nosefilters. Too bad, he would have to take them out one by one. There were only three left anyway.

He landed on the side of the house and ran around to the front. He spotted one of the soldiers coming towards him, armed with a rocket launcher. Before the merc could even aim it, Dominik had shot a net out of a cannon on his forearm. It covered the victim and automatically drew tight, immobilizing him in a less than a second.

Another enemy took him by surprise and started firing. Every bullet exploded on his armor, testing its limits. Dominik realized that their enemy had taken the necessary steps to fight a superhero. He smiled, thinking that they were going to be surprised to find not one but two heroes!

Meanwhile, a second round of gunfire erupted; as it might cause some real damage, the young Nero reacted. He launched another net, but his opponent avoided it by rolling away. The merc came up on his knee and took aim again.

Dominik shot up to avoid the second round, but in his rush, he forgot his main enemy who cut him down in mid-air with a cloud of explosive bullets. His armor started giving way and pieces of it fell with the shrapnel. The young Dark Flyer pushed all the power of his jets into the night sky. It was time to change tactics. Luckily, there was no major systems damage. When he figured he was out of range of the mercs' weapons, he used his targeting system to spot his enemies. He then sent three self-guided missiles rushing toward the targets.

Unfortunately, Rico had charged the front door and managed to smash through the armored shutter and get inside the house. It protected him at the last second from the missile that demolished the porch. The two other missiles reached their targets, seriously damaging the mercs' protective suits. They were thrown away onto the grass, wounded and knocked out.

The new Dark Flyer synchronized his armor's computer with the home automation system. The cyborg was winded by the explosion and slow to get up, but soon, he was ready to explore the house. The young hero had no choice. He headed for the burning porch to follow him into his family home.

Two of the soldiers had been wounded in the jump and could not move. Taos gathered the other three quickly and ran through the tropical forest towards the Nero mansion. She heard the gunfire and explosions coming from the other side and saw the new Dark Flyer rising into the night sky, then heard the three missiles hit her first attack group.

A few hundred yards away ,the original Dark Flyer landed his jet in a grotto, jumped out of the plane and onto a four-wheeler, a vehicle he had especially equipped to defend his island: fast, all-terrain and, above all, armed to fight all types of threats.

The vehicle sped into a secret tunnel that came out in the jungle not far from the wreckage of the stolen jet that had just crashed. The detection system he had installed on the island allowed him to locate his four enemies who were running through the trees.

He caught up with the two slower ones, who heard him, turned and fired at him. The armored windshield of the ATV held up against the first shots, but started cracking under the explosions of the special ammunition.

Cletus neutralized both shooters by launching nets like his son had done. The mercs were immobilized immediately, wrapped in the nets that kept squeezing them, cutting through their suits.

Taos waved an order to her last man. They split up and went in different directions. The lethal woman jumped on a vine and shimmied up toward a high branch. Then running from branch to branch with unnatural agility, she rushed toward the house. She managed to avoid detection for a few seconds, but the first Dark Flyer spotted her and decided to chase after her. He turned right, sped around some bushes and was once again close to his foe.

Just then, the other merc came out of hiding and tossed a handful of fragmentation grenades at him. Cletus had barely time to lower the grill in the front of his vehicle. The grenades bounced off it, exploding a split second later. The ATV barreled through a cloud of flames and of metal, but its driver was protected behind the armor.

The shockwave from the explosion had thrown the mercenary to the ground. He was just getting back up when the vehicle hit him, driving him into the trunk of a palm tree, unconscious. Just in case, the Dark Flyer threw a net that nailed the thug to the tree; then, he took off at full speed.

The mansion was very quiet when the new Dark Flyer landed his armored suit on the ruined porch. He let loose an army of sensors, but the gadgets hidden in all the household objects disrupted the search. He had forgotten to ask his father to connect him to the building's security system. He decided, therefore, to call him.

"Flyer 2 to Flyer 1, do you read me?"

"Loud and clear, Flyer 2. I'm coming in the back of the house. There's a kind of ninja woman in front of me. I think she just got in through a window."

"And I'm looking for a cyborg muscleman. I'll go up to the boy's room and hope they're not already there."

"OK! I'll join you as soon as I can. Over and out."

Cletus switched the engine to silent mode and skidded to a perfect stop in front of the window Taos had used to enter his fortress. He scanned it.

"Acid. I don't know where she got that compound, but it worked like a charm."

He, too, climbed through the opening and landed in the huge kitchen located at the back of the house. He tiptoed out, holding an electrified tonfa and a multi-bullet handgun of his own invention.

When he reached the hallway he saw his son in his armor standing stock-still in the doorway of Ricky's room. Staying close to the wall, Cletus snuck up to the door.

A woman's voice was barking orders:

"Don't move, Dark Flyer, or Rico will tear off the kid's arm. I'd rather carry him out of here in one piece, but I'll do whatever it takes to keep you both out of our way."

Dominik had seen his father coming up. He raised his hands and backed into the hallway, heading toward the entrance hall.

In the bedroom, Taos was holding a katana with the blade against Ricky's throat as he was held firmly by the cyborg. The child was squeezing his bear and crying a river of tears.

The two criminals headed for the exit, keeping a close eye on the armored superhero. When Taos stepped through the door, the original Dark Flyer hit her wrist as hard as he could with the tonfa.

Surprised and shocked, the woman dropped her katana, but swung around swiftly to launch a kick at her attacker. She caught him in the face, and the older man thought he would pass out from the blow.

Rico sneered and pulled his minigun off his back. Holding Ricky by the wrist, he started shooting.

Dominik kept his hands up and in a clear, calm voice said: "Colm, activate!"

Instantly, the teddy bear being cradled in the child's arms came to life, wiggled around, and then jumped on the giant's arms. The clover unsnapped, freeing the toy's hands, and rolled a little farther up the left arm to become some kind of shield. Four metal claws shot out of the fingers and the bear used them to tear at the cyborg's arm.

Rico let go of Rocky when the metal muscles started springing out of his lacerated arm. Using this moment, the boy ran down the hallway and through the young Dark Flyer's legs. When he was safely out of range, Dominik fired his plasma projectors at the cyborg warrior, who raised his now useless arm to protect himself.

The teddy bear had turned into a self-guided combat device. It jumped to the ground, landed perfectly, and slipped between Rico's legs while the cyborg was busy trying not to get toasted. Colm snuck up behind Taos as Cletus was struggling to get up. Despite his advanced knowledge of fighting techniques, he was almost completely powerless against Vega's female bodyguard—she was as good as Kit Kappa!

Cletus vaulted into the air to get back to his feet. His arms were in defensive position, ready to block or grapple the next martial art attack.

Just when Taos was throwing a kick, harder than ever, the fluffy robot planted its metal claws into the ankle of the foot she was standing on. She screamed in pain and lost her balance, thereby missing her target—Cletus' face.

Meanwhile, Rico had his minigun back in his good hand and sprayed the hallway, shooting at the armored Flyer. The superhero backed away, using conventional bullets to attack the cyborg, making sure his father was out of range.

Colm stood firm in front of the older Flyer with its shield out before him, a rather ridiculous-looking gesture given its small size. The teddy bear's black plastic eyes were challenging the formidable Taos, who was having trouble putting her foot solidly on the ground.

She looked worriedly at Rico.

"That's enough, let's get out of here!" she ordered.

With this, she threw a little ball on the ground that exploded in a bright light, blinding both Cletus and the sensors in Dominik's armor. They heard a crack over their heads and, when they could see again, there was a huge hole in the ceiling, courtesy of their departing foes.

The young Dark Flyer took off through the opening, trying to catch the kidnappers, but artillery fire was waiting for him outside, damaging his flight systems.

He dropped onto the flat roof and saw his enemies running on the beach toward a boat, the one that had first made his father suspicious. He launched a few plasma shots at them, but had to take cover from the gunfire from the yacht.

Oh well, he thought, *at least Ricky's safe, that's the main thing.*

The two Dark Flyers had swapped their costumes for Bermuda shorts and were tanning on the beach in their lounge chairs. Nearby, in a monokini, Sweet was playing in the water with Ricky. The quiet beach was disturbed only by the sounds of the construction work taking place a hundred yards away where NeroTek was working around the clock to rebuild their owners' tropical mansion.

"Tell me everything, Dominik," said Cletus. "What is that bear?"

"It's C.O.L.M.! Cybernetic Organism Leisure Mammal. The real Colm is still on a shelf in my room. I got the idea of a teddy bear bodyguard while working on my new alloy, Hexagonium. After another unsuccessful test, I ended up with a very flexible alloy that could contract like muscle fiber under electrical impulses. I started working on artificial muscles using this new metal. One thing led to another and I made a small robot to test the movements and strength. As a result, my twelve-inch cybernetic organism is unbelievably strong.

So, I just improved the prototype in my spare time and I added a state-of-the-art mini-computer, the best sensors around, and all the necessary coding for it to react to its environment. Of course, I added a few weapons, both offensive and defensive, as well. For the outside, I used the latest fibers being developed."

"Incredible. It's hard to believe it's so light with everything you stuffed inside it."

"It weighs almost seventy pounds, but I put in a little anti-gravity unit that lightens it up. In time, it will be able to jump super high and even fly. But that's with some extraterrestrial tech I picked up on a mission to Zhud. Anyway, it's a one-of-a-kind."

"Well, it won't be easy to make a duplicate."

"Yes. I think the hardest thing will be to give Ricky a ordinary copy when we send him back to his parents. t there's good news there: the trial's over and they testified. Vega has no more reason to blackmail them now. Let's hope he won't seek revenge later on."

"We'll have to invite them here. A little vacation would do them good. And it'll give you time to get a new Colm ready!"

Ben Leonard (aka Ra) by Roberto Castro

Young American journalist Ben Leonard is the reincarnation of the Egyptian god Ra, once the ruler of a tribe of Immortals, descended from Atlantis, who gave birth to the Egyptian pantheon. Since the awakening of his soul, he fights his evil brother Set, who plots to conquer the world. This story takes place long before his recent recruitment into the Hexagon Group...

Alex Nikolavitch: *The Return of Apophis*

The pick-up truck bumped along a bad road covered in rocks that was putting the old suspension to the test. The five men in the bed hung onto their AK-47s and mumbled at every jolt as they watched the vibrations of the metal crate strapped down to the corrugated metal with old ropes. None of them knew how to read the European characters painted in black on the sides, but the red symbols all over it were clear: the contents of this box were explosive. The road ran around a huge rock, a solid block of limestone eroded by the winds of sand.

One of the men in a *keffiyeh* was turning the knob of a transistor radio trying to catch a station but could not find anything but static.

"You can stop playing with that machine, Karim? Even if you find something, you'll only get western music and you'll just defile your ears and your heart with seeds of Shaitan."

"Be quiet, Marid, I'm trying to get news!"

"Crusader's vomit!"

Marid tore the radio out of his hands and threw it into the sand. Karim shrugged his shoulders. He was used to this kind of crisis of authority from the boss.

The driver turned left and the pick-up dove into a narrow ravine that cut through the mountain. A horrible gnashing sound was a constant reminder that the truck was scraping against the rocky walls.

All of a sudden the rift opened up and they came out into a small cirque, like an amphitheater. One of the walls had been sculpted. On both sides of a door, half-hidden behind a huge slab, stood two huge stone sentinels staring into eternity with their empty eyes, two men whose dress and hairstyle indicated their Egyptian origins. But unlike their brothers guarding the entrance to the temple of Abu Simbel on the banks of the Nile, these here were standing and their hands were gripping spears.

The pick-up pulled up to a stop and Karim opened the case. It contained blocks of plastic explosive perfectly wrapped, which he handed out to the others. They placed them at the feet of the statues and a few around the ankles. Climbing over the slab that partly obstructed the entrance Marid set a few explosives inside the small temple.

When he came back out he turned around and said:

"We're going to destroy the idols like our Afghan brothers! They will fall before our eyes, symbols of our fight against the infidels!"

Karim cleared his throat, "Before our eyes? You know, with so many explosives in a confined space like this… My advice is not to wait around here to watch."

Marid gave him a nasty smile and handed him the radio-controlled trigger.

"That's true but one of us has to stay here to press the little red button. It won't work outside."

Karim examined the box. "Couldn't we set a timer?"

"They wouldn't synchronize. Everything has to blow up at the same time. And the honor has fallen upon you, brother."

The others climbed into the pick-up leaving Karim alone, holding the trigger, facing the stone giants. Born in Egypt, unlike most of his comrades, he knew how ancient idols looked. These suddenly seemed different. Rather than kings or impious gods, these were strangely more like guards whose mission was to forbid anyone from entering the temple.

Or exiting.

The truck had only made it half-way out of the ravine when one of the men asked the boss, "Marid?"

"Yeah?"

"Do you think it's a good idea leaving Karim behind?"

"He's sacrificing himself for the cause. Besides, I really don't trust him. I don't like people who listen to the radio. While doing so, they can't listen to me."

"But he's the one who knew where to get the explo..."

An enormous explosion cut him off and the shockwave flipped the truck over before burying it under the rocks.

A plume of smoke dust rose above the mountain like a volcanic eruption and cast a dark shadow over everything around.

Maybe even a little too dark...

The open space was bustling. Photojournalists receiving orders for their jobs or bringing back their pictures, editors on the phone with families of crime victims to make them give up a few photos from the happy days for the tearjerker, and grumpy reporters typing up their dispatches while mumbling under their breath.

Out of habit, Pipp reached for the plastic cup of coffee and sipped, but it had been empty for a long time. He crumpled it and threw it in the trashcan full of others before searching his pockets for spare change.

A hand offered him another steaming hot, plastic cup.

"Oh, thanks, Lucy."

"I can read you like a book. What are you breaking your back over there?"

"The Queen of England at the derby. Nanousse brought in some bad snapshots that he asked me to caption."

"And you've been on it for two hours without writing three words, right?"

Pipp swallowed some of the hot coffee. "How'd you guess, gorgeous?"

"Feminine intuition, of course. And my intuition tells me you've completely lost your motivation."

She handed him some paper pulled out of the laser printer from a foreign news agency accompanied by a few black-and-white photos. Still holding his cup Pipp spread them out on his cluttered desk.

"Have you spoken to Ben? He might like this."

The aerial photos, maybe coming from a military source, showed a small, rocky, mountain cirque whose walls had long, black gashes. One of the walls had collapsed, revealing the entrance to a gigantic cave. Succinctly the text spoke of an ancient Egyptian temple blown up by jihadists operating in the Sinai Peninsula.

Pipp threw away his empty plastic cup and picked up the telephone. "Hello, Ben? Get down to the *Globe* and hurry."

A few minutes later, Ben Leonard entered the newsroom. He was welcomed with a roar.

"Leonard! My office!"

As usual, he had barely walked in the door before the chief called him. It was in the tight space called the "fishbowl" because of the big window that separated it from the open space. Pipp and Lucy were already waiting for him.

When he entered the little room, the chief was shuffling papers and looking disgusted, "Your colleagues have a passion for defending ancient ruins, you know."

"Huh?"

Ben sat in a swiveling armchair made of frayed leather but that was once luxurious, a souvenir of the better days of the *Globe*. When the crisis had passed, this piece of furniture was never replaced and became a relic of a distant golden age.

"Here, look, Leonard."

Ben took the bundle of paper that he held out and examined it glumly.

"Where is this?"

"It's written right there, Leonard! Sinai, Egypt! You've heard of it, I hope?"

Pipp winked at his colleague. Ben gave the bundle back to the chief.

"Sure. I see exactly what it is. An ancient temple that's been stricken with taboo since the Middle Kingdom. The zone was holy, sacrosanct, and dynasty after dynasty respected the prohibition until it was forgotten."

"Mystery, old stones, all that should make a good subject, Leonard. I've booked tickets for you three for Cairo but no messing around, kids. You meet up there, find contacts to evaluate the situation in the country, and if you can, talk to the Director of National Antiquities but don't set foot in Sinai, you hear me? It's too dangerous. You're not war correspondents."

"We're not war correspondents only because you don't want to pay us the going rate for the work, chief," Pipp said.

The editor sneered, "If I paid you for your competence, Pipp, you'd be getting minimum wage."

He put his glasses on the pile of papers and rubbed his eyes with his thumb and index finger. He was tired.

"Go on, scram."

The hotel was not much to look at. Far from the posh quarters of Cairo, and farther still from the tourist areas, to get there one had to twist through narrow, crowded alleys, side-step the donkeys and peddlers, then climb some slippery stairs polished by the ages. The *Globe* no longer had the expense account it once had to send its great reporters all over the world. Or maybe the price of hotels had gone up significantly, even in poor countries.

Pipp was contemplating these things over his Turkish coffee in the bar when Ben and Lucy came back from the French Consulate.

"The chief called the Consul before we got here to make a formal prohibition against giving us visas for Sinai," the young woman announced.

"And that surprises you?" Pipp sipped his coffee. He put down the cup with a thick layer of grounds in the bottom. "The fortune tellers could make a fortune in this dump with coffee like this."

Ben sat on an ivory-inlaid, wooden stool on the other side of the low table that was covered with an intricately carved, brass tray. "I don't think they could predict what's going to happen now."

Pipp answered with a wink. "Are you going to change, Ben?"

"And quick. According to the rumors around town, they've lost contact with some villages in the peninsula lately, around the destroyed temple. Something bad happened out there."

Lucy frowned. "Tell us about it."

Ben leaned forward and whispered like a conspirator, "The forbidden temple isn't a temple but the memorial of a very serious incident involving the Immortals of Heliopolis, dating back to time immemorial. I don't have all the details because it's sometimes hard for me to probe the memories of Ra and I don't even know if he was there at the time."

"But didn't you fuse with his soul?" Lucy seemed genuinely surprised.

"It's more complicated than that. Plus, Ra doesn't know everything. These things go back before the time he became king of Heliopolis, and they were already not talking about it by then, I think."

"Yeah," Pipp grumbled. "Your temple is like the uncle gone to South America who the family stops talking about at the dinner table."

"You must have had an interesting family, Pipp."

"In fact, as an adult, I found out he'd just followed a dancer. It crushed all my dreams of the narco godfather or treasure hunter. He died a janitor in Buenos Aires, but..." Seeing the blank stares of Ben and Lucy he cut it short. "Sorry, Ben. What do you think we should do? Ra wants to go investigate the place?"

"Consult Atum first of all. He could fill in the blanks of the story. I'll go to the Sinai but there's no need to go rushing in blindly without knowing more."

185

Ben got up and looked over at the shady patio of the hotel, in fact, just a rear courtyard where a few potted plants had been placed. The area was deserted and at this hour there was nobody at the windows. He went over, looked up at the sky and his body emitted a bright golden light. In the next instant he was gone.

Pipp muttered, "He could've at least warned us. I would've put on my Raybans.

The hidden, secret city of Heliopolis was in a panic when Ra landed softly before the huge columns of the temple-palace. A crowd was gathered between the sparkling obelisks and the beryl sphinx. Ra, giving off a warm light, stood before the half-animal statues. Anyone else would have been blinded. They welcomed him with timid remarks.

"Ra, you came! You, too, are you taking refuge in our stronghold to await the terror that will certainly destroy us?"

Ra raised his arms to demand silence, which he got. Still, he had to speak over the nervous murmur of the crowd.

"As you know, I am the depository of some of the memories left behind by your brother Ra when his Ka was ripped from his body. But no matter how hard I try, I can find no trace of what this distant, secret temple contains. Only the warning to never enter it. But Atum will provide what's missing."

The crowd suddenly went quiet, then parted to give him access to the narrow passage between the two columns of stone. Suddenly, he really felt his double nature. Although he carried the soul of an Immortal, the king of the city, he was not at all one of them. As Ben Leonard, he was human, all too human. The preoccupations, desires and fears of the inhabitants of Heliopolis were completely alien to him.

He walked in between the huge columns and was welcomed by two of the Immortals who ran the city in his place.

"Greetings, O great Ra," said the enormous man with a white beard and hair while the woman with strangely slit eyes bowed reverentially with her hands raised, palms forward.

Ra bowed in turn, letting the halo of light surrounding him fade away out of respect for the ageless shadow of the temple palace. "Take me to Atum, wise Osir."

"Atum is already working on resolving this crisis, Ra."

"But what is its nature, Osir? What is the thing coming out of that temple that scares the Immortals so much?"

The elder of the two looked saddened, pulling on his robe embroidered with stylized animals in profile. Ra had never seen him so feeble. Osir was older than human civilization but this was the first time he looked like an old man.

"You are aware, I believe, of how Aru, the founder of our tribe of Immortals, disappeared."

Ra nodded. "Wicked Set took advantage of a moment of weakness to destroy him."

"That's right, young Ra, but do you know what that weakness was in a being otherwise endowed with cosmic power?"

Ra shook his head.

Osir told him, "The world is nothing but cycles. The cycle of the sun producing the day and dragging the night in its wake, the cycle of seasons, the cycle of the rising and falling of the Nile, the cycle of birth and death. We Immortals often believe that our special nature is that we exist outside the cycles. Nothing is more false, and a force of destruction appears over the ages to remind us of this. Apophis is its name, the serpent whose rings limit the cycle of the gods themselves. Aru was painfully aware of this and he tried to comfort his people about this burden. The last time Apophis awoke from his sleep of ages, Aru went to meet him and challenge him. Our king held a large part of his vital power in the Scepter and the Flail, royal symbols of this earth washed by the Nile. He pushed the monster back toward the desert and mountains by striking him continuously but at the same time being blown in the face by the breath as hot as the desert wind and as noxious as the swamps."

Remembering this, Osir looked like he himself was in the throes of that agony once suffered by his king and mentor.

For a moment he leaned on one of the cyclopean columns covered in carved hieroglyphs.

"With a mighty blow of the Scepter, Aru threw Apophis back onto a mountain which collapsed under the impact. Aru pushed all the debris into the crater which became a steep-sided cirque. Aru was victorious, but he did not go to lick his wounds before first breathing some extra vital power into the magic seal and the stone sentinels who would signal the alarm. The inscription closed the mountain around Apophis and it was only an earthquake, thousands of years later, that opened the rift giving access to the rocky cirque."

Osir's voice was weak as he continued.

"The earthquake happened when the Immortals were all frozen in sleep under the spells cast by Set. For, the evil one had used Aru's weakened state to attack him by surprise and destroy him before taking control of the sacred city."

"Then, to destroy Ra, its defender, whose wandering soul ended up incarnating in me," Ben mumbled.

Bastet took his hand and led him deep into the temple, leaving Osir out of breath after his story.

"What's wrong with Osir?"

"He breathed in part of Atum's vital force in looking for a solution," the cat-eyed woman responded.

"And?"

"To no avail so far."

"Take me to the computer, Bastet."

The grainy, ochre stone was deeply carved with furrows in crisscrossing geometric forms inside of which shined with pale gold and also deep blue enamel. In front of the elaborately carved wall stood a real titan, massive, with bulging muscles. Next to him hung a broadsword the color of polished bronze and contoured, big enough to cut a hippopotamus in two.

"Greetings Ra," the stentorian voice boomed.

"Salutations, powerful Anhur."

The Immortals of Heliopolis were known among the tribes of beings like them, as particularly pacifist. But that did not mean they left themselves defenseless, and Anhur could scare off most invaders. Nevertheless the colossus looked worried. He put his hand on the carved stone, the interface of a huge computer whose slightest vibrations could be sensed.

"Atum talks to me, my friend, and his oracles would make you tremble."

The vibration got stronger. The gigantic warrior closed his eyes to soak it up.

"We cannot conquer Apophis, he tells me. What Aru did is to delay the fulfillment of the cycle and the price was too high. Pushing him into a cave cost all his vital energy, however considerable it might have been. And despite all my power, I won't last half as long as he did."

"And the Scepter? The Flail? What became of them?"

"They were piously preserved, Ra. But who can wield them?"

"How could we know if nobody tries."

With infinite sadness the giant looked at Ra, then he gestured to follow him. Bastet let them go with bowed head.

In the desert outside of the city stood a gray mastaba made of age-worn basalt. Anhur put his hand on one eroded stone that looked no different from the others but it tilted backwards with a muted hiss.

A flight of steps descended into the dark depths. Ra lit himself up so that his inner light spread into the narrow passage. Step by step he went down, followed by the gigantic warrior who had to turn sideways to fit between the rocky walls.

The stairs ended at a corridor in which Anhur had to bend over but it soon grew bigger until it reached a vast, cubic room. The back wall had a door whose two panels of bronze and ebony were closed. Anhur opened his sack and took out a golden key that he stuck in the lock. A quiet click followed by a whisper of air and the door opened onto the arsenal of the Immortals.

Anhur pointed at a stone sarcophagus whose heavy lid was covered with a thick layer of dust. "Go. I cannot touch these weapons that contain the remains of Aru's power."

With awe, Ra lifted the granite cover. Inside the stone lay the Scepter and the Flail, the emblems of royalty in Egypt. His hands trembled as he grabbed them, lifted them before his eyes. The golden surface, even after all these millennia, was still stained with the ashes of combat. Ra closed his eyes. All the way to the depths of his being he felt the brute power of these two weapons vibrating through him.

"I... I will try to prove worthy, Anhur."

"Try not to suffer too much. You have to make them yours and fight like their creator fought, holding nothing back, no blows, no energy, no strength, and not be weakened by it."

When Ra left the arsenal, the crowd around the temple had become reverentially, heavily silent. Deathly even, which was a bad omen.

Bastet and Osir bowed their heads to salute him.

Ra preferred not to wait around. With the weapons in hand he went to fulfill his mission.

The mountains and the desert looked like they were burning. At least there seemed to be jet-black fumes or mists rising from them, slowly waving plumes and coils. For miles around a blanket of night, almost solid, hungrily swallowed all light coming from the sky. Nothing could really be seen except a swaying, a bubbling maybe or else it was a vibration.

"A palpitation" Ben thought to himself, being a journalist used to searching for exact words for a headline. But he was not here as Ben Leonard because he bore the appearance of Ra, protector of the Immortals, holding the emblems of the royal power of Heliopolis. His body irradiated a bright, solar light, standing out against the black desert. The dark palpitation, he realized, reminded him of something organic, almost alive, like the slow crawl of amoebic jelly under a microscope.

The black amoeba started quivering more vigorously, with unexpected energy, then it shot out a pseudopod of the same color, which sprang up toward the sky and straightened out like a huge snake. The image was made stronger by a dim shimmer at the rounded end of the thing, on the dark snout as if two eyes had just opened.

Ra fell back, stupefied.

The thing made of night turned its gaze his way and it went right through him. He felt his soul stripped bare by the essential, primordial blackness and his shield of light start to crack around him. Soon he was exposed to the depths of his being, scrutinized by those eyes that were nothing else but an abyss of the dark and eternal chaos of the world before the world. While the abyss gazed on him he watched the nothingness elsewhere, the great frozen exterior, the negation of everything. Ra was nothing now and the monster's malevolent attention was peeling away layer after layer of what remained of Ben Leonard under the borrowed rags of the Immortal—some journalist for a dying paper, a young man who had been a restless child, a little snot, a...

"Aaaaaaaaaahhhhhhhrrrrrr!"

Ben's soul struggled to escape the vision's clutches. He searched inside himself for the remnant of Ra's light and he lit it up, dimly, then he mustered all his strength to soar into the skies.

Escaping from the cloud of dark influence, he bathed in the sunlight, drank in the warmth and felt a little better.

Then he looked down. Far below him, coiled around the mountain, the dark shape was still there. The beast lifted its vile snout and Ra could not stand it. He left for the south as fast as his power could propel him.

Ra collapsed onto the summit of a dune in the middle of nowhere in the Nubian desert, the arid strip of land that extends from the Nile to the Red Sea.

When he regained his senses night had fallen. He realized that he had dropped his weapons. He looked around for them and reached out for the Flail. For a brief moment the gentle, warm energy from it comforted his soul still tortured by the memory of the creature made of night.

But the Scepter was not there. He looked around and saw a pair of feet. He raised his head and immediately recognized the massive, bald Immortal staring at him from on high and holding the Scepter.

Ra sat up straight, alarmed to see such power in the hands of his eternal enemy, a fierce and determined adversary come back to Heliopolis—Set!

However, the evil god did not look hostile. His smile and his eyes were a little teasing, mocking, but his way of wielding the holy weapon left no doubt of his intention to use it. Therefore, Ra was stunned when he ended up handing it to him.

"Here, I think you haven't finished with this yet."

"I… Thanks, but…"

"But what?"

The glint of mockery in Set's eyes was unbearable. Ra clutched the two weapons to his chest like a surprised woman wrapping her nudity in a robe before the lecherous stare of an intruder.

"You… I…"

Set burst out laughing. "That's why I can't take you seriously as an Immortal, poor Ra. There's too much of this Ben Leonard in you, this puny human afraid of everything bigger than him. However…"

"However?"

"However, I have decided to help you, poor little creature. Apophis is threatening me as much as you. He's threatening Heliopolis."

"But you're the enemy of Heliopolis."

"No," Set shook his head. "I'm the enemy of the puppets who govern it. I want to rule in their place. But what's the use of being king of a pile of ashes? Heliopolis has to survive if I want to rule. You can understand that, can't you?"

Set turned to the north.

"This thing is threatening all of us, Ra. You have been chosen to fight it and protect us. To be frank, I don't think you can do it. Not alone in any case. Not as long as you make these stupid mistakes."

"What mistakes?"

"Not looking at Apophis. You don't stop to measure the void. You have to strike, strike relentlessly. Put all your energy into it. The fire of the sun is in you, Ra. It alone can dispel the darkness of elementary night."

The renegade Immortal held his hand out and touched Ra's forehead. A shock ran through both of them.

"To prove my good faith and to help you in the battle, I'm transferring some of my vital power to you. It will be useful against the beast."

Reeling under the shock Ra tried to stand up. Finally, he looked a little skeptical at his old enemy who gave him a shove to face north.

"Your enemy is in that direction."

Ra trembled, then soared off, brandishing his magic arms.

Set watched him fly northward and then, more calmly, followed him.

In the dim light of the rising dawn, neither Ra, nor Set, had seen the graceful, silent figure leaning on a rock nearby. Two eyes with vertically slit pupils blinked then disappeared in the fading night.

This time Ra did not give his enemy time to notice his arrival. He veered off to come in from the east with Kepri, the rising sun, at this back, encircled by the light. Then he dove into the thick night that clung to the desert, which had swollen with darkness.

Ra yelled and struck with the Scepter and the Flail, one after another, breaking up the murky cloud. The plumes suddenly grew thicker and tried to grab him, his limbs and weapons. Ra called upon the power contained in the latter and the black pseudopods recoiled. This small victory emboldened the Immortal as he headed for the sooty mass and started hammering away with strong blows.

Two eyes opened in the dark wall. Two openings that were darker than the darkness itself, staring at him.

Ra screamed and looked away, attacking another part of the thing. Here also a pair of eyes opened up. Then others all around him.

Ra swung frantically at the air around him. The light emanating from his body was pulsating less and less as the dark eyes sucked it away from him, drained him, emptied him of his vital power.

Feeling himself fainting Ra used his last strength to break the Flail over his knee to extract a little more power. A sphere of light surrounded him, illuminated the desert and cleared a passage all the way to the ground with the vivifying rays of the sun.

Ra felt the rejuvenating warmth and cast aside the broken weapon. The last dark plumes clinging to the ground scurried away in fear.

"Ha, ha, ha! So, you're not so terrible, Apophis, you who make the masters of Heliopolis tremble, as well as evil Set!"

The Immortal raised the Scepter like a torch destined to light up the world. Then, seized by doubt, he turned around.

Behind him stood a dark column of cloud, widening at the top like the hood of a cobra. Its evil eyes were fixed on him.

"Oh…"

The creature stuck and swallowed him in one gulp before righting itself again, leaving nothing on the ground but a perfectly round crater of sand vitrified by the explosion of light, along with the two fragments of the sacred Flail.

Drowning in a thick mass of coagulated darkness Ra was suffocating. He opened his mouth to scream but the night poured in. All at once he let loose the remainder of his vital power, the soul of Ra the immortal, the power given by Set and that which he had absorbed from the sacred weapons, even the tiny spark that had been Ben Leonard, the adventurous journalist.

The dark quivered but held fast against this last, desperate effort.

Apophis remained alone, standing tall over the desert being consumed again by the darkness.

Ra felt himself parting. He saw before him the realm of Shadows, the strange, other place where the souls of Immortals went to rest when by chance their name betrayed them. The dismal territory called out to him insistently.

The colossal creature hesitated in the air and opened wide a black mouth to spit like owls do to get rid of the remains of a mouse swallowed the night before. When Ra's body fell on the ground, twisted up, the last remnants of his light were fading away. The monster leaned over and sniffed as if make sure that his Ka was really gone for good. Now that his mission in this world was accomplished, that the Immortals had once again been confronted with death, the monster had no other reason to exist. Its night-colored form dissipated in the morning glow and when the sun rose nothing was left of Apophis.

From the summit of the mountain where he had sat and watched the battle Set clapped his hands gloriously. "Well, the show turned out better than I hoped."

Calmly he went down and trampled the plain. After a short, casual walk he came before the bloody, contorted body of his old adversary.

"I scorned you, Ra, but I have to admit at this dismal time that you lived up to your task. It has always been in the order of things and of the world to see the Sun disappear and leave the night behind."

As if to prove him a liar, the sun approaching the zenith shot its rays over the sands and rocks making a white vapor rise up.

Set looked around for the Scepter of Aru. "Ah-ha!"

He dashed over to the foot of a rock where the weapon had fallen but when he leaned over to grab it, a slender hand sprang from behind the rock and snatched it away. The scepter hovered with its hooked tip aimed at Set's face.

"Bastet!" the Immortal blurted out in surprise, "You, too, want to take over Heliopolis? You're finally fed up with being a subordinate? We can reign together, you know? The throne is big enough for…"

He did not finish his sentence. The woman with cat eyes flicked the weapon and sent him flying fifty feet away. "The thread is holding that binds his Ka to his corporal envelope, Set, and Heliopolis still has a legitimate sovereign."

She strode over to Ra.

"You did good work and served the Immortals well, but you received a meager reward. I'll have to remedy that."

Bastet pointed the Scepter at the sky, then with all her strength she planted it in Ra's mangled body, chanting ancient words in the language of Misraïm, the same language that Atum the computer of stone and enamel transformed into vibrations to express its profound thoughts. The weapon glowed, then flashed a blinding light. In the corrosive flash it dissolve until nothing was left.

Ra coughed, a spasm that was unworthy of an Immortal and would have given Set more reason to mock. But Set was lying at the foot of a cliff with a bloody face and would not awake for days to come.

"Slowly, Ra. You're still weak even with all the power you've just absorbed."

"A… Apophis…"

"Aru's error was to want to control him, to imprison him. A primordial creature like that cannot be pacified for long except by a sacrifice. Yours in this case."

She helped him stand up.

"I'm going to bring you to Heliopolis. Our doctors will examine you and…"

"No! My friends are waiting for me in Cairo. I…" Ra hesitated. Then he continued in Ben Leonard's voice. "I don't mean to be ungrateful or anything, Bastet, but no. If Osir knew what he sent me into, I don't want to see him right now. Heliopolis can count on me to defend it, but I'd prefer if the Immortals played fair with me."

"As you like, Ra, but…"

"But you're suspicious of my human part."

Bastet looked away with sadness in her eyes.

"I want to spend some time with the humans," he burst out. "There are some of them with powers, too, and they can help me control mine, which I feel is always controlling me. That Set tries to manipulate me, I can understand, but you, who call yourselves my friends…"

The cat woman took his hand. He did not pull back but he still felt a distant coldness that contrasted with the warmth emanating from her.

"Who was that girl?"

The question came out of both mouths at the same time.

Ben plopped down into the embroidered pillows on the big armchair made of black wood inlaid with mother-of-pearl.

"Bastet? One of the Immortals. She kindly brought me back. I'm not sure I could've made it alone."

"Poor thing," Pipp joked. "Well, speak up!"

Lucy took out her notebook like a professional but Ben held out his hand to stop her.

"First of all I'm going to tell you what really happened. But that's not what the chief is going to print, of course. We'll call the local Interior Ministry this afternoon to get the official version and then we'll take off."

"OK," Pipp said, "but I want to know everything about that gorgeous thing there…"

Lucy elbowed him in the ribs.

"Ouch!"

Sunk into the cushions Ben smiled as he watched his colleagues joking around. This human teasing was innocent and soothed his soul. Then he sat up, took a glass of mint tea from the copper engraved table and started in on his story.

"In the beginning of time, when Aru was still ruler of Heliopolis, a danger arose like they had never seen before…"

Count Saint-Germain by Manuel Martin Peniche

A member of the Twelve, a secret society of Immortals who originated in Atlantis, Count Saint-Germain (sometimes known as Germanus) lives on throughout history, putting his great wisdom and his occult knowledge to the service of good. He has become much more active in our era, guiding and advising many other heroes with an affinity for the occult. His arch-enemy is Maleficus, a renegade sorcerer from the Twelve...

Yohan Odivart: *The Man Who Couldn't Die*

2017

The sound, amplified by the echo in the vast, rectangular room, reminded Saint Germain of the priest's solemn steps in the temple of Horus in Hierakonpolis. But it was only one of the museum guards—and a tired one to boot.

Still, this did not stop the Count from seeing in his mind's eye all the details of the procession of Horus' clergy, from the banks of the Nile all the way to the mud brick temple, carrying in their arms the majestic statue with a falcon's head. Behind them came the quicker steps of the barefoot children who were bubbling over with excitement at the thought of seeing their protector god.

He saw again the boys' frizzy hair, their dark skin and their eyes lined with green. The smell of lemon carried along the Nile was stronger than all the other smells—the sweat and the oil rubbed on to protect the skin of the men and women. He could still count the mosquitoes buzzing loudly in the sky behind the procession like a storm cloud.

At that time, already a member of the Twelve Immortals of Atlantis, he could compare the mass of humanity, with their existence so brief, to those clouds of mosquitoes. But he already knew the danger that awaited anyone thinking like this:

it was the path taken by his enemy, Maleficus, when he had betrayed them, and declared himself high priest of Baal, Otar and the Sphinx, and servant of evil. Count Saint Germain saw himself as the protector of humanity, a dedicated guardian, constantly vigilant against the darkness.

"I was hoping you would enjoy this visit, not sink into a deep trance."

His companion's charming voice pulled him out of the depths of his memory. "I'm really glad to be here with you, always, as you know," he replied.

Sometimes, her face reminded him of others, and he had to concentrate hard to remember her name—and that was when he knew he loved her. Sibyl was the one who kept him in the present and anchored him in physical reality, constantly reminding him of the importance of humanity when he was in danger of disappearing in the maze of the Great Mystical Work in which he was a master. The other faces were from a past sometimes centuries-old: Marie-Anne, with the curly red hair; Drusilla, who loved reciting poetry; Meriré, whose fascination with magic had cost her her life... His feelings for them still existed in some corner of his mind, protected by the mnemonic magic inherited from mighty Atlantis.

He tore himself away from this maelstrom of memories, looked up and focused acutely on his surroundings. The walls were papered with *fleur-de-lys*, faded by the years. To his left was a magnificent, marble fireplace above which hung engravings of coats of arms that bore the symbol of French royalty.

"The banquet hall," he pronounced clearly in a desperate effort to keep from slipping back into his memories...

He remembered the serious face of a troubled king on the eve of his coronation by the archbishop, distrustful of his entourage, asking him under his breath: *Saint-Germain, which of them is really worthy of my trust?*

The Count put his hand on Sibyl's arm. He wanted to grab her with all his strength, but instead, he barely touched her. But this time, it was enough. The room was empty and cold; but her arm was warm, alive and solid.

"Let's keep moving," he said. "Didn't you want to see the treasures of the King's Coronation? We're almost there. I can feel the energy from some of the objects."

She looked at him curiously, as usual whenever he mentioned his ties to magic. There was also a glimmer of envy in her eyes that he was never sure whether it was of him or his power. But he willed away these unworthy thoughts.

The museum guard was slumped in a chair and staring at nothing, unaware of the visitors. A couple, however, went up to ask him a question. Saint-Germain turned his back to them and walked under a vaulted ceiling to the treasure room. Then he led Sibyl into a small chapel full of liturgical items and old jewelry, some of it centuries old. A little inner voice told him that nothing here was older than him and he would have been a perfect addition to the collection, given the number of French kings he had seen crowned. And married, and conquered or conquerors in battle, and died...

He had personally handed Charlemagne's sword, Joyeuse, to Philip the Fair, but this room only had a reproduction, much newer and more richly decorated.

There were many gold rings and chalices; crosses and necklaces; centuries of history dead and buried—except for him, Saint-Germain, the Immortal.

And one gold ring with a black, roughly cut stone—a piece of meteorite. Sibyl was talking to him but he was already far away.

1307A.D.

Count Saint-Germain, his face under a leather hood to protect it from the pouring rain that soaked his horse and the land around him, was leaning over his vision mirror.

He was lagging behind on purpose, hoping not to alert the evil creature he was chasing. But not wanting to leave his allies alone, he had come up with this plan: to use the silver mirror engraved with Atlantean runes and activated by commands that he was muttering quietly after the long ride.

On the other side of the mirror, Guillaume, his faithful squire, recognizable by his stooped posture, was going down the steps of the jail whose existence the Templars had never acknowledged. But their arrest in Paris had led to some troubling revelations, and the name of Baphomet had been uttered.

As soon as Philippe the Fair got word of this, he had summoned the Count, whose connection with the occult—and his battles with certain demons—he had heard of, or at least believed he knew. He had given to him the confession of the Templars arrested in Paris, who had worshipped the "idol" Baphomet at the command of the founder of their Order, the famous Hugues de Payens, who had accompanied Godefroy de Bouillon on the First Crusade two centuries ago.

The Count, along with Guillaume and fifty knights, obeying the king's order, had set off immediately on the water-logged roads, when the gray day had barely risen, in order to get to the Count de Champagne and try to stop Baphomet before the news of the arrests reached him. It was to keep the element of surprise and fool the demonic creature that Saint-Germain had stopped in front of the Payens church, a good distance from the commandry. He was aware of the risk he was making his companions take, and only at Guillaume's insistence had he been persuaded to rely on this dangerous plan. Faced with normal humans, his companion had said, Baphomet might reveal himself more readily, and not think of fleeing. Then it would be easier for the Count to confront him.

In the meantime, Saint-Germain watched from a distance, his mystical power hidden behind an ancient amulet with the seal of Horus. Guillaume had made it to the bottom of the stairs and, in the torchlight, was gazing at the cages where grim forms lay dying. Emaciated, disease-spotted arms reached out to him. Cracked and coughing voices begged for his help. One of the knights, a big man with a mane of tangled red hair, came forward with the keys to free the prisoners.

"Thank God, you came to save us!" a high-pitched child's voice said.

The ten year-old, who had stood up when they had arrived, explained: "The master, Ponsard, he's going to kill us all. For the idol!"

In the midst of their sorrowful groans, while some were stretching out their limbs, other prisoners agreed:

"They worship the demon! They made us spit on the cross and they laughed…"

Guillaume was shocked, but stayed focused on his task. He motioned to the knight who opened the last cage and brought out a young, blonde girl in rags whose arms were covered with bleeding scars. Her legs were so weak they had to carry her.

"The monsters," Guillaume hissed. "Come on, little one, you have nothing more to fear."

In the huge grange, the royal knights held at bay a small group of soldier-monks of the Temple who had not really resisted. They were very few, hardly ten in the commandry. Their master, Ponsard, in spite of everything, stood proudly against his enemies. Standing around six and a half feet-tall, he looked down scornfully on them, even though he had been caught, like his brothers, in the middle of a ceremony in the chapel—and therefore was unarmed.

"What are you accusing us of?" he thundered. "We are under the protection of His Holiness Pope Boniface himself! No layman, even the king, can judge us or lift a hand against us. Fear our wrath!"

Guillaume walked straight in. The knights then brought in the tragic victims from the underground prison, all of them squinting in the light. Barely able to contain his anger, which kept him stiff and tall, glaring at Ponsard, he said:

"And what right do you have to keep these peasants and children in cages? What crime did they commit to be treated like this, these good people who are under the protection of His Majesty King Philippe himself?"

Ponsard looked at the freed prisoners and his face crumbled.

"Prisoners? Cages? We have nothing to do with that!"

He turned to the other Templars and murmured:

"I know nothing of this. I was... ill. What have you done?"

The soldier-monks remained silent, statuesque. Some lowered their eyes.

Guillaume was turning red.

"You will answer for your crimes. But not here. First, you can confess in the church in Payens, then you will be brought to Paris for judgment."

Ponsard feebly closed his ring-laden hands and looking powerless, which contrasted dramatically with his attitude before the prisoners arrived.

"I don't remember anything that happened these last few days," he said. "No, for weeks now... the fever... I was probably the victim of witchcraft. I swear it, I'm innocent!"

Several of the king's knights looked away to hide their contempt. Guillaume seemed sickened by the whole scene but did not try to hide it.

"Come on," he ordered, "Let justice be done!"

Later, while he was watching these events in the little Atlantean mirror, Count Saint Germain wondered about the rumors that had sent him here. It was more than likely that Baphomet, one of his old enemies, had already fled and left this puppet to his sad fate.

As soon as Ponsard arrived he threw himself at his feet, wringing his hands, and begged:

"Save me father, for I am a sinner!"

The fallen master of the Payens commandry had mistaken him for a priest when he saw him standing before the church. Saint-Germain watched him carefully. It was highly unlikely that an individual possessed by Baphomet would not recognize him, even if their last meeting dated back centuries ago. Was he just playing with him? Mocking him? Or had Baphomet really left the body of the Templar?

This cat and mouse game was lasting too long, the Count told himself. He glanced at the other Templars in their wet, muddy garb but felt no threat, neither mystical not human. These monks were just tired and mostly felt ashamed.

Turning his head, he saw the former prisoners being led into the nave of the church where they would be protected from the pouring rain.

Finally, he took Ponsard's hands and lifted him up. Both hands were heavy with rings and signet rings, all in gold. So much for the poor knights of Christ, the Count thought. But none of the rings had the black stone that served as a refuge for the essence of Baphomet. One finger, however—the index finger of the left hand—was bare with a pale band that bore witness to what it recently lost.

"Where is the ring you wore on this finger?" the Count asked.

"I don't know. I really don't remember anything of late. I took the ring out of the reliquary where my predecessors had kept it. The ring of Hugues de Payens, a priceless relic, a secret of the Order... Is that what you're looking for, father, that holy object? Our first Grand Master brought it back from Jerusalem. We must find it no matter what lest it fall into the hands of heretics!"

"Calm down. Trust me, we'll find the ring. But to do so I need to see your back."

"What do you mean?" Ponsard looked lost.

"Do as I say if you want to save your soul," Saint-Germain insisted, playing on his fears.

Still on his knees the Templar took off his tunic ignoring the cold rain that kept falling,. His chest was criss-crossed with old scars. He leaned forward, bowing down, prostrate. The Count, with no great surprise, saw the red pentacle topped by a pair of horns in the middle of his back. As expected, it was the mark left by Baphomet on the puppets he abandoned.

A pentacle topped by little goat horns looked engraved in the back of the naked old man. His olive-skin corpse lay on top of other bodies in the midst of the columns of the temple of Amun, the holist of places.

"He was the high priest of Amun," Meriré muttered in a flat voice before this carnage that Saint-Germain (who then went by the name of Shed) and she were staring at.

He scowled as his mind tried to calculate the number of victims. The strong, bitter scent of magic filled the air. Meriré smelled it too, because he saw her wrinkle her nose before wiping away any emotion from her face, as if she were a statue, with perfect make-up, dark red lips and emerald green eyes in a copper-colored face. He found himself more and more distracted by her presence, and this even when the scene before them should have occupied all his attention.

"Twelve victims," he said aloud. "Most of them temple servants. It's an abominable sacrifice to satisfy the worst demon."

As if to confirm his statement, Meriré picked up a blood-stained papyrus written in hieroglyphs and ornamented with a bull-headed demon. It was a ritual dedicated to Baal who was always thirsty for human blood. This explained the stench of black magic.

"We have to stop the one responsible for this massacre as soon as possible," he continued, "because he won't stop before Baal is incarnated. This could be the act of an Initiate—maybe Ba-Peph himself!"

Saint-Germain walked away from the massacre, being careful to respect the bodies of the guards who had been efficiently eliminated before the intruder had committed his dreadful bloodbath.

Meriré followed him, her eyes glistening in the middle of her impassive face. This type of magic disgusted her and he knew that she, like him, would not stop before finding the author of this reprehensible act. It was one of the reasons he had stopped trying to keep her away from the world of the occult: he knew that it was bound to fail. She was much more determined than he. That was why he was sure she was going to become an excellent Initiate once all the secrets of Atlantis were revealed to her. Thus he was hoping to be able to convince the other Twelve to share their knowledge with her when he returned to Hierakonpolis.

They left the main temple and found the sun almost at its zenith. The heat was much stronger outside than in the shade of the temple, but at least here it smelled of stone and sand instead of rotting flesh. The other priests of Amun entered the temple, no doubt to purify the bodies and prepare them for burial. They knew that Shed would do all he could to find the guilty party and punish him. That was the only reason they had called upon him. After all, he had had victories in the past in his battles against evil.

It was far from the eyes of the temple servants, in a rectangular chapel of white limestone, ornamented with brightly painted statues, that Saint-Germain began the ritual to invoke one of the avatars of the god Horus. On his knees he chanted and repeated the ritual until a man with the wings of falcon appeared in a halo of light in the middle of the chapel. He had begun when the sun was high in the sky, and now it was setting, coloring the sand dark red. He had to hurry because the ritual to invoke Baal could only take place at night, under the conspiratorial light of the moon.

"I am at your service, Atlantean, as agreed in the ancient pacts that bind us," said Horus. "Speak and I will obey."

"Here, Mighty Horus, is a papyrus used to practice evil magic," Saint-Germain showed the bloody papyrus that Meriré had given him in the temple. "Lead me to the one who wrote it and created this spell so that I can put an end to his nefarious deeds."

The Egyptian God spread his wings and sniffed the twilight air. Its black eyes stared unblinkingly beyond the horizon.

"Follow me," it said. "Such magic leaves strong traces for one who knows how to look."

Horus made him cross the entire city of Ouaset, alley after alley, following the course of the setting sun, before stopping before a mud brick construction that no decoration or symbol distinguished from its neighbors.

Saint-Germain heard the lapping waters of the Nile in the distance, but the river could not be seen from this spot. Concentrating on his goal, he thanked the God who had started to disappear. Then, he swung open the wooden door and jumped into a dark room, lit only by a torch hanging on the wall.

Meriré came in right behind him. He had just enough time for his eyes to get used to the dark and recognize the hateful figure of Ba-Peph, sitting cross-legged on a reed mat. The villain's face had not changed; it was still bitter and cruel. A simple garment of white linen over his shoulders down to his feet hid his hands.

"Welcome, Shed," his old enemy said. "I've been waiting for you."

"It's always so hard for you to admit defeat, Ba-Peph. Did you think your schemes would go unnoticed and your plan would have the least chance of success against me this time? Have you learned nothing from our past encounters?"

He heard Meriré close the door behind her to shut off any escape for the evil wizard, who burst out in uncontrollable, unsettling laughter.

"It's touching to see how much you respect your superior, but you forget that I, too, have been initiated into the Atlantean mysteries. Besides, this time, I have an ally. For it wasn't I who created that spell you hold in your hands."

"So, who have you corrupted?" Saint-Germain asked.

"No one. I just allowed an old... creature... to come to life out of some stone where it had been trapped by the ancient Danaians. First of all, in the body of Amun's high priest, but it had to die in order to complete the ritual. Its spirit, then, was transferred into the body of the closest person, a young woman who had come to spy on the most secret rites of the Amun priesthood…"

Saint-Germain heard Meriré step forward and turn around. Her eyes shined as bright as burning coals and her hands had grown claws in a despicable transformation. On her left hand, a gold ring set with a black stone reflected the torch-light.

"I'd like you to meet… Baphomet," Ba-Peph declared.

Saint-Germain took two quick steps to the side to dodge the claws, but he knew he also had deal with the evil sorcerer. His situation was critical.

Calling upon his memory of Atlantean spells, he chanted some ancient words of power in a choppy rhythm like a Kerma tambourine, summoning the master of the forty-nine serpents, Baktiotha. In an instant, giant snakes appeared out of nowhere and attacked Meriré and Ba-Peph, winding them in their colorful coils. They struggled furiously to get free, but in vain.

Saint-Germain thought fast, trying to remember a spell to banish a creature like Baphomet, but failed to find one. He knew there was no way to get rid of this monster without killing Meriré, which he refused to do. Maybe defeating Ba-Peph would give him enough time to find a solution.

His enemy was already shaking off the snakes that were supposed to hold him. In his hand was a dagger covered with runes that gave off the stench of dark magic.

Ba-Peph ran at Saint-Germain yelling curses. All the Atlantean could do was to fend him off, being careful not to get scratched by his foe's evil blade. Out of the corner of his eye, he glimpsed the creature possessing Meriré freeing itself from the snakes. He desperately mustered all his strength to summon back Horus, screaming his invocation and praying that the god had not yet returned to Heliopolis.

Suddenly, Saint-Germain thought the sun was rising in the middle of the night. His enemies backed away, blinded by the aura of the falcon god.

"Get me out of this trap!" he commanded, hanging onto Horus' body.

The god rose up and they crashed through the roof of the building that collapsed under his power. He soared off at a terrifying speed—and soon, the city of Ouaset was but a dark point on the horizon.

In his head Saint-Germain kept telling himself that he would find Meriré and save her. But Ba-Peph had other plans that required Baphomet's ring to be worn by other people. By the time Saint-Germain was dropped off at the temple of Hierakonpolis, Meriré was already dead.

The sixth year of the reign of Neferkheperure Akhenaton (1349 B.C.)

The two enemies looked tiny in the shadow of the pyramid that hid their confrontation from the eyes of the world.

Gripping his bronze sword, which had been forged in the flames of a volcano in the middle of the sea, Saint-Germain faced off against a daunting desert warrior.

Tall and thin, the man held a sharp spear in his right hand and wore a gold ring set with a black stone on his left.

The second year of the reign of Hamilcar Barca (235 B.C.)

Posted on the heights of Carthage, Saint-Germain was watching the behavior of a big woman dressed elegantly, which showed she belonged to the aristocracy, during a religious ceremony in honor of the soldiers who died in combat.

Although she enjoyed an excellent reputation in the city, she was really a priestess of Moloch. who regularly performed human sacrifice.

And Baphomet's ring was on her index finger.

The tenth year of the reign of Nero (64 A.D.)

In the midst of the flames that ravaged Rome, Baphomet reveled. He was close to opening a passage that would allow not only Baal, but his two cohorts, Otar and the Sphinx, to rule over the entire Roman Empire—and soon the world.

But when the pentacle it had traced on the ground with the ashes of its burnt victims started to glow more brightly, it heard the voice of Saint-Germain already chanting the words of power that would put an end to the fiery tornado that was indispensable for its ritual...

685 A.D.

Baphomet caught its breath as Saint-Germain's magic forced it back.

"Not this time!" the creature howled, brandishing a heavy axe that a frail young woman like her should never have been able to lift...

988 A.D.

"And yet, you will always find me across your path, Baphomet," Saint-Germain said while his enemy vanished in a baleful mist...

1307 A.D.

In front of the Count, the sweet face of the Madonna smiled at her pure white child. In his mind, she wore a thousand faces, but he could think of only one—Meriré. He shuddered instinctively, still soaked by the rain and frozen by his memories. Over his head, the broken arches protected him from the downpour, but not from the clinging mists of the past.

Saint-Germain had abandoned the soldier-monks of the Temple outside in order to look at the bare back of their fallen master and the mark that Baphomet had left there. '

Taking refuge in the church, the prison victims looked like deathly specters that a tenuous breath of life, a mere thread, separated from a destiny that still eluded Saint-Germain. He chanted a brief spell in the sacred language of ancient Egypt—a simple extract from the Book of the Dead. The fragile existence of the poor beings before him was revealed in all its tragedy: their wounds, their nearness to the beyond. Everyone was so close to death… except one of them, who was much more *alive* than the others.

He looked into the eyes, now full of irony, of the young blonde woman saved by Guillaume. She had recognized the spell and understood what it meant.

"I shouldn't be surprised," Saint-Germain spoke as if they were in the middle of a normal conversation. "You have always preferred being clothed in some kind of purity, after all."

"To think that Meriré had more influence over me than over you," Baphomet replied in a child's voice.

The Count approached the young girl, making a very discreet sign to Guillaume to get away and hoping that his old friend would obey without question this time. One thing, however, was incomprehensible: the child wore no ring. Again, the monster possessing her seemed to read his mind.

"You're not the only one to learn new tricks over the centuries, Shed. I was hoping that this would be enough to evade you and vanish into the dark. I had other plans, you see, rather than having to face you again. This fight is your obsession, not mine."

Saint-Germain's laughter echoed under the vaulted ceiling of the church. The other former prisoners had stepped away from the girl when they had noticed his strange behavior. They watched the Count, convinced that he had become mad.

"You're right," Saint-Germain managed to sputter between fits of laughter. Finally, he was able to control himself and he shrugged his shoulders. "You're not worth the trouble. In that ridiculous body, it's obvious that you're powerless."

And like a challenge, he turned his back and started walking toward the exit.

Baphomet's reaction was quick in coming. The girl jumped up, despite her wounded legs, and the odor of black magic quickly reached the Count. He felt the creature running toward him and, at the last second, he sidestepped, hitting one of the huge stone columns that supported the vaults. He felt his right shoulder dislocate, but he kept his left hand closed over the stone that he had taken out of his coat.

Slowly turning to face his enemy, he could see that Baphomet had completely transformed, revealing his true essence for the very first time. In front of him stood a gigantic creature, ten feet-tall, with arm and leg muscles so bulging they were deformed, ending in thick, black claws. Two goat horns stood atop its three inhuman faces. The metallic scent of blood and, more earthly, of rot, were so strong that the Count was sure that everyone could smell it. To top off this abominable scene, the three mouths vomited their curses at the same time in a triumphal cacophony.

"You wanted it! I'm going to finish you off once and for all! Nobody mocks Baphomet and gets away with it! For Baal! Otar! And the Sphinx! Die!"

The monster came toward Saint-Germain, looming over him, and with all the brutality in its being, it swung its arm at the enemy who had barely gotten up.

With superhuman speed, the Count shot up his left arm to block the blow. Baphomet was stunned when Saint-Germain locked his fingers with its own, heedless of the claws tearing at his arm. He felt an object between their two hands that started to burn. Not its body, but a new sensation, its mystical essence.

213

When it tried to pull away from the Atlantean's grip, it felt it was already drained of strength. The Count stared with an intensity that was unusual, even for him.

"There was a member of the Twelve I located in the deepest desert of Arabia after decades of searching for her. She told me of the djinns who were locked up in black stones since time immemorial. And of their pride, their vulnerability when they manifested all their essence rather than using a human body as a puppet. You have to admit, Baphomet, that is useful knowledge, isn't it? Oh, I see that you're in no condition to answer, so allow me to enlighten you on how you were defeated. What you are feeling is the philosopher's stone in my hand. It's capable of changing one essence into another. Lead into gold, for example. Or the essence of a djinn into lead—cheap and. above all. lifeless. Good-bye Baphomet. Our paths are separate now. just like you said."

The monster could not hold back a pathetic groan while its essence was absorbed and changed by the philosopher's stone until it shrank into a small ball of lead.

Saint-Germain caught the girl's body when it fell forward and bent double in a violent coughing fit. After a few painful minutes, she spit out a gold ring set with a black stone, covered in bloody bile. The ring no longer gave off the smell of magic. The Count picked it up, weighed it in the palm of his hand for a moment, then turned to the royal knights who had entered the church, too late to be of any use. He held out the ring to the closest of them.

"You will give this ring to your king on my behalf and you will repeat these words: Baphomet is gone, but this gold ring will remind the kings of France that they must fight evil for all eternity."

"Aren't you coming back with us? His majesty would like to see you, and hear of your deeds in your own words, My Lord Count."

But Saint-Germain's mind was already far away in the forests of reeds on the banks of the Nile, along with Meriré of the copper skin and iron will...

Sibyl shook his arm, her face wrinkled with worry. The Count became aware of his surroundings again. He was in the Palace of Tau, in Reims, the city where the kings of France were crowned. With his good friend Sibyl. She seemed on the verge of panic.

"You froze there for a minute, and then you turned pale as death. What happened?"

He looked at the ring of Baphomet, lying lifeless and harmless in the display case, and he cracked a little smile.

"No worries, Sibyl. It was just an old memory. Nothing important."

Taking her arm, Count Saint-Germain, Immortal of Atlantis, founding member of the Twelve, master of the mystic arts, left the room, keeping his eyes off Meriré's face as it was reflected in one window after another, all the way to the exit.

Stormshadow by Manuel Martin Peniche

Stormshadow, aka Stormalong or Sturmaloon, is the shaman of the Twilight People, a race of gods and monsters who came from another universe and were hunted by the powerful galactic entities known as the Towers long ago. They eventually found refuge on Earth during the era of Atlantis, and played a role in its destruction. Stormshadow's natural form is that of a gigantic dragon. He serves the descendents of King Gal, who was murdered by his evil brother, Kruge...

Frank Schildiner: *The Wanderer's Nightsong*

Warte nur, balde
Ruhest du auch.
-- Goethe

The diner was the old-fashioned variety, complete with the sheet metal walls, formica countertops and tiny juke boxes at each table that play an endless array of top 40 music hits from 1948-1959. Yes, this was a classic New Jersey diner, the kind used by Hollywood and as much a part of state's the culture as Frank Sinatra and jokes about freeway exits.

Of course this one was on the Autobahn in Germany and the average meal costs more than most people's car, but that was not an issue to Stormshadow. A tall spare figure with a long fringe of brown hair that fell to his shoulders, he possessed a sharply lined face and deep set brown eyes that seemed almost black in color. Currently he was ignoring the very expensive hamburger in front of him and was concentrating, head down, on the New York Times crossword puzzle.

"What did you get on seven down?" The ancient vampire asked, his accent clearly Sabine Italian as he sat down across from Stormshadow. He did have a copy of the paper in hand and was smiling easily.

"Nick's dog," Stormshadow said, repeating the clue from the paper. "Asta. Name of the dog from *The Thin Man* book and each of the *Thin Man* films."

The vampire seemed surprised by Stormshadow's lack of interest, but decided to remain casual as well, "I believe I've seen those movies. Dick Powell and Myrna Loy were the stars?"

"William Powell," Stormshadow corrected, looking up and placing down his fountain pen. "William Powell and Myrna Loy were a classic film team, making thirteen movies together and often playing spouses. Their chemistry was considered so good, they were believed to be a real life couple. They weren't in fact, but when I met them on the set of Shadow of the Thin Man, they did demonstrate a genuine affection for each other."

"I need to talk to you Shaman Stormshadow," The vampire stated, dropping the paper and unable to hide his intentions any further. He was using the ancient title Stormshadow held with the Twilight People before his exile by the usurper king, Kruge. As the wizard-priest of the Twilight People, he was known as a powerful mage who's true form was that of an enormous dragon.

"And your six friends?" Stormshadow asked casually, looking at each of the vampires that were seated in various places around the room. He'd spotted each as they entered the diner, but had remained disinterested at the time. Sometimes the Duke of the Vampires sent them his people out on missions, sometimes for the usurper Kruge, but more often for his own purposes.

"They are to guarantee your compliance. Place this on your wrist, if you please. Otherwise my comrades will kill every human in this building. Your love of humans is known to us, Shaman." The vampire sneered, dropping a large jeweled bracelet on the table.

Stormshadow picked up the bracelet, shrugged and placed it on his wrist, "The Band of Hecate...you fear I will stop you by placing a spell on you and your cadre? Or do you call yourself a horde?"

The vampire looked ready to pounce, his face becoming skull-like and his teeth elongating, "Cadre? Horde? You seek to insult me? Only ghouls call themselves a cadre! And ogres are hordes! How dare you?"

Stormshadow chuckled slightly and shook his head, "Typical vampire, all vanity and appetite. Only Duke Vittorio has anything approaching nobility."

"The Duchess Elizabetta rules the vampire clan now. She is the consort of the great and mighty King Kruge." The vampire spat, his elongated sharp fingernails cutting into the table's surface.

Stormshadow frowned and shook his head, "Too bad, I liked Vittorio. Crude at times, but a gentleman of honor. The Twilight People are less by his loss. I assume Elizabetta murdered her father and assumed the title...yes, I can see that on your undead face. How...typical of her. She and Kruge are an excellent match, monsters the both of them. Now, what do you want, vampire? I'm close to completing this puzzle and still have the London Times waiting."

The vampire smiled, rows of serrated teeth shining in the bright light. "King Kruge wishes to see the Shaman of his people as well as the distant blood of his late brother. He wishes you and the ancestors of Gal to return to his side."

"In other words," Stormshadow replied with a smile, "He has a means of locating the ultimate weapon of the Twilight People, Kera, and requires the blood of a king and a dragon. And being a coward, he will not risk his own blood. Correct?"

If a vampire could flush, this ancient Italian one would be bright red. But he did look embarrassed for a split second before returning to his sneering pose. "No matter. We have captured you and will you bring you before the King, helpless. You cannot transform or use your magic unless you take off the bracelet. And if you do that, my brethren tear these useless humans apart."

"Helpless am I?" Stormshadow asked and was suddenly on his feet, a pair of enormous LeMat revolvers appearing in his hands. He fired quickly and coldly, each shot catching the vampires filling the diner in the heart or head, causing them to crumble into ash instantly. The people in the diner began to scream, some ducking, other trying to hide or flee. The vampire seated before Stormshadow was frozen in place, realizing the huge guns spat instant death to his people.

Seconds later Stormshadow removed the bracelet from his wrist and spoke a few words in an ancient lost language. His eyes pulsed blue as he spoke, the humans in the diner suddenly turning silent and resuming their seats. The sounds of laughter and other conversation could be heard as Stormshadow returned to his seat, guns still in hand.

The vampire tried to speak, realizing he had vastly underestimated the ancient wizard-priest. "You use those human weapons well." he managed to blurt out.

"I was once known as the gunfighter Stormalong, Ghost of the South. I keep in practice just in case. Now, send this message to the usurper and his father murdering consort. Stay away from myself and the blood of Gal. Or there will be consequences. Understood? Good. Now, flee...run away little vampire."

Returning the pistols to their holsters, Stormshadow picked up his fountain pen and read the next clue. A Swiss River, three letters beginning with the letter A...

Kit Kappa by Alfredo Macall

Janet Marson was the only survivor of a plane crash in Tibet in the 1940s. Her baby son, Kit, was raised by the monks of Mohenjo Dar, who live a secret existence in the hidden valley of Kappa, protecting the occult lore of Atlantis. As an adult, Kit was sent by the Great Lama into the outside world to fight the renegade, Darma. Kit is a master of martial arts, and enjoys exceptional vitality and strength...

Krystoff Valla: *Every Journey Begins with a Single Step*

A loose stone on the wall fell off when Kit Kappa put his foot on it. With this sudden loss of support he fell backwards into the dizzying abyss. The young man, however, managed to grab onto a small handhold and stop his fall. Hanging in the air with a faint smile on his face, Kit looked around calmly.

At this late hour, the circle of perpetually snow-capped mountains gradually cast their shadow over the narrow Kappa valley down below. Hidden away in the middle of Tibet for centuries, this place was the secret refuge the community of monks of Mohenjo Dar. Even further down, already in the dark of night, the buildings of the great monastery clung to the gray wall, melting into it as if they had always been there. As the sun at this end of summer was sinking behind the ridgeline, the sky was turning purple. An eagle screeched and drifted a few yards away from Kit, eyeing the intruder curiously, before soaring back to its inaccessible eyrir. Nearby, behind a needle-like spur of rock, water sprang out of the cliff and exploded in mist on the rocky chaos one hundred yards below. A fresh wind swept over the narrow valley, bringing with it the faint odor of smoke.

With his heart delighting in this majestic sight, Kit took a deep breath of the pure air. He loved this place. He had grown up here, become the young man that he was today. He had no desire to leave. But a fleeting expression of anger crossed his face, so he chased away the dark thoughts in order to concentrate on the situation at hand. The smell of fire meant that he was almost there. On the ledge that he saw a little ways above him, his friend Tapley, was waiting for him with a good meal, and all they needed to spend a calm, cozy night in the grotto that had been their lair since childhood. Tomorrow, at the crack of dawn, they would go back down to the valley by the old path on the other side of the mountain.

Kit pulled himself up with all the strength of his powerful arms and resumed his careful ascent. He felt a little tired and hungry. The long excursion on the steep wall, a way for him to commune with the valley, was an interesting test of his skills. Kit was glad he had succeeded, and he was eager to celebrate the victory with his friend. Tomorrow the Grand Lama of Mohenjo Dar would tell him again about the need for him to go out into the big wide world. But tomorrow was another day. Tonight, he wanted to enjoy Kappa.

Kit swung over the ledge and stood above the abyss. The wind was stronger, gusting in spurts and kicking up piles of snow on the mountain. Here, he was halfway to the summit, but the narrow platform at this height looked over the whole valley—a stunning and serene view for the brave climbers able to reach it. Even the western path that climbed out of the monastery, although much easier, required excellent physical condition, if you wanted to make the trip in less than half a day. The natural cave, hardly more than a deep hole in the bare rock, was open before him. A twig fire was burning down in the middle of a small circle of stones. Food was unwrapped on a white cloth near the big backpack that Tapley had packed in the morning. The sleeping bags were still rolled up off to one side. But there was no trace of his friend.

Immediately on alert, Kit hunkered down and looked around more carefully. Tapley could not be far, maybe just behind the rocky peak in front of the path, out looking for wood to feed the fire for the night. Still, his warrior instinct whispered to Kit to stay vigilant. With his eyes open, he let his mind embrace the surroundings, trying to become one with his environment. The smell of smoke filled his nostrils. But his sharpened senses noticed that it masked another scent, more subtle. The scent of oil and metal: *a firearm.*

In a superhuman reflex, Kit threw his chest backward. The gunshot echoed like a clap of thunder in the mountaintops. The bullet grazed his chest and flew off into gray mists over the valley. A second shot rang out, but he was already gone. The young disciple of Mohenjo Dar had rolled on the ledge into the camp and the meager shelter of a low rock. He quickly got up, squatting near the fire and holding a rock that he had snatched up in the same movement.

The shooter hiding in the shadows of the grotto did not have time to adjust his aim. With a dexterity that had been trained by long practice, Kit threw his rock and struck his adversary on the forehead. It was hard enough to knock him out. Vibrating in unison with the mountain, Kit felt the danger before seeing it. Other men came running in from the path, sweating fear and hatred.

One of the many lesson of the Great Lama had taught him in the monastery's training room was: "Always avoid a fight you have not chosen. But if you must fight, then take your enemies down quickly."

Determined not to let them get the upper hand in the battle, Kit attacked two of the assassins.

The first one did not see him coming. Kit stuck close to the wall and surprised him when he appeared at the end of the path. An atemi of his elbow to the chest, then a forearm blow to the throat, and the attacker collapsed without a sound, falling back onto the ledge, which kept him from tumbling into the void.

His partner stopped right away. He pulled forward the machine gun that was strapped to his shoulder, but too slowly. Kit was already on him. He kicked the gun up, unleashing a round of fire that did nothing but break the silence. A second kick, just as swift, knocked the wind out of the attacker who stumbled back. As he was trying to catch his breath and fire again, Kit grabbed the gun and snapped it out of his hands, breaking the leather strap. Then he tossed it into the abyss.

His attacker used this brief reprieve to counter-attack. Wearing a tight, black, military outfit, his big muscles rippled under the shiny fabric. A real giant, he was a head taller than the young warrior and looked proud of his strength. He opened one of the pockets on his uniform, pulled out a long knife with a notched blade and pounced.

The glistening metal split through the air a few inches from Kit's face as he backed up to dodge the blow. One more pushed him to the edge of the precipice. For a moment, he almost lost his balance and toppled over, but he caught himself at the last second. An evil grin twisted the brute's thick lips. A shiver ran down Kit's spine. Of fear? His enemy was sure he had already won the fight and was playing with him, swinging the knife in front of him like a cobra ready to strike its helpless victim. The young man forced himself to control his breathing. As he calmed down, his martial spirit got back in control.

"When the tiger is too confident, it bares its fangs too soon."

The Great Lama of Mohenjo Dar knew a fitting proverb for every step of his training. Strangely lucid now, Kit realized how much more affected he was by the teachings than he had thought, so much so that it came back spontaneously at this critical time.

The soldier bluffed a high swing, then plunged the steel blade toward his target's chest. With his body and mind in total unison, the Kappa disciple watched the attack in slow motion. He dodged it easily and grabbed the wrist of his enemy as it passed by him. Then, he spun around to accomplish his offensive move, to amplify it. With one knee on the ground, he felt the joint crack between his fingers. His attacker screamed. He was thrown forward and tripped on the edge of the path into the void. His cry of terror echoed for a long time.

Kit got slowly back to his feet, staring down into the valley. He did not know this man, and yet he had tried to kill him. Of course, he was only defending himself and all his years of apprenticeship had paid off. But Kit stood still as if his blood had frozen in his veins. He had just taken a life…

The loud hum of propellers snapped him out of his morbid reverie. Two big twin-engines were drilling through the clouds, skirting the snowy mountaintop above him. The planes started a sharp turn, seemed to hesitate a moment, then dove toward the monastery on the side of the mountain, like eagles after their prey. Kit watched on in a daze at this sight that was not only out of the blue, but completely out of place.

The planes flew over once, then a second time, and dropped a string of bombs on the ancient buildings. A series of explosions razed the red tiled roofs, sowing panic in the courtyards where the monks were finishing their last exercises for the day, or were just relaxing. Orange flames sprang up behind windows and columns of black smoke rose into the sky.

Before Kit's horrified eyes, the two bombers flew once more over his home. Fifty men dropped out of the gray machines. Parachutes opened right away, guiding the mercenaries over the wall of the grand monastery of Kappa. The staccato notes of machine guns in the hands of the attackers made the young adept tremble all over.

"Emotion that overwhelms you hides your senses like a wave crashing and drowning a beach under its fury. Let it flow back over you and free your mind."

Another teaching of the Great Lama came back like a litany. With his body paralyzed, and his eyes closed, he breathed deeply again and again. The icy air burned his lungs, pushed the pain out of his head to bring it to his chest. The sounds of battle faded. Slowly, his tight muscles relaxed one by one; his shoulders slumped a little; his back became less stiff; his fists opened. The vital energy was once again circulating normally through him, opening up his awareness and projecting it toward the horizon.

Kit snapped open his eyes. They focused on the bottom of the valley. Wounded, scared, his friend Tapley was running toward the monastery. Without the slightest hesitation, the

226

young initiate of Mohenjo Dar started running down the steep path.

The patches of snow thinned the farther down he went, but he had to stay alert because small sheets of ice dotted the descent. The sun had now totally disappeared behind the summits. Despite the bright full moon visibility was decreasing every minute and the temperature was falling fast. With effort Kit could ignore all these details. The mastery of his body, which he had worked hard on over the years, helped him adapt to the conditions. Forgetting the darkness and the cold, he sped down the mountain concentrating on his only goal: reaching Tapley.

He felt their presence long before seeing them. Kit had got off the winding path, cutting across the hill to save time. He came out, therefore, above the three mercenaries waiting for him in ambush, hiding behind some fallen rocks that were partly blocking the way. But the sound of his footsteps on the rocky slope had attracted their attention. Surprised, they turned in his direction, their guns held out in front of them.

Kit measured the distance of the jump. Too far to avoid the bullets. Unless...

The disciple of Mohenjo Dar let his instincts take over. He jumped feet first as the metal cannons aimed at him. With a thud, he fell into a snowdrift, kicking snow at his enemies a few feet below him. Bullets whizzed blindly through the white cloud, missing their target. The leader ordered them, in broken English, to stop firing. He did not have time to finish talking.

Kit jumped out of the snow cloud like a jack-in-the-box. With all his strength and energy behind it, his kick broke the leader's jaw. The soldier fell back onto one of his men and brought both of them down.

The young man landed on the edge of the path, rolled between two rocks, leaped to his feet, and continued scrambling down the path at breakneck speed. The third merc, completely caught off guard, stood frozen to the spot.

Maybe they had a radio transmitter, Kit was not sure. If so, other men would be waiting for him at the bottom of the valley, ready to block his way to the monastery that was perched on the side of the mountain. Among his other teachings, the Great Lama had insisted that his disciple study the classics of Chinese literature. First, the famous Sun Tzu and his magnificent *Art of War*. A saying of his master seemed particularly fitting to his current situation: "If you are greater in number than your enemy, attack hard. If your forces are equal, work it to your advantage. If you are outnumbered, take them by surprise."

The young warrior of Mohenjo Dar knew exactly what he had to do.

Few people still took the tunnels. Although the underground rooms above them, dug directly under the main buildings, were still used for training, the deeper zones remained deserted and surrounded by mystery. Some of the old monks claimed that these natural caves had once been home to creatures born out of the bowels of the earth, but Kit doubted it. He imagined that, like most of the ones near the surface, these caves must have been used as storerooms for the first inhabitants of Kappa. As a child, he had explored several levels with Tapley without ever finding anything, but some remnants of wooden objects rotted by the humidity. Therefore, he was moving through passages that he believed he was the only one, except his friend, to know about.

The memory of his childhood friend brought waves of memories into Kit's mind. A bunch of images flashed by, happy and studious moments, and harder ones when the Great Lama had taken him, a young orphan, under his wing. He had grown up here and thought he would never leave, rightfully considering Kappa his home. Until two days ago when the master of Mohenjo Dar had mentioned his desire to see the young man rejoin the outside world—"To face the universe that you belong to without knowing it and that needs you!" the old sage had said—and Kit could not believe his ears.

He had left in silence, stunned, crestfallen. He did not want that future! Who could possibly need him? He was just a simple adept of Mohenjo Dar. He still had so much to learn and his talents were too weak to change the world. Or worse, to save it.

Another of the Great Lama's adages echoed in his mind, "Every journey begins with a first step."

In the dark grotto, lit only by a pale reflection off a huge stalactite dripping clear water, Kit clenched his teeth and fists, getting a second wind from his new resolution. Yes, a first step was always needed. For him, it meant saving his own people.

"Move it, little maggot!"

Tapley was thrown off balance when he was shoved hard in the back. He almost fell down the stairs into the humid basement, but, despite his bound hands, he managed to stay standing by leaning on the wall streaked with saltpeter. Still, the blow against his shoulders caused him to grimace in pain. When he had been caught, he had defended himself well, which the cuts and bruises on his face bore witness to. But all his efforts had been in vain. He was outnumbered, subdued and brought back to the monastery. Above them now, in the exterior buildings, the sounds of battle were fading away as each pocket of resistance was defeated, one by one, by the weapons of the mercenaries. Tapley, however, had not lost hope.

"So, where is it?" the first of the two guards barked with a strong German accent. "If you mess with us, you'll be sorry!"

At the bottom of the stairs, the young man pointed to a corridor to the right with a low ceiling. They pushed him toward it. The trio entered the passage and the two soldiers turned on their flashlights. Only ten steps later, they came into a long, narrow, natural cave. Thousands of sandstone jars sealed with wax were lined up on old wooden shelves.

"The wines of Kappa valley," Tapley announced. "Some of them are hundreds of years-old. A special nectar, one of a kind, kept for special offerings."

His guards burst out laughing.

The bigger one, a blonde brute with bulging muscles, kept smiling,

"We did good not to kill you right away."

The second groaned and became serious again,

"Stop joking around. The boss said to keep this one alive until we get his buddy. In case we need him as a hostage."

"Ha! They're just monks! You'll see how fast they fall on their knees before our machine guns!"

The second mercenary did not look convinced and kept a firm grip on the weapon strapped around his neck. His partner went to look at the shelves. He grabbed a jar at random, blew off the dust, and tried to pop the cork with his combat knife.

"Tell me, little monkey, your gods, spirits, whatever they are, they won't mind sharing their drink with us, right? What do you think?"

His guffaw echoed through the rocky vault.

Tapley recited a teaching of the Great Lama, "If the enemy is too strong for you, submit to fate and fight when conditions are favorable again."

"What?" the more serious guard (more worried, too) leaned toward the prisoner.

The blow hit him sharply on the back of the neck. He tried to steady himself against the wall next to him, but a series of precise, powerful hits doubled him over and dropped him to the ground unconscious. In the dim light, his acolyte had no idea what was happening. All he knew was that they were under attack. He threw away the jar and tried to pull up his gun.

Despite his tied hands Tapley managed to grab a jug of wine in his fingers and throw it as hard as he could at the mercenary. The pottery struck him on the head and exploded on impact, splattering him with its contents. The young monk knelt down right away. He felt more than saw someone jumping over his head.

Kit landed on the uneven ground in front of the merc. With a loud *kiaï*, his lightning quick attack struck the man's chest, throwing him back against some shelves where he collapsed, out of action. Kit then turned to his friend and smiled.

"Well done, Tapley," he said.

While Kit picked up the knife off the ground to cut his friend free, Tapley shook his head sadly.

"What a waste. Such good wine..."

They went through the deserted corridors of the main monastery as cautiously as possible. They were lucky. The route they took missed the few patrols set up by the invader.

Kit and Tapley heard it at the same time—the sound of pounding boots coming their way. They jumped through a narrow opening in the wall, which they remembered being used for storage for the training rooms on the ground floor. They waited in the dark, huddled between the wooden dummies and punching bags, until the sound faded away. Silence was restored and Tapley let out a sigh of relief.

"And now what are we supposed to do?" he whispered.

Still keeping a close eye on the doorway, Kit rubbed his chin as if deep in thought.

"Surprise effect. That's how these men took over the monastery so easily. Who here was expecting to see enemies falling from the sky?"

Tapley nodded and joked: "You, maybe. You did the same to get here."

"That's not funny!"

"I know... Sorry, Kit. But you're right. The Kappa valley has lived in isolation for a long time. Locked away in its ancient traditions. Nobody could've foreseen this. Planes, bombs, machine guns..."

A brief silence fell over them while they contemplated the situation.

"Who are these guys?" Kit finally asked. "And what do they want?"

"I don't know," his friend replied, "but I know one thing for sure: they're really well organized and knew exactly where to strike. They're familiar with this place."

"What do you mean?"

"The ones jumping out of the plane landed exactly on the esplanade, or so I was told, and knew exactly which buildings to enter. Apparently they headed straight for the most vulnerable places."

"They attacked at twilight when the monks were resting, spread out, alone in the sanctuaries, or preparing dinner. It's hard to organize an effective defense like that."

They understood each other.

"What else, Tapley? What else did you notice when they brought you here?"

Tapley scratched his head with a funny look of concentration on his face. "It wasn't as easy as that, of course. Our brothers did defend themselves. One guy, who looked like a small mountain, and was obviously their team leader, said they'd suffered more losses than planned. Another answered that there were still at least thirty of them. And he laughed when he said they all had enough bullets to deal with the little monkeys."

"Where did they take them?"

"Sorry, but I don't know. If I had to guard a hundred prisoners, I think I'd lock them up in the…"

"The Testing Arena," Kit blurted out excitedly.

"Are you sure about your plan?" Tapley asked nervously.

"No, but do we really have a choice?"

His friend must have seen that they did not, because they continued in silence through the maze of buildings. They were going up a long corridor along the exterior wall. Small windows, taller than they were wide, were opening onto the void, letting in the cold air from the snowy summits. They stopped at the top of a wide stairway and saw on the landing the big double doors closed with a heavy wooden beam.

"This way?" Kit asked again.

"If you'd kept up with the meditation sessions of Master Kwang, you'd know the building better," his friend scolded him.

Kit furrowed his brow. "Yes, this way. We cross the Rooms of Inner Peace, go back down to the Bridge of Contemplation, and right behind..."

"The arena, OK, let's go. Once our companions are free, we can organize a counter-attack and get the monastery back. Let's hope the goddess of luck gets smiling on us."

But it must have been the day when said goddess was busy elsewhere...

The two young men were in the middle of the impressive bridge when things got seriously complicated.

In the very heart of the monastery, in a big room with a vaulted ceiling, a gaping hole, not too long or too wide, but very, very deep, plunged into the heart of the mountain. A rush of warm air rose up from the bowels of the earth in a steady, breathing rhythm, as if a forgotten giant had decided to sleep there for eternity. The peaceful, strangely supernatural spot used to arouse a feeling of harmony with the world in the minds of those who passed by. Centuries before, the monks had decided to build a wooden bridge over this abyss, fifty feet long, with sculpted railings that looked like interwoven dragons. Four huge columns carved out of giant tree trunks from the bottom of the valley, framed the construction and held up the high ceiling. The bridge was wider in the middle than at its ends and often caused monks to meditate on the union of man and the forces of nature.

Kit and Tapley had to cross this vast, open space to arrive at their destination. Afterward, they just had to run down a short hallway to reach their goal. The old, red, wooden bridge creaked under their weight, the sound echoing down into the bottomless pit.

The mercs stumbled out of a side door leading to the teachers' rooms. They came from the same side of the abyss as the two adepts of Mohenjo Dar. Kit and Tapley counted at least fifteen, most of them carrying wooden crates full of precious objects—the spoils of war. On seeing the two young men, they dropped their booty and grabbed their machine guns.

233

"Run!" Kit yelled to his friend.

The two of them broke into an all-out sprint for the opposite side. The first bullets whistled by their ears as they hid behind the huge lacquered pillars carved into imaginary creatures and curling lines.

"Cease fire!" the leader shouted, a short guy with big arms covered in tattoos. "The chief wants them alive."

Somewhat reluctantly the mercenaries exchanged their firearms for combat knives.

On either side of the parapet the two young men stared at the closed doors of the arena only 50 yards away.

"Go free the monks!" Kit said. "I'll hold them off!"

"What? How are you going to do that?"

Kit smiled confidently at his friend.

"Don't worry about it. I have an idea."

With a determined look in his eyes, Tapley took off. A little gunfire echoed mournfully, but the leader shouted his order again not to shoot.

Kit saw his friend disappear down the dark hallway. In a few minutes, the tide would turn in their favor and the guardians of the monastery would get the upper hand—if they had a few minutes. The young warrior was determined to give it to them.

He heard the heavy footsteps of the thugs treading cautiously over the bridge. They seemed hesitant. Good! They had obviously heard about what had happened to their comrades who had confronted Kit.

With his fists in front of him, the young man felt the energy flowing through his body. Short breaths, eyes closed, he tried to control it, to channel it to his goal. Of course, he had seen the Great Lama do this many times and he had tried to imitate him—with mostly disappointing results. But this time, he did not have the luxury to fail.

All of a sudden, he noticed that his temples were beating in unison with the chthonian wind. He felt the energy, the *chi*, building up in him like a flood pouring into a narrow canyon. His frozen arms seemed made of stone. His clenched fists heated up like they were held over burning coals. Behind him, he knew that the mercenaries had reached the middle of the bridge.

With a pang of regret for what he was about to do, Kit stepped out of hiding and stood before them.

Stunned by this move, the mercs stopped. Kit's face twisted crazily with all his concentration. His eyes were wild. Mystical, spiraling plumes and incandescent sparks shot out of him. His hands were like two pieces of red-hot steel.

"Master of my body and mind as one, I am invincible!" Kit chanted and with the sound of thunder he struck his two fists on the age-old bridge.

The crash shook the foundations of the building. Tapley had to hold onto the heavy door handle to keep his balance. He turned around briefly to see the Bridge of Contemplation explode into a million pieces and the men on it disappear into the depths of the mountain.

"By all my ancestors!" he panted.

Shaking himself out of his sudden daze he hurried to unlock the huge double door.

The half dozen overconfident mercs watching the arena were no match for him. The first two stood near the main entrance and were not expecting to see the door open and Tapley rush in all fired up. With a series of expert atemis, he put them out of action before they even had time to point their weapons.

The monks were ready to react to the intrusion and in a few seconds, the four other mercs were overpowered and disarmed.

"Where's the Great Lama?" Kit asked when he joined them in the room reserved for ritual combat.

An old monk put a gentle hand on his shoulder.

"He said that we could put our trust in you, young disciple. He was right."

"OK, but where is he?" Kit was getting impatient.

"Six bandits took him to his rooms," another monk broke in. "To meet their leader, I think."

Kit breathed deeply. The last few minutes had given them a certain advantage over their enemies, who were too sure they had won and were off plundering. Even alerted by the noise of the collapsing bridge, they would be easily surprised and defeated one by one. In a split second, Kit made his decision.

"Tapley! Organize the resistance with the venerable masters. We have to flush out and capture all the mercenaries here. I'll take care of freeing the Great Lama."

To his surprise Kit met hardly any opposition scrambling up through the monastery toward the private rooms of his mentor. Only once did he have to fight a merc who had come to investigate the sound that had shaken the buildings. The enemy might have been an excellent shot, but he was no match for a warrior trained in the finest techniques of hand-to-hand combat. The fight ended as quickly as it had started, and Kit went on his way. Again, there was only one guard posted outside the Great Lama's rooms. He crumpled under one expertly executed atemi without knowing what hit him.

The young adept of Mohenjo Dar moved forward very carefully. He tiptoed through the antechamber with their walls covered with heavy, scarlet drapery. For one brief moment, he wondered how many hours he had spent in this place receiving his master's teachings full of wisdom. An explosion made him jump. He went to a window and looked outside.

In the inner courtyard of the monastery, the monks had apparently surrounded the last members of the airdrop, barely a handful of men. A small group led by Tapley were holding the captured weapons and threatening the mercenaries. It only took a few seconds for them to throw down their machine guns and surrender.

Kit smiled in relief. He could always count on Tapley. Once again, his friend had proved his loyalty and his ability to help him.

Free of worry on seeing his companions out of danger, Kit went back to exploring the rooms and their simple but warm furnishings where the master of Kappa lived. The bedroom was empty and undisturbed. However, a cold breeze was coming through the cracked open door that led to the workroom. Kit headed for it.

The dark room was ice cold. Here, in one corner on the top floor of the monastery, big windows opened onto a narrow balcony that ran along the entire room. The windows were open and the purple curtains danced frantically to the rhythm of the wild winds. Pages of manuscripts were flying all over the place; furniture was lying overturned on the soft carpet where there were traces of frost.

Kit froze in the doorway. His heart sank at the sight.

In the middle of the room the Great Lama of Mohenjo Dar was sitting in the lotus position on the top of a black lacquer low table. His face looked pale and golden in the moonlight. His eyes were closed, serene, sunk in deep meditation. However, a strange and complex device was all around him.

Eight hand grenades were attached to the legs of the table. A cord passed through each pin, hooked up to pulleys in each corner of the room where Kit could see vials of acid in sealed glass boxes dripping their contents onto the cords, threatening to snap a counterweight at any moment that, he was sure, would cause a lethal explosion. If he broke the transparent boxes, he was afraid he would just speed up the process. The wires looked so tight that the least pressure would no doubt release the mechanism. Then he saw the ropes around the wrists and ankles of the old monk. The slightest movement would blow him up.

Kit called out quietly to the Great Lama. The eyes of the old man opened slowly and a kind smile brightened his age-old face.

"You still have time," he whispered.

"Time? Time for what?"

"To find a solution."

Despite his doubts, Kit felt reassured by the old man's serenity. He started thinking as fast as he could. The acid was gnawing away at the cords, narrowing the margin of error by the second. He checked the four big pulleys stuck in the walls just above each box. Everything started from there.

"I have to block the pulleys," he announced with more confidence than he really felt.

He started searching among the objects lying on the ground for something that might help. A handful of various paintbrushes were scattered over the thick wool carpet. Their white wooden handles could do the trick. He whisked them up and knelt down in the first corner. He stuck a brush gently into the pulley, forcing it carefully, slowly (more slowly than he cared to) until it locked the rusted metal into position.

He let out a long sigh. "One down, three to go."

Behind him the reedy voice of his master made him shudder.

"In the absolute, there is no good or bad choice as long as your actions coincide with what is just."

The sound of an engine suddenly filled the room. Kit jumped up to see a huge helicopter hovering before the big windows. The jagged mountaintops disappeared behind the ugly shape as its spinning blades made the wind blow stronger into the room.

A figure walked toward the machine, standing out against the gray body of the huge aircraft. Kit cursed himself for not thinking of it, for fixating on the Great Lama's jeopardy, for not checking to see if anyone was hiding on the balcony.

He squinted in the ray of light that the helicopter projected into the room. Stunned, the young warrior only then recognized the brains behind the attack.

"Darma!"

Darma! He, too, was a former disciple of Mohenjo Dar. Kit had known him as a child, and he remembered envying the man for his mastery of the martial arts and his advanced warrior skills. But his soul turned out to be as dark as his fighting technique was brilliant. The Great Lama had to expel him out of Kappa valley, to exile him far from those he could never again call brothers.

"Darma!" Kit cried out again, feeling rage boiling in his blood.

The traitor's laugh sounded as cruel as it did amused. His strong voice was barely heard over the noise of the helicopter.

"Oh, look, isn't that the new protégé of the senile old fool? What are you going to do now?"

With an angry sneer on his face, Kit locked his blue eyes on the traitor. He instinctively went into the tiger's stance and silently challenged Darma to a fight. The attitude only made the villain laugh more as he openly mocked the young warrior.

"Little doggie got his hackles up! Think you can handle it?"

"I'll make you pay for your treachery!"

"And let your venerable master die? Tsk, tsk. That would surprise me."

The words of the old sage, spoken just a few seconds ago, came back to the young man's mind. He was furious! Darma was right. Kit had a choice, but being a good disciple of Mohenjo Dar, he would do what was just.

His muscles slowly relaxed and he dropped the fighting stance. He squeezed the brushes and headed over to the second corner. While working, he yelled out:

"Why?"

The former monk looked like he was fully enjoying the moment. He was on the edge of the balcony, gripping the rope ladder thrown out of the helicopter.

"Revenge, boy, revenge. Today, you think you've won a round, but you only postponed the inevitable. I will never leave you in peace! I will strike again! Whenever I want! And you will taste the bitterness of tears and despair… Sooner or later!"

The traitor's sinister laughter faded as the helicopter sped away toward an unknown destination in the night still bright with the full moon.

Without stopping his work, Kit watched the helicopter until it disappeared in the shadows of the mountains.

"Run away, Darma, run as far away from Kappa as you want. I will search the world over if that's what it takes to find you, and I will stop you from doing any more harm."

Kit repeated this promise to himself until he had saved his master from the trap he was imprisoned in.

When he was free, the Great Lama stood up, rubbing his painful wrists. The smile on his face said all that needed to be said about how satisfied he was—and proud of his disciple.

Ozark by Luciano Bernasconi

About the Authors

Brought up reading the adventures of Phileas Fogg and Captain Nemo (his father was a Jules Verne fan), it was quite natural for **Cédric Burgaud** to enjoy reading, then writing, fantasy fiction, first for himself, then for his family and friends. He has had several stories published in Rivière Blanche's thematic anthologies, including those devoted to the Hexagon Comics universe.

Nelly Chadour has been writing since she learned how to handle a pencil, and became a professional writer in 2011. Her works have been published by Editions Malpertuis, Céléphais, Le Carnoplaste, and Rivière Blanche, including (for the latter) a full-length Hexagon novel starring *Sibilla*, which is currently scheduled to be translated and published by Black Coat Press.

Fabien Clavel was born in 1978. After studying classical literature, he became simultaneously both a teacher and a writer. He has had about thirty novels published in various genres, including *Furor*, based on the Roman defeat of Teutobourg, and *Feuillets de Cuivre* [Copper Leaves], a steampunk detective story. He has also authored thirty short stories.

Tepthida Hay is an accomplished novelist who has worked in many genres, having written more twenty stories published in various anthologies and magazines. She likes folklore and mythology, and also steampunk fiction.

Julien Heylbroeck comes from the world of role-playing games, having worked on many successful products, including *La Brigade Chimérique*. He loves pulp heroes, super-heroes, and more particularly *luchadores* from Mexico. His stories have appeared in anthologies published by Malpertuis, Le

Carnoplaste and Rivière Blanche. He collaborated with Romain d'Huissier on this volume.

Romain d'Huissier also comes from the world of role-playing games, having worked on *La Brigade Chimérique*, and designed and written an RPG based on the Hexagon Comics Universe for French publisher Les XII Singes. He has published a number of short stories and novels for Malpertuis, Le Carnoplaste, Critic, Trash and Rivière Blanche. For the latter, he has written two novels featuring the Hexagon group of super-heroes, *Dark Matter* and *The Immortals' War*, and assembled four anthologies devoted to the Hexagon Universe.

Born in 1970, **Jean-Marc Lainé** was editor at Semic (the predecessor of Hexagon Comics) in the late 1990s. He then edited a line of comics for publisher Bamboo. He has written several graphic novels including the *Omnopolis* trilogy, the second volume of the series *42*, and the two-volume *Grands Anciens*, which describes the meeting between Hermann Melville and H.P. Lovecraft. He has also written several acclaimed non-fiction books about the art and history of comics.

Jean-Marc & Randy Lofficier have collaborated on five screenplays, a dozen books and numerous translations, including *Arsène Lupin*, *Doc Ardan*, *Doctor Omega*, *The Phantom of the Opera* and *Rouletabille*. Their latest novels include *Edgar Allan Poe on Mars*, *The Katrina Protocol* and *Return of the Nyctalope*. They have written a number of animation teleplays, including episodes of *Duck Tales* and *The Real Ghostbusters*, and in comics, such popular heroes as *Superman* and *Doctor Strange*. Randy is a member of the Writers Guild of America, West and Mystery Writers of America.

Ghislain Morel discovered comics at age six in a box that belonged to a cousin of his, filled with French editions of Marvel titles. Born in 1971, he is old enough to have bought and read the original black and white mags which featured the heroes of the Hexagon Universe. He has written games, short stories, articles, played music in the groups Maigh Tuireadh, Skøll and Naheulband, and chaired the musical and literary collective, The Deep Ones.

Alex Nikolavitch is a jack of all trades when it comes to writing. He is a translator, a lecturer, and has written countless articles, comics, short stories and novels (*Eschatôn, L'île de Peter [Peter's Island]*). He is the author of the non-fiction book *Mythes & Superheros*, and is delighted to put his theories in practice by contributing to the Hexagon Universe.

Yohan Odivart is a history teacher and a fervent gamer. He discovered the Hexagon Comics Universe through the RPG designed by Romain d'Huissier. His predilection for short fiction and his interest in history motivated him to create a tale featuring the mythical Count Saint Germain.

Frank Schildiner has been a pulp fan since a friend gave him a gift of Philip Jose Farmer's *Tarzan Alive*. Since that time he has written *The Quest of Frankenstein, The Triumph of Frankenstein, Napoleon's Vampire Hunters, The Devil Plague of Naples, Irma Vep and the Great Brain of Mars* and *The Spells of Frankenstein* for Black Coat Press. Frank has also been published in numerous other anthologies. He works as a martial arts instructor and resides in New Jersey with his wife Gail who is his top supporter. He is a regular contributor to *Tales of the Shadowmen*.

Fascinated by fantasy since his childhood, **Kristoff Valla** is now a professional writer who expresses his love for the genre through various RPGs and novels, even though he sometimes feels he never has enough time to tell all the stories he would like to recount. He is, among other things, the author of the trilogies *Coeur de Jade* [Jade Heart], *Lame du Dragon* [Dragon's Blade] and *Kath*.

EXPLORE THE WONDERS OF THE HEXAGON
UNIVERSE AND ITS HEROES IN OUR COMICS:

Bob Lance #1: The Round Table. Carpi & Bernasconi. 64 pages b&w. $12.95.

Bob Lance #2: To Seek the Holy Grail. Carpi & Bernasconi. 54 pages b&w. $12.95.

Bob Lance #3: The Ghost of Rasputin. Carpi & Bernasconi. 54 pages b&w. $12.95.

C.L.A.S.H. Frescura & Trevisan. 248 pages b&w. $20.95.

Dick Demon: Vanishing Point. Lofficier, Arden & Peniche. 108 pages color. $26.95

Dragut/Scarlet Lips. Lofficier & Macall. 68 pages color. $19.95

Galaor, Warrior of Mû. Lofficier, Macall, Xavier & Peru. 68 pages color. $19.95.

Guardian of the Republic #1. Mornet & Roncagliolo. 48 pages color. $12.95.

Guardian of the Republic/Barbarella. Lofficier & Ruiz. 48 pages color. $12.95.

Guardian of the Republic/Dragut/Scarlet Lips/Time Brigade.

245

Lofficier & Macall. 48 pages b&w. $9.95.

HEXAGON COMICS: THE FIRST 70 YEARS. Lofficier et al. 300 pages b&w. $22.95.

Hexagon novel #1: Dark Matter. D'Huissier. 300 pages. $22.95.

Kabur #1. Legrand, Lofficier & Bernasconi. 252 pages b&w. $20.95.

Kidz. Lofficier & Macall. 52 pages b&w. $10.95

The Lunatic Legion. Lofficier, Bouquet & Lafuente. 52 pages b&w. $10.95.

The Partisans. Thomas, Lofficier & Guevara. 48 pages b&w. $9.95.

Phenix #1. Lofficier, Bernasconi & Roncagliolo. 248 pages b&w. $20.95.

Scarlet Lips. Wolfman, Lofficier & Guevara. 48 pages b&w. $9.95

Strangers Origins: Homicron. Buffolente, Lofficier & Dzialowski. 364 pages b&w. $24.95.

Strangers Origins: Jaydee. Grossi. 260 pages b&w. $20.95.

Strangers Origins: Starlock. Legrand & Bernasconi. 256 pages b&w. $20.95.

Strangers #0: Omens & Origins. Lofficier & Various. 128 pages color. $29.95.

Strangers #1: Strangers in a Strange Land. Lofficier & Various. 160 pages color. $34.95.

Strangers #2: Of Blood and Fire. Lofficier & Various. 160 pages color. $39.95.

Strangers #3: Of Gods and Men. Lofficier & Various. 160 pages color. $39.95.

Tales of the Twilight People: Dr. Despair. Lofficier & Agapit. 148 pages b&w. $12.95.

Tiger and The Eye. Lofficier & Ruiz. 136 pages b&w. $12.95.

Time Brigade: The Grail Wars. Lofficier & Green. 48 pages color. $12.95.

Wampus #1. Frescura & Bernasconi. 232 pages b&w. $20.95.

Zembla #1. Oneta & Oneta. 280 pages b&w. $22.95.

TO ORDER: pay by credit card/paypal direct from our web-site: *www.hexagon.comics.com/shop.html*
or pay by check to the order of BLACK COAT PRESS sent to:
BLACK COAT PRESS c/o Mr. Greg M. Seigel,
18321 Ventura Blvd., Suite 915, Tarzana, CA 91356.
E-MAIL INQUIRIES: *info@blackcoatpress.com*

www.ingramcontent.com/pod-product-compliance
Lightning Source LLC
Chambersburg PA
CBHW060352030726
47497CB00003B/679